EAST RENFREWSHIRE

✔ KT-167-077

EFFIE'S
WAR

Also by Philip Paris

EFFIE'S
WAR

PHILIP PARIS

BLACK & WHITE PUBLISHING

First published in 2018
by Black & White Publishing Ltd
Nautical House, 104 Commercial Street
Edinburgh EH6 6NF

1 3 5 7 9 10 8 6 4 2   18 19 20 21

ISBN: 978 1 78530 195 7

Copyright © Philip Paris 2018

The right of Philip Paris to be identified as the
author of this work has been asserted by him in accordance
with the Copyright, Designs and Patents Act 1988.

All rights reserved.
No part of this publication may be reproduced,
stored in a retrieval system, or transmitted in any form,
or by any means, electronic, mechanical, photocopying,
recording or otherwise, without permission in
writing from the publisher.

This novel is a work of fiction. The names, characters and
incidents portrayed in it are of the author's imagination.

A CIP catalogue record for this book is available
from the British Library.

Typeset by Iolaire, Newtonmore
Printed and bound by Nørhaven, Denmark

For Catherine

Berlin, 1930

On the day their visitor was due at the apartment, even Walter's self-assured father was on edge, constantly pacing around the luxurious rooms to check that the cleaner had been vigilant, as if the poor woman dared ever to be anything else. There would be just the three of them for dinner. No witnesses. The cook would leave once everything had been prepared. Rolf Möller himself would serve the food.

Walter had given up enquiring who was coming, but when their mysterious guest arrived he wished he had been more prepared. The man was physically unimposing, yet he dominated the space around him in a way that Walter had never experienced. The plethora of influential businessmen, politicians, academics and artists who had walked through their front door over the previous five years paled into insignificance.

Walter stood awkwardly nearby while his father took the man's coat, before making the rather one-sided introduction.

'May I introduce my son, Walter.'

Walter shook the offered hand and was startled at the steely grip. Likewise the eyes that bored into him were steely and cold. He'd recognised their guest immediately. Everyone knew Adolf Hitler.

The meal was a minefield of intense, probing questions, many of them utterly bizarre and apparently unrelated. However, the silences were worse. Hitler would stare at Walter as if trying to see inside him, to verify that his answers matched what he was really thinking. It was obvious to Walter that his father had previously spoken about him in some depth.

'Walter,' said Hitler, pushing away his dessert plate and at last getting to the real reason for his visit. 'I can see that you're a young man of honour, one who can be trusted never to repeat anything revealed during this meeting.'

Walter knew he was being flattered – 'buttered up' as his aunt Iris would have said – but he couldn't help feeling pleased, grateful even. Despite his discomfort at the grilling, Walter hadn't been able to prevent himself from hanging on to every word that Hitler uttered, as if those words had somehow become the most important things in his life.

'Walter,' his father said softly.

Walter felt that he had fallen under a spell; the gentle prompt made him realise he was meant to respond – to confirm that he would indeed keep everything strictly confidential.

'Of course, sir.'

'Good. Europe will one day be at war again and when that time comes the Fatherland will need people living among the enemy, people who are totally loyal to Germany and willing to sacrifice their lives for the greater glory of our victory. Your father feels that you are such a person and, having now met you, I agree.'

'I don't understand, sir.'

'I am selecting a unique group of men and women who will be trained vigorously in many skills before they start a new life in another country, one that the Fatherland is certain to fight in the war that will sweep Europe again.'

War? thought Walter, but all he said was, 'Spies, sir?'

'More than that, but let's use the term for now. Tell me ... why do you think spies get caught?'

Walter had no idea. The entire evening had been surreal, and this line of interrogation was making it even more so.

'Because they are careless, sir?' he tried, summoning up the courage to meet the dark gaze from across the table.

'Perhaps.'

Walter withered under the stare. His father kept quiet. He had been uncharacteristically subdued and subservient during the entire 'interview'.

'Because they are unfortunate ... encountering bad luck?'

'People make their own luck in this world.'

Hitler spoke quietly yet with such fierce intensity that Walter was suddenly chilled. Rolf Möller scratched his lip, as if it was itchy or just a habit of his. The movement was completely casual, yet it was enough to catch his son's attention. Walter's mind whirred. Was it meant to be a clue? If so, what did it mean?

Hitler sat back in his chair, a sign that he was not going to speak until he heard the answer he wanted. The question posed the biggest test so far. Walter frantically tried to work out a solution to something he had never given a moment's thought.

Lips ... What had his father said to him all those years ago, when they were leaving Scotland? Something about creating false perceptions ... making others do what you want them to but without telling lies. Walter began to glimpse fragments of an answer; however, he had to speak the words aloud in order to start making sense of his jumbled thoughts.

'Spies get caught ... because ... because they have created a perception about themselves that is too far from the truth.'

Hitler banged his fist on the table. Cutlery clinked and several items jumped, as did Walter.

'Excellent! That is exactly right!' Hitler was agitated with excitement. A muscle in his cheek twitched. 'Spies are nearly always found out because they pretend to be something they are not. That is why you will be the person you appear to be and why you will never be discovered. This is how you will serve Germany. You are to find me a secret ... something that will make your enormous sacrifice worthwhile.'

'But how will I know this secret, sir?'

'You will know. When you learn it ... you will know.'

PART ONE

1

Edward Ross sat at the large kitchen table and chewed his favourite pipe with such force that it was pure luck that neither the stem nor his dentures broke. He had read the letter once in total confusion, twice with a growing dread and a third time with a smouldering anger that few people would have believed possible of the quietly spoken elder of the kirk. His wife, Martha, was washing the breakfast dishes without any knowledge of the despair growing only a few feet away.

'Damn ... damn!'

Martha turned around in surprise at hearing such language.

'Edward! Whatever is the matter?'

Ina had just walked through the doorway and stood open-mouthed at her father's utterance. He saw her staring.

'Where's Effie?' he said.

'Upstairs,' replied Ina.

'Fetch her.'

'What's happened?'

'Fetch her! You need to hear this together.'

Ina had never seen her father so distraught and rushed to get her sister, who, at seventeen, was almost three years younger. Mr Ross slid the letter across to Martha. It was only right that she should have the chance to read the contents before they were discussed. She was still trying to understand the implications when their two daughters burst into the kitchen in a way that would normally have resulted in them being chastised sternly. Mr Ross looked at the sisters standing side by side, as exactly alike as an apple and pear can be.

'Father,' said Effie. 'What's wrong?'

'Sit down.'

The girls sat at the table while their mother collapsed into the nearest chair.

'We've received notice from the authorities that we must leave the farm by the twelfth of December.'

'Leave?' said Effie. 'Why? Who's going to look after the livestock?'

'We'll have to get rid of it… cattle, sheep, pigs, even the hens.'

Martha put a hand to her mouth and laid down the letter. Effie reached over and snatched it, scanning the text frantically while Ina looked on.

'There must be a mistake,' said Effie. 'They're giving us one month to move or sell everything, in addition to processing the crops. It's not possible in such a short time. We would need a small army of workers.'

'Why do they want our home?' said Ina, close to tears. 'What possible use is it to them?'

'We could move the stock until we return,' Effie cut in. 'This letter seems to imply it's temporary.'

'It's not just our farm, so there'll be a surplus of animals and no one in the area will have the capacity to take on other people's,' said Mr Ross. 'We might find someone to look after the horses, but as for the rest ... And it'll be a sad day indeed when we lose Alastair and his family.'

'Barbara will be heartbroken,' said Martha. 'Their boys were born on Kirk Farm. Our cottage is all they've ever known as home.'

'Alastair will have to find new employment at the end of the term,' said Mr Ross, shaking his head. 'He won't have any choice.'

They fell silent, reflecting on the enormous changes that were about to be forced upon their lives. Effie eventually broke the stillness by jumping up and pacing around the kitchen in a state of great indignation and irritation that was so ... Effie.

'This is not right,' she said.

'It's the war,' said Ina.

'I know it's the war!'

'The letter says there's a meeting this afternoon at Inver hall, so perhaps we'll get some answers there,' said Martha.

Effie turned to her mother. Martha was a practical, down-to-earth woman, not given easily to weeping, yet she looked close to tears now. Effie's father, grandfather and great-grandfather had meticulously bred the best livestock possible. The careful records they had kept meant they could trace the lineage of some of the cattle and pigs for more than eighty years. They were a part of the land as much as the ancient horse chestnut tree that overshadowed the drive.

'If we sell the stock then so much will be lost,' said Ina.

'People are losing sons, brothers and husbands,' replied her father, sitting up straight in his chair as he began to pull himself together. 'If we survive this war and only lose our animals, then we should thank the good Lord.'

'Can't Christopher do something?' said Effie, never one to back down without a fight. 'Surely it must be some use having an officer living here.'

Captain Christopher Armstrong had been billeted with the family for three months. Mr Ross had been horrified when he had been informed that they would have to provide accommodation for a young British officer. He readily acknowledged that plenty of other families in the area had been ordered to give room and board to military personnel, but with two beautiful, trusting daughters in the house the idea of a stranger living in such close proximity made him very uncomfortable.

The move had been a double-edged sword. Christopher had been polite and respectful, behaving like a caring older brother to seven-year-old Hugh, who had taken to him immediately. In fact, everyone liked him; Ina a little too much. She had fallen hopelessly in love, ignoring the advice given during their father's frequent lectures on the subject of 'hasty wartime romances', and how uncertainty about the future was putting too much pressure on couples to commit.

He liked to remind them that there was a lot of wisdom in the saying '*Marry in haste, repent at leisure*' and how, when he was young you courted for months before you even held hands with a girl – and as for kissing! His daughters always listened politely without comment, and the advice had been easy to follow while there was no one to fall in love with.

'I don't see how Christopher can help, it's nothing to do with him,' said Ina bristling, yet there was a hesitance in her words. Effie guessed she was thinking the same thought – that surveying the surrounding land for this evacuation was precisely what Christopher had been sent to the Tarbat peninsula to do.

*

That afternoon Effie accompanied her father to the nearby village of Inver.

They entered the packed hall to be greeted by the grim faces of neighbours and friends and got the last two seats together. Effie knew everyone, by sight if not by name; other local farmers and crofters, people from Inver, Constable MacKay, the postman and Doctor Gray, who had last called four months earlier when Hugh had been ill.

Her gaze rested on the imposing figure of the Reverend Smith. As her father had often commented, the minister was a tower of strength in these worrying times, a true man of the cloth who worked tirelessly on behalf of his parishioners, as willing to chop firewood for someone as he was to sit by their bedside, with a prayer or a blessing, when they were dying.

Effie saw the minister turn his head towards her, as if sensing he was being watched. She smiled and he nodded, his expression appearing sombre. She thought that the huge responsibility he already had for his flock was about to increase significantly.

Christopher sat to one side of the small stage, normally used by the local band on dance nights. He also looked nervous, staring at the floor as if trying to avoid having to make eye contact with anyone. On the stage were two strangers. One of them stood up and the hall fell silent.

'Thank you for coming at such short notice. I'm Lord Rosebery, the Regional Commissioner for Scotland, and this is General Sir Andrew Thorne of Scottish Command. We're here to explain the situation and answer questions as much as we are able. You should all have received a letter, instructing you to vacate your properties and land by the twelfth of December at the latest.

'I understand that this great upheaval may be very upsetting for some. However, I can assure you that it is vital to the war effort. If required, help will be provided with accommodation, although it is hoped that those affected will find somewhere close by with friends or family.'

This idea caused a murmur throughout the hall. Didn't Lord Rosebery know that finding room and board was already extremely difficult?

'I know this has been a huge shock,' he went on. 'The area being evacuated will extend from just south of Portmahomack and Rockfield to the outskirts of Fearn and Hilton. Around nine hundred people will need to be rehoused and this includes the entire community of Inver.'

At this the murmur rose to a chorus of disgruntled voices, a hubbub which took several minutes to die down.

'Those living north of the affected area will not be required to leave, although access through the restricted zone will be limited to twice a day, at times specified by the military. Farms that have to sell their livestock will be provided with transport to the nearest market.'

'What about the crops?' Effie suddenly shouted. 'They

might be gathered, but it's impossible for them to be processed in the time we've been given.'

'It's a good question, young lady ...'

'Don't "young lady" me! I've worked this land ever since I was a child!'

Mr Ross put a hand on Effie's arm, a signal that she was crossing the line from being firm to rude.

'We appreciate the difficulties,' continued Lord Rosebery. 'Additional manual labour will be supplied by Italian prisoners of war stationed at the camp in Kildary, as well as the Home Guard and Women's Land Army. The country desperately needs the food you have grown and you can be assured that whatever aid required will be provided.'

'Will the military live in the houses once the owners have left?'

This query was put by the minister and several of those present stressed their concern about this point. From his irritated, somewhat flustered expression, it appeared that Lord Rosebery would have preferred to leave questions until he had finished his explanation, but feelings were running high and he had no choice but to tackle them as they arose.

'No, properties will remain empty,' he assured everyone. 'Help will be available to move and store furniture. We suggest that when you leave you take all your valuables and those possessions that you may need in your places of temporary residence.'

'How long are we going to be evicted for?' asked the postman, a man in his fifties. 'My mother's over ninety and there are lots of other elderly folk in the parish. This forced move is going to be incredibly upsetting for them,

13

particularly if we can't say for how long it will be. There'll be more than one who will fear they won't live to return home and be able to die in their own bed.'

Despite the postman's plea, the two officials could not give any firm date for a return. However, they provided what details they could. The evacuation would mean the closure of the primary schools at Inver and Geanies, along with the telephone exchange at the latter. Information centres would be opened at each school and people would be able to call over the coming days to request assistance. Assurances were given that the authorities would pay for any damage occurring to property.

The meeting lasted for nearly an hour and when it came to an end the Reverend Smith rose from his seat and asked everyone to join him in prayer for those facing danger far away and for those closer to home who were about to endure these unexpected difficulties.

People mingled afterwards in an atmosphere of frustration and resignation. After all, families throughout the country were making huge sacrifices and there were a great many who had lost homes and loved ones to German bombs. So far, the enemy hadn't appeared interested in the Tarbat peninsula, tucked away in their corner of the Scottish Highlands. There wasn't anything nearby to warrant a bombing raid apart from the small military airfields at Tain and Fearn.

In the midst of the complaints and anxieties being expressed all around her, Effie spotted Christopher slipping out of a side door. She forced her way through the throng at the main entrance so she could run around the outside of the hall and cut him off.

'You knew about this!' she said, barely managing to stop herself from poking him in the chest. 'How could you have lived with us for all these months, eating at our table and sweet-talking your way into my sister's affections, while all the time you were sneaking about, planning to have us thrown out of our home!'

Christopher towered above Effie, yet she stood her ground inches away, which meant that she had to tilt her head to meet his gaze. The wind whipped her hair into even more of a tangle than it normally was and she had to push it out of her face to maintain her angry stare.

'I'm sorry,' Christopher sighed. 'You're right. I simply couldn't tell anyone. This project is top secret and I had strict orders.'

'And did these orders include making my sister fall in love with you?'

'No. And they didn't include me falling in love with Ina. And I do love her, Effie. She's true and loyal and dearer to me than anything in the world.'

2

Walter shut the front door. He took a deep breath, letting it out slowly in order to control his excitement.

Hitler ist ein Genie.

He certainly didn't speak these words or even consciously think them. Instead he felt them, deep in his heart. He stayed where he was, leaning against the heavily varnished wood of the door, and recalled, as he often did, his first meeting with Dieter Stein.

Stein was part of a team that had been handpicked by Hitler to train spies who were destined to become so deeply embedded within British society that their existence was to remain unknown even to Germany's military intelligence organisation, Abwehr. They were a secret within a world of secrets, reporting and responsible only to Hitler via a small group of trusted personnel.

Stein was a sadistic thug who Walter would grow to fear and hate, but he didn't know this at that initial encounter, when this stranger had started barking orders the instant they met.

'From now on you speak only in English, you think only in English, when you take a shit you do it in English and when you come your cry of ecstasy is in English.'

Walter smiled at the comment, a mistake he never made again. Despite Stein's vast bulk, he moved so fast there was no time to react and Walter doubled over from the force of the punch to his stomach. Stein reached down, grabbed his jacket and pulled him upright so that their faces were inches apart, forcing Walter to inhale his stale breath.

'I'm not joking!' he snarled. 'And if someone hits you in a fight then you swear at them in English!'

Walter was barely able to speak and desperate to prevent the tears he could feel forming. It took all of his willpower to reply.

'You ... fucking ... bastard.'

Stein grinned. It was the most frightening expression Walter had ever seen on a person. Yes, there was little doubt the man was a psychopath, but in the years following, Walter had been forced to admit that the thug knew his business. The advice he had driven into Walter was ingrained into his psyche and had no doubt helped to save his life on more than one occasion.

Walter forced his mind back to the present, to focus on the immediate issue – why were the British authorities giving hundreds of people a few weeks' notice to move off their land in a remote part of Scotland? He walked into his small study, pulled out a map of the Tarbat peninsula and laid it on the table.

The officials at the meeting that afternoon had announced that the land was needed for battle practice; Walter thought most people would simply accept the statement at face value. However, it didn't ring true to him. He felt sure there must be many more places around the country that could be used without causing such disruption. Feeding the population was a major problem and the British government wouldn't do anything that took so many farms out of action unless it was absolutely vital.

Walter knew the landscape intimately, but by marking out the boundaries he could more easily visualise the evacuation zone. Making some quick calculations, he estimated it consisted of around fifteen square miles. He slowly moved his finger backwards and forwards across the paper, trying to spot what it was that he was missing.

The nearby military airfields fell outside of the designated area. Yet all that remained was farmland, crofts, a few tiny hamlets and the village of Inver. There were plenty of fertile fields, but he couldn't see anything else of specific value.

Walter paced about the study as he went through various possibilities in his head. Unless the authorities planned to build a secret factory, why would they want somewhere so out of the way? He discounted the idea of a building of some sort.

A new airfield, much larger than the existing ones?

He stopped walking and stared at the map from the middle of the room, as if he might reveal the answer by sneaking up on it. The east coast consisted largely of cliffs and stony beaches. He had explored there many times, enjoying the sight of some of the few cliff-nesting house martins in the country.

Next, Walter's eyes were drawn to the yellow band of beach along the west coast between the fishing village of Portmahomack and the town of Tain. A section of this was included within the land to be vacated. He moved closer, his heart beating fast as he felt he was getting nearer to understanding an important piece of the puzzle.

He had placed a pencil at Balnabruach to mark the eastern boundary and a penny to the left of Inver, indicating the western edge. The yellow strip between seemed to beckon, swirling in front of his eyes as if it was real sand blowing in the wind. For a moment he felt slightly light-headed.

Walter stood on the verge of the secret, the one he had sacrificed so much of his life for, the one he would take personally back to the Führer, who would make him a hero throughout Germany. The answer was so near he could almost taste it, like the saltiness of the sea air on a windy day.

'The sea air,' he whispered, his words echoing the random thoughts in his head. 'The sea,' he repeated, as he focused on the large area of blue on the map. It came to him then, with such clarity that he didn't know why it hadn't been immediately obvious.

'Of course ... that's why they want us off the land.'

A slow smile spread across his face. He, Walter Möller, was going to unearth one of the greatest Allied secrets of the Second World War.

3

The Italian was big, but he wasn't an instinctive fighter and he staggered as Mirko's fist hit him again, the blood now running down his nose, joining that from his split lip. Mirko was enjoying himself and had no desire to hurry, so he let the man recover rather than finish him off too soon.

It was the same argument that had been going on since Italy's capitulation two months earlier. Until that point the eighty POWs at the Kildary camp had worked together with only the frictions and irritations that could be expected when men are forced to live in such a confined space.

The announcement at the beginning of September that Badoglio's government had effectively swapped sides and was now opposed to Germany had at first been dismissed by some as British propaganda. However, within days the details that had emerged on the radio and in newspapers forced even the most die-hard Mussolini supporters to accept the news was true.

And the revelations had split the camp. The majority were relieved to be out of the fighting and simply wanted the war to end so they could go home to their families. But about twenty were determined to remain loyal to Mussolini and arguments had soon flared up. Allegiances mattered. It quickly became apparent that there was no middle ground, you either whole-heartedly backed Il Duce or you were totally against him.

Men who had known each other for years found their friendships torn to shreds in acrimonious debates about not just the politics of the situation, but also the rights and wrongs of what they should do next. The atmosphere in the camp became so charged that some POWs changed huts; only the occupants of hut 3 were those who remained true to Il Duce's cause and Mirko was their leader.

He stepped closer to his opponent, disdainfully blocked a wild swing and punched him full in the face. His action was greeted by wild shouts of warning and encouragement from the large circle of POWs around them, the raw energy of which simply fuelled Mirko's desire for violence. The fight had begun almost immediately after the men had returned from clearing ditches, mending fences and other labour-intensive tasks. They hadn't even had time to clean up.

Only a handful stood in silence. One of them was eighteen-year-old Antonio 'Toni' Mario, something of a comedian who was always getting into one scrape or another. He understood that the men needed to let off steam. They'd been stuck in this cold, windy, desolate land for seven months and forced to eat, sleep, work and wash in unnaturally close conditions. Most of them hadn't been near a woman in years. It was no wonder they fought.

Toni and Mirko had been captured during the North African campaigns and later ended up in the same camp in Egypt. The much older man had subsequently looked out for him, once preventing a severe beating when an

21

aggressive brute took offence at the fact that Toni was pleased to have never fired his rifle before being captured.

One night in Egypt Mirko had revealed that he had a young brother of a similar age and he hoped there was someone protecting him too. Toni, taken aback by such candour, was very grateful, yet his loyalty was also tempered with wariness. As he watched Mirko brawling now, he suspected that the hardened brick-maker from Florence was fighting not because of his principles, but because he liked the sense of power that came from hurting people. He was good at it.

Toni looked over to where two British army privates, McIntosh and Atkinson, watched from the entrance to the administration hut. The POWs had learned to avoid Atkinson. The private wanted revenge for the death of his brother, who was killed during the spring in Italy. But he was stuck in this remote part of Scotland just as the Italians were, so he took every chance to make their lives as miserable as possible.

Toni returned his gaze to the centre of the ring and almost called over to Mirko. This one-sided volley of punches was barbaric. The other man seemed nearly unconscious, but at last he was saved from any further punishment when a British officer strode into view and ordered the two privates to put a stop to the disgraceful display and get the injured man seen to.

'Watch their eyes,' said Mirko later on. 'If you're facing a lumbering fool like that one you can be sure they'll give themselves away by glancing at where they intend to strike.'

Toni remained silent, amazed at how unmarked his

friend was. Mirko often tried to teach him the basics of fighting, but the advice was inevitably wasted. It had been the same during Toni's army training, when the sergeant had bellowed at him on the parade ground one day that he would be more effective turning his rifle around and beating the enemy with it. Toni hated violence, and he reckoned many in the camp felt the same, and lots of British and German soldiers too.

'Are you even listening to me?' Mirko snapped.

'Yes, I heard everything you said.'

'It doesn't bloody go in there, though, does it?' said Mirko, reaching over and knuckling Toni on the head, using significantly more force than necessary.

'Ouch!'

With a speed that took him completely by surprise, Mirko grabbed hold of Toni and lifted him across his shoulder as if he weighed little more than a child, then he started running around the hut.

'Hey! Has anyone seen Toni?' he shouted. 'I can't find him anywhere.'

'Put me down, you great fiorentino oaf.'

'Giorgio! Have you seen him?'

'No,' replied Georgio, laughing. 'What's that you've got?'

Mirko looked at Toni's backside, inches from his face.

'Oh, I've found his arse,' he said, slapping it with his free hand. 'It's the rest of him I've lost.'

Toni tried to lever himself upright by grabbing Mirko's belt. Instead, he suddenly felt a hard slap.

'Giorgio! Just you wait.'

Then Mirko started running again and soon all the men

in the hut were in uproar at the ludicrous sight. And Mirko and Toni were laughing the loudest because for those few brief moments they were simply friends messing around – they knew nothing of the events on Kirk Farm that would soon tear their relationship apart.

4

The atmosphere on the farm that evening was subdued. Only Hugh, who had not heard the news about the evacuation, chattered away as usual while Effie washed him in the old tin bath, which had been put in front of the fire in the living room.

'Fee,' Hugh said, using the name he'd called her since he was young. 'Will you make me another puppet?'

'Another one! You've already got hundreds... thousands... actually, I think you've got millions.' She stopped scrubbing his back, lifted his arm and washed underneath, which made him giggle. 'It's a wonder you can fit in your bedroom.'

'I don't have millions. There's space for one more.'

'It's funny how there's always space for one more.'

'Yes, but there is. I can show you where it would go.'

Effie had begun making these toys when she was a child and would write short dramas to perform with Ina in front of their parents and brother Duncan. At twenty-three, he was now in the army somewhere in England. The family hadn't seen him for months and hadn't heard much from him either.

'And who have you got in mind this time?' asked Effie.

Those that she made now usually represented a specific person. Hugh would then insist that she wrote a new story for the latest addition. The two sisters would get down behind the settee, as they did when they were young, moving the puppets along the top as everyone else watched from across the room.

'The minister.'

'The Reverend Smith? I'll have to include him in a play. Do you think he'll be happy with that?'

'It depends what you write.'

Effie dried Hugh, helped him into his pyjamas and dressing gown then took him upstairs. He slept in a tiny room and if he woke during the night he would usually pad along the corridor and end up squeezing between Effie and Ina in their shared double bed. The sisters thought it would be simpler to put him there in the first place, but their father insisted he should be in his own room. When Effie returned, Ina was in the bath.

'Hey, I was going to get in there!'

'The water was just sitting here going cold. Anyway, you can get in after me.'

'Thanks.'

'While you're there...' Ina held the soap in the air, indicating that she would like her back scrubbed.

Like almost everything else in their lives, soap was rationed. Once a sliver became too small it would be put in a jar and when there were sufficient Ina would stick them together to create a new bar of multi-coloured odds and ends.

The sisters were sick of the shortages. Almost all foodstuffs were rationed, along with everyday items from clothing to coal. Living on a farm meant they were better off than many as regards fresh food and there was plenty of wood for the fire, while their mother was a miracle worker in the kitchen and on the sewing machine.

However, there was a limit to the number of times a bit of ribbon or frill could be added to a faded dress to improve it and although neither sister was vain, they missed not being able to buy a new outfit more regularly. Their lives were dominated by the official coupons needed to buy products, while the government had reduced the clothes allowance more than once since the start of the war.

'What are you going to say to Christopher when he finally has the nerve to return?' asked Effie as she rinsed her sister's smooth back.

The officer hadn't been to the farm since that afternoon's meeting at Inver hall, so Ina had been unable to tackle him about his involvement in the evacuation. Effie could feel her smouldering with contained anger, and she didn't envy him their reunion. She didn't usually keep secrets from her sister, but she hadn't mentioned that she had cornered Christopher after the meeting.

'I'll ask him calmly and politely ...'

'Calmly and politely?'

'Yes. I'll ask if the evacuation was the reason he was sent here in the first place.'

'Then what?'

'I'll enquire ...'

'Still calmly?'

'Of course. I'll enquire whether it was actually his recommendation to use the Tarbat peninsula.'

'What if he says yes?'

Ina hesitated, her emotions clearly a whirlwind of conflict.

'I can't tell you what will happen in that case … you're too young to hear.'

★

By the time Christopher arrived, everyone had gone to bed apart from Mr Ross. The farmer, sitting in an old wicker chair pulled up close to the range, was smoking his pipe. When he inhaled, the bowl glowed red in the surrounding dimness; the only other light in the room came from two paraffin lamps.

In one corner Nip, the family Border collie, was asleep in his basket beside a large grandfather clock. The clock had been a wedding present from Mr Ross's parents and no one else was allowed to touch it. He always kept it five minutes fast, so the family should never be late for Sunday service.

Mr Ross heard the front door open and close, and a few moments later the officer appeared in the kitchen. He started slightly when he saw the farmer; it was obvious he'd hoped everyone would have gone to bed.

'Martha left some stew, but I doubt it'll be edible now.'

'That was kind of her. I'm sorry it's gone to waste.'

'Worse things have happened … especially today.' Mr Ross put his pipe down. 'For goodness sake, stop standing there in the doorway and get warmed up. It's wickedly cold outside.'

'I'm sorry about what's happened,' Christopher said, sitting at the table near to his host so that their voices wouldn't carry and he could benefit more from the heat.

'It's not your fault. You were only obeying orders. No one can expect anything else ... including Ina. She's planning to give you a roasting when you next meet. My advice is to stand up to her.'

'I think I'd rather be on the front line than face Ina's wrath.'

'It's only because she thinks so much of you,' said Mr Ross. 'You're decent and honourable, we all know that.' The last said as a warning as much as a compliment.

'I don't know if you've been told that military personnel based in Britain can apply for compassionate leave to help their families with the evacuation,' Christopher said, as a peace-making gesture after his apparent betrayal.

'Can they?' Mr Ross said. 'We would love to have Duncan back, even if it's just to help move us off the land.'

'If you like, I'll make a few enquiries. I might be able to get a message to him quicker than you.'

The two men talked amicably late into the night until the farmer decided it was time to turn in. Taking one of the paraffin lamps, the officer went to the bottom of the stairs and removed his shoes. He was using Duncan's bedroom and he knew that Mr Ross had given the family strict instructions that absolutely no one was allowed to enter. As Christopher climbed the last few steps he saw Hugh coming along the corridor. The boy had his eyes closed and didn't appear to realise that he was there. Christopher watched as Hugh went into his sisters' bedroom and quietly shut the door.

5

Despite the late night, Mr Ross woke early the next morning, as he did every day. The Ross family had owned the surrounding two hundred acres for generations. Over the years improvements and new ideas had been implemented gradually, but since Britain entered the war huge changes had been forced upon farms in a frantic effort to significantly increase food production.

Every strip of land had been brought into use and extensive ploughing had resulted in much greater mechanisation, although Kirk Farm still managed with its five Clydesdales. Everyone's favourite, Bertie, was rather old to work the fields but he could still pull a cart and was handy for short trips here and there.

Mr Ross was considering who he could contact to take in the horses for the period that they would be evicted as he went out with Nip to the field to fetch their two dairy cows. It was a twice-daily ritual and when he called their names the animals readily followed him to the shed for milking.

Martha appeared minutes later carrying a spotless enamel bucket, which she placed in position before straightening up to look at her husband over the top of the cow's back. It was one of those rare moments in the midst of farming life when they had the luxury of just stopping for a moment and doing nothing. He forced a smile, although he could feel that the sadness settled around his eyes and didn't go away.

'I remember the night Jessie was born,' he said, running his hand over the beast's broad neck.

'I was there, helping you deliver her.'

'Yes, and the three calves she's had since.'

'Don't forget the birth of Jessie's mother.'

'That was a bad time.' He sighed at the memory. 'We nearly lost both.'

Martha reached over and took his hand. They stood quietly, resting their arms on the cow, which waited patiently to be milked.

'We've seen a lot of life and death on the farm over the years,' she said.

'All the same, it's been a privilege to work the land.' He squeezed her strong fingers. 'I couldn't have done it without you.'

'And I'll be by your side when we return. We might not have a date but we will come back, Edward, one day. Then we'll buy what stock we need and start again. And when this dreadful war is over Duncan will come home to help run the place and you can start to take life a little easier.'

This time when he smiled the sadness left his face completely.

'Now that is a nice thought. And look at Hugh. He's got a real interest in every aspect. Some of his questions are so deep at times that it's hard to believe he's only seven.'

'Almost eight, as he likes to remind me. Effie is using

fabric from your old overalls to make him a pair. He'll look like a proper farmer and will be in his element.'

They laughed, relaxed and at ease in each other's company. He squeezed her hand again and was about to speak when Jessie mooed, reminding them that she was still waiting.

★

For the first time ever, Hugh was accompanied to school that morning by his father, who took the opportunity during the half-hour walk to explain that they would have to leave home for a while. Hugh wasn't the least concerned; in fact, he seemed pleased to learn that classes would cease the following Friday, so there would be three weeks' holiday before they left.

'Where will we live?' Hugh asked, as they turned into a lane bordered either side by tall hawthorn hedgerows.

'I don't know,' Mr Ross said with his usual honesty; he knew he had a fine line to tread between being open and not frightening his son. 'But you needn't worry. We'll be together until we return.'

He didn't mention that their entire livestock would go. He thought that sometimes it was kinder to impart information bit by bit and let the implications sink in gradually. The previous day the farmers at Inver hall had agreed to meet the relevant officials to discuss livestock issues and when Mr Ross entered the allocated classroom he found men from neighbouring farms already there. It didn't take long to decide that the cattle, sheep and pigs destined to be sold should be taken on three separate days to the Dingwall auction mart, an hour's drive away. Animals to be butchered would be sent to the slaughterhouse in Tain.

Some of the men present stressed that they wanted to keep their horses, although they knew how difficult it would be to find suitable homes locally. Most of the hens would end up in the cooking pot or be handed over to places outside the evacuation zone, on the understanding that when people returned there would be some support in restocking.

Mr Ross found it a lonely journey back to Kirk Farm without Hugh chattering by his side and he was glad of Nip's company. When they arrived his wife insisted that he sit in the kitchen while she made some tea and called in Ina and Effie. They were soon gathered around the table, eating scones, plain but still warm from the oven.

'So ... the cattle will be gathered from the designated area on Thursday and taken to Dingwall for sale the next day,' he said, relaying earlier conversations. 'The pigs will be taken on the Monday of the following week and the sheep two days after that. The horses will be the last to go.'

'Not Bertie!' said Effie.

'No, even if I have to pay for his stabling. But from what I heard this morning we may have to sell some of the others, despite their years of faithful service.'

Everyone simply assumed that Nip would go with them wherever they went, so his future was never in doubt. As they sat eating the last of their scones, even Effie struggled to find something to say that was positive or, in her eyes at least, helpful.

'I'm sorry, Father,' said Ina, eventually breaking the silent gloom they had fallen into.

'There's no time for sentiment,' he replied. 'It's going to be all hands on deck right up until the deadline. Apparently, the POWs will arrive tomorrow. Let's hope they can at least tell a cockerel from a cow.'

★

That evening the family sat quietly in the living room, Mr Ross smoking his pipe and throwing the occasional log on the fire. Ina and her mother were knitting and Effie was finishing off the overalls she'd been making. Hugh sat on a stool, cutting up a newspaper into squares and using a pencil to put a hole through the corner of each one.

'Fee.'

'Mmm?'

'Do you think I should make some squares larger?'

'What for?'

'People with bigger bottoms.'

The three women stopped what they were doing to stare at the boy. Mr Ross tried to hide his smile, but Effie simply dissolved into a fit of giggles and couldn't reply.

'And did you have anyone in mind?' asked Martha.

'Doctor Gray has a big bottom. If he used our dunny then these might not be the right size,' said Hugh, indicating the pile he had already threaded on to a length of string.

Ina, unlike her sister, tried to maintain a mature composure as the question had been a genuine one. However, when she spotted her father looking flushed as he

34

attempted not to laugh, she had to put both hands up to her face.

'I think you're on thin ice, young man,' said his mother, who was the only person not amused. 'Perhaps you would like some very small pieces?'

Hugh considered this as a serious possibility and his expression of deep concentration was too much for Mr Ross, who suddenly found that the fire needed a great deal of attention.

'No, I don't think so.'

'Here,' said Effie, trying to steer the conversation on to safer ground. 'Come and try these on.'

The newspaper squares forgotten, Hugh came over and was soon proudly showing off his new overalls. As his mother had predicted, they did indeed make him look like a proper farmer and the fact that they had been made out of material from a worn-out pair of his father's seemed to instil even more pride in the boy, who strutted around the room like a fashion model.

'Right, they're lovely, but it's way past the time when someone should be in bed,' said Martha, feeling that her son had had more than enough attention and praise for one evening. She put down her knitting and picked up the nearest paraffin lamp. Hugh gave everyone a hug and followed her upstairs.

'You've certainly made him happy,' said Ina. 'I can see it's going to be impossible to get him to wear anything else for weeks.'

Effie nodded in agreement, although didn't comment. She was already involved in the next project, selecting scraps of material to make a glove puppet representing the minister. It wasn't so easy, as her store had become ever more depleted over the last few years.

At her feet was the sewing box that Duncan had made for her sixteenth birthday. He had done the same for Ina when she reached that age so that his sisters, both skilled at a range of crafts, could each be more in control of what they made. At the time everyone had commented on what a very thoughtful gesture this was ... everyone except Martha, who had suggested the idea.

When she returned to the living room her husband was tuning the radio to catch the evening news. As ever, it was dominated by the war, along with information from the government outlining the latest advice on how to make supplies go further.

'If we make things go any further they'll be so out of sight we'll never see them again,' said Effie, without looking up from the material she was cutting.

'Maybe that's the idea,' said Ina. 'If you lose it, you can't use it.'

'I always knew there was a poet lurking somewhere behind that stern exterior.'

'Just you wait until you want to be warmed up in bed tonight ... I'll give you "stern exterior"!'

An item then came on the radio about Italy and the confusion over the position of prisoners of war held by Britain and its Allies. Italy's capitulation in September had created a situation to which there was no obvious solution and the Geneva Convention had no guidance about what to do when a country changed sides during a conflict.

The recently appointed Badoglio government had to be

granted some sort of new status after the change in allegiance, yet Italy couldn't suddenly become an ally, particularly when thousands of British servicemen remained captive on Italian soil, even if these POW camps were now manned by German soldiers.

'That business with Italy sounds like a mess,' said Martha, once the radio was turned off. She was unravelling wool from an old jumper and winding it into a fresh ball, from which she would make socks.

'It is, like most of war,' said her husband.

'You girls be careful when those men arrive tomorrow,' said Martha. 'Are you listening?' she said more sharply, when neither of her daughters replied.

'Yes, Mother,' said Effie. 'We must be careful with the Italians tomorrow.'

'And on every other day.'

'They're probably no different to Mr Romano and we've been buying his ice creams for years without any concerns for our safety,' said Effie.

'That's different, Mr Romano is Scottish,' said her mother, which made the sisters laugh.

'Take heed,' said Mr Ross, his tone making it clear that his daughters had to take the threat seriously. They had been brought up to be decent and respectable, but these young men had been away from home for years and ... Mr Ross didn't like to think any further about the implications. 'You will likely end up working side by side, sometimes having to show them what to do, but never let yourself be alone with them. You keep close to each other or you make sure that Alastair or I are nearby. Are you taking notice, Effie?'

'Yes,' said Effie, visibly bristling that her father had singled her out. Just because Ina was nearly three years older and had Christopher on a hook didn't mean that she was about to throw herself at the first foreigner to stroll on to the farm.

★

Later that night, Effie lay with her head on Ina's chest and her arm across her tummy as the sisters tried to get warm in bed. The upstairs of the house was so cold in winter that they always ended up cuddled into each other, their hot water bottles merely keeping the chill off their feet. It was no wonder Hugh so often came to join them.

'So, when do you think Christopher will ask you to marry him?' said Effie, in a belligerent mood after her father's lecture earlier that evening.

'Whatever makes you think he would ask such a ridiculous question?' said Ina.

'For goodness sake, it's so obvious how in love the two of you are that the rest of us can almost hear wedding bells.'

'There's nothing obvious about anything.'

'Considering you're the one who's meant to be endowed with boundless common sense, you certainly talk daft at times.'

'I do not! And don't you go making up such ... tales! Save your fanciful stories for Hugh and your puppets.'

They fell silent. In one ear Effie could hear Ina's heartbeat while in the other she heard the wind howling beyond the blackout curtain that hung across their bedroom window. The sounds were so utterly conflicting that she was fascinated by their contrast. For the last week the temperature had been dropping daily, warning of the approach of winter. She had thought that their conversation was over, when Ina spoke once more.

'Do you think he might ask?'

Effie laughed and pulled her sister closer in the darkness.

6

Ina, Effie and Hugh watched as the army truck trundled along the drive towards the house. They could see about a dozen Italians on board and when the vehicle stopped the two soldiers at the back jumped down and read out the names of six men who, almost reluctantly, disembarked and stood around staring at the unfamiliar surroundings.

The soldiers resumed their positions as one of the Home Guards in the cab got out before the truck turned about and set off to drop men at the next farm. The sisters looked with surprise at the man who walked over. It was Mr Lawson, a retired schoolteacher.

'Hello Ina, Effie, Hugh,' he said cheerfully. 'Well, here are the POWs from the camp. Most of them are just lads. You won't get any trouble, although I don't know how much work you'll get either. I'll stay until they're collected this afternoon and returned to Kildary.'

'Crikey, what a bunch,' said Ina. 'A sudden gust would blow the whole lot over.'

'To be frank I think you might have been better with half a dozen land girls,' said Mr Lawson with a nod.

'I should let Father know,' said Ina. 'He's in the top field.'

Her departure left them all standing about, uncertain what to do. Hugh tugged on Effie's dungarees and when she bent down he whispered in her ear. His sister straightened up, looking at him in mock horror.

'Please,' he said.

Effie paused to consider her brother's suggestion, then walked over to the Italians.

'Does anyone speak English?' she said loudly, as if expecting that their hearing might be defective in some way. One of them stepped forward.

'My name is Antonio Mario. Everyone calls me Toni.'

The young man removed his cap, saying something to his comrades as he did so. They followed his example and when he bowed so did they. Hugh, standing beside his sister, started to giggle.

'Each group has one person who can translate for the others,' said the Italian.

Effie was so fascinated by his beautiful smile and kind eyes that it took her several seconds to regain her thoughts.

'Right, well you can't hang about doing nothing,' she said as she set off briskly. 'Come with me.'

'Get going lads,' urged Mr Lawson when they hesitated. 'It's not me who'll be telling you what to do on the farm.'

They caught up with Effie, as she arrived at a pen where several pigs were happily rooting around, entirely oblivious to the sudden audience.

'Toni, I want you to move that pig,' said Effie, pointing, 'into the building over there.'

'That one?' Toni confirmed in dismay.

'Yes.'

'He's very big.'

'It's a sow.'

'Is that bad?'

'You shouldn't have any difficulty. The secret to getting her to do what you want is to … sing.'

'Sing?'

'Love songs.'

'I don't know any English love songs.'

'No matter. It's the sentiment that counts.'

Toni turned to his comrades and spoke in rapid Italian, gesturing at the huge sow as he did so. There was a lot of muttering and shaking of heads, but after a few moments he handed his coat to the man next to him and gingerly stepped over the low wall.

'Does it bite?' he asked Effie.

'Only when hungry. Oh, and she likes you to tickle her behind the ear.'

'Now I think you're pulling my foot.'

The pigs began to sense this was someone they didn't know and started to shift nervously. Toni moved closer, then took a deep breath. For a moment everyone was stunned by the rich, deep quality of his voice. However, when the Italians realised he was actually serenading the massive, muddy sow they roared with laughter and lined up along the wall to watch and shout encouragement, any apprehension forgotten completely.

Toni walked slowly towards his target. Hugh had to hang on to his sister to stay on his feet, while it required an enormous effort for Effie to maintain her composure. Suddenly Toni made a dash and the pigs scattered either side, leaving him alone and surprised at his failure.

Undeterred, he rushed forward again, dodging left and

42

right every time the selected animal looked as though she might go in that direction. Then he dived, wrapping his arms around her neck before being dragged along the ground. Ear-piercing squeals competed with hysterical shouts from the spectators. The sow's body inexorably slipped through Toni's hands until he was hanging on to one short leg, then that too was gone, leaving him sprawled face down.

'Oh no,' whispered Effie, realising that the joke had gone too far.

'What on earth is going on here?'

Everyone turned.

Mr Ross was striding towards them with Ina close behind. He surveyed the scene, his face flushed with increasing anger, as Toni slowly stood up, staring at his uniform with disbelief. It was clear that he'd never been so dirty in his whole life.

'Effie?'

'I'm sorry, Father,' she said. 'It was just a bit of fun.'

'We don't have time for fun. I need these men working and I won't have a man spending his entire day covered in filth. Take him to the tap then fetch him some overalls. As you think it's so funny you can clean his clothes.'

Effie looked completely crestfallen and her father couldn't help but regret his harsh response. He would never admit it, not even to his wife, but Effie was his favourite child. And, as the good Lord knew, there was enough misery without him adding to it.

'Make sure you do a proper job,' he said still stern before giving a huge wink only for her and turning to the Italians.

'They don't speak English,' Hugh told him.

'Don't worry, son. They'll understand well enough. You lot,' he said pointing his finger back and forward across the group, 'this way.' He jerked his thumb in the opposite direction and they followed him without a murmur. After a brief hesitation the Home Guard set off after them.

The entertainment over, Hugh strolled off to play on the tractor tyre that hung from a rope on the horse chestnut tree. After a moment's consideration, Ina walked back to the house, leaving Effie and Toni looking at each other in silence over the wall.

'I'm sorry ... about your uniform.'

'I'm sorry you got into trouble.'

'That's all right. My father's not really angry with me. It's just that we have to leave the farm and it's very upsetting.'

'Where will you go?'

'We don't know. But you're here to help get everything ready.'

They fell silent once more, with neither of them making any attempt to move. While they remained they were alone and each of them felt a desire to see what might happen. The sow that had caused so much amusement moved near to Effie, so she reached down and scratched it behind the ear.

'It's leg,' she said.

'I'm sorry?'

'You said that I was pulling your foot. What you meant is "pulling your leg".'

'Oh ... thanks.'

'Although ... it was really the pig ... that had her leg pulled.'

The situation suddenly seemed overwhelmingly ridiculous. Effie found herself laughing uncontrollably, her joy utterly unrestrained, and she soon had to put a hand on the wall to steady herself. Toni watched with a mixture of bemusement and sheer delight on his face. Then he laughed too, until tears streamed down his cheeks and he had to join her at the wall.

'You smell awful.'

'Mirko won't want to sleep in the next bed to me tonight,' he said, reaching down to scratch the pig behind her other ear. 'This beast is smiling. I never knew a pig could look so happy.'

'Come on. Let's get you cleaned up.'

When Effie emerged from the house Toni was standing by the outside tap in his underwear, dripping wet and shaking with cold.

'You'll catch your death,' she gasped. 'Use this sacking to get dry. It's clean. I've brought you a pair of my brother's old trousers plus a jumper and some overalls.'

Once he was dry, Effie handed him the items one by one. As he put them on she couldn't stop herself from admiring his body. He had a narrow, sculpted build – well proportioned and a lot stronger than he had appeared in the ill-fitting uniform, which now lay on the ground waiting for her attention.

'Why does your uniform have red circles?' Effie asked, having noticed earlier that there was a large circle on the back of the jacket, with a smaller one on the outside of one arm and one leg.

'So people can see we are prisoners of war,' he replied. 'The material underneath is cut away to prevent anyone from removing the target discs.'

'Target discs?'

'That's their other purpose. They make it easier for British soldiers to shoot us if we try to escape.'

★

There was a gentle knock at Christopher's bedroom door.

'Just a minute,' he called, putting the folder of documents he'd been studying into a leather briefcase. Quickly he closed and locked it, before placing the case at the bottom of the wardrobe. The key went on top.

He opened the door to find Ina pacing up and down the corridor. All of the pent up frustration, the angry phrases and accusations Ina had rehearsed in her head, evaporated in an instant upon seeing him. She threw herself into his arms and he held her tightly.

'I'm sorry,' he said. 'I've been so busy with the army camp and ...'

'Shhh,' she said. 'I know.'

'I wish there had been another way.'

'It's not your fault. People have to make all sorts of sacrifices, much worse than this.'

'I've hated keeping a secret from you, but at least one good thing has come out of all this.'

'What?'

'Can't you guess?'

But before Ina could reply his lips were upon hers in a passionate kiss and she felt herself melting into his arms. These feelings were still so new to Ina. Christopher was the first man she'd ever kissed, mainly thanks to the watchful eyes of parents, members of the kirk and the community at large. Ina had always known that any perceived transgression would be reported far and wide with astonishing speed and that retribution from their father would be equally swift.

But the truth was there had never been any local men whom Ina wanted to spend time with. On the few occasions when she'd gone with Effie to the Saturday night dance they usually spent the evening dancing together.

When Christopher eventually pulled back, Ina buried her head into his chest. They had so little opportunity for privacy that they didn't move for several minutes.

'Will you leave,' she asked, 'now this decision has been made?'

'You don't get rid of me that easily.'

'I don't want to get rid of you,' she said, looking up at him.

'I'll stay at least until everyone has been moved safely out of the area. After that I could be sent anywhere.'

'How I wish this dreadful war was over,' she murmured. 'There seems to be no end in sight.'

'The sacrifice everyone is making in the Tarbat peninsula is vitally important in helping to make the end come sooner.'

'Christopher, now you sound like a politician.'

'Oh no, that bad? There's only one way to stop that.'

And then a kiss more passionate than the last marked the end of their conversation.

7

Mr Ross was struggling to explain that underneath the large mound of earth in front of him was a pile of potatoes. Nearby was a machine that consisted of a hopper with a long conveyor belt, at the end of which two empty hessian sacks hung limply from round metal hoops. As Effie and Toni came into view, the Home Guard, standing beside the farm's outdoor weighing scales, raised his eyes at the sight of an Italian in civilian clothes, but he remained quiet and let the farmer take the lead.

'About time!' Mr Ross exclaimed. 'Can this man explain to the others what we need to do?'

His daughter looked at the POWs, then picked up a spare potato graip.

'Right,' she said and showed them the rounded prongs of the graip, designed to reduce the risk of damage to the crop. 'When we gather potatoes we store them by digging out some earth and putting a layer of straw over the depression we've made, then we pile the potatoes on top to make the shape of a cone and cover them with more straw before shovelling earth over the whole lot to seal it.'

Toni looked at her in total disbelief.

'This is not like singing to the pig, is it?'

'No, it's not, and if your men don't get to work soon my father is going to be angry. Now, you need to explain to your friends that if they watch me I will show them what they have to do.'

Toni did his best to give a running commentary in Italian while Effie carefully removed the soil from a small area of the mound. She could feel the men's eyes on her as she worked.

'Have they understood?' Mr Ross suddenly asked, aware too of the Italians' appraisal of his daughter.

Toni questioned his comrades and was greeted with enthusiastic nods.

'Yes, sir. They're very understanding.'

'Thank the Lord. There's been enough time lost this morning.'

The men were given tools and they began to remove the soil and pull away the straw. Once it appeared that everyone knew what they were doing Mr Ross went off to check on the cattle, leaving Alastair, his two daughters and the Home Guard with the POWs.

'So, I take it you want to be a farmer when the war is over?' Effie asked Toni as he worked next to her.

'A farmer? No, I want to build cabinets.'

'A cabinetmaker?' said Effie, slightly surprised that he was decided on such a specific career. Her future felt so vague.

'My father is a joiner and I love anything to do with wood. My uncle Luis is a cabinetmaker and that's what I want to do. But this war means I have lost the years when I would normally have been learning my craft. Who knows when I will return to Italy and what I will find when I get there.' Toni sighed, pulling away some straw before he went on.

'I might be an old man before I have learned my trade. Yet I'm fortunate to have the chance to grow old ... so many are dead before their lives are begun. I will always be grateful to at least reach my aim.'

Effie was taken aback at such honesty and the depth to this handsome Italian. She had already witnessed his outwardly cheeky, personable nature, but she now wondered about the rest, the man underneath.

'And what about you?' he asked. 'Will you become a farmer?'

'Me? I'm not sure. I was almost fourteen when war broke out and since then I've spent most of my time helping my parents. I never saw this as my future. My older brother, Duncan, will eventually run Kirk Farm.'

'What do you want to do, in your heart?'

'Goodness, you don't waste any time.'

'Waste time?'

'You get straight to the point.'

'That's partly because I'm Italian.'

'What's the other part?'

'Seeing friends die.'

They looked at each other for a long moment in silence, as if no one else was around, and an understanding passed between them before they continued.

It didn't take long before there was a sufficiently exposed area for Alastair to start the small petrol engine that drove the conveyor. Effie asked Toni to tell two men to stand with her and Ina on either side of the belt and observe what they did. After several minutes of instruction and arm waving to the other POWs, Alastair started to feed the contents of the pile into the hopper and seconds later this emerged on the belt.

Ina and Effie deftly removed stones and damaged potatoes as they moved along the conveyer and the two Italians soon joined in. When she was confident they were proficient, Effie went to the end of the line where the first sack was filling up. Once this reached a certain level she pushed across the wooden slat to divert the potatoes into the other sack and got the full one carried to the scales to check it was the required hundredweight.

After about fifteen minutes, Alastair handed over the task of loading the hopper so that he could oversee the 'dressing' and help move and weigh full sacks. The men fell into a rhythm, taking away earth and straw, filling the hopper, removing unwanted items and carrying full sacks to the scales.

'Come with me,' Effie told Toni, before setting off briskly towards the farm buildings.

'I still don't understand everything we're doing,' he said, once he had laid down his graip and caught up with her. He was amazed at how she would make an apparently snap decision and then set off so quickly to do whatever she had thought of.

'We produce mainly seed potatoes, which are sold to farms in England for them to plant and grow their own crop,' she explained. 'They're transported by train, but the wagon won't be at the station until Monday so we have to put the sacks in the storage shed for now. That means we're going to see Bertie.'

'Who's Bertie?'

'You'll find out,' she said, smiling.

A short while later they were standing in the barn by the stall of a Clydesdale, its sleek black coat a complete contrast to its legs, which were pure white from the knees down.

'It's a horse!' Toni exclaimed. 'A big, beautiful horse!'

'See how much you've already learned? We'll make a farmer of you yet.' Effie laughed. 'He's worked this farm since I was a baby and may be a bit past his best, but we love him,' she said, stroking the horse's muscular neck. 'Now we need to hitch Bertie to the bogie.'

'That doesn't sound nice,' said Toni, as he watched her, liking her natural affinity with the livestock as well as her pleasing figure beneath the rough dungarees she wore.

'Fixing the horse to the cart ... the former in front of the latter.'

Effie led Bertie outside and over to one of the carts, then demonstrated how to fix the harness and traces. Toni was interested in how the beast and the wooden structure came together to form one harmonious entity and Effie answered his many questions with an impressive confidence.

'Come on, we get to ride back to the field.'

He got up beside her on the seat and with a flick of her wrist they set off to join the others.

'You're skilled at this,' he said, squashed up agreeably next to her.

'Well, I can't take all the credit. Bertie knows where to go. I bet if he could speak he would tell you that we're going to fetch potatoes.'

'Imagine if the animals could speak? Wouldn't that be something?'

'They would certainly have a few tales,' said Effie

chuckling, and when Toni didn't get the joke she laughed even more.

The downside of their journey was that it was only a few minutes before they stopped by the sacks lined up next to the scales. Ina had sealed the tops with binder twine, creating a lug in the corners to make handling easier.

'Now comes the hard bit,' said Effie, getting down. 'Let's get this lot loaded and when we've got enough we'll take them to the storage shed.'

'Where we'll unload them,' said Toni.

'I knew you were quick,' she said, smiling at him.

*

Food was nearly always eaten in the fields where people were working and around mid-morning Martha walked over from the house with a tray on which there were an assortment of glasses and jugs of milk. She was followed by Hugh, who was carrying, with great concentration, a large plate piled high with a mound of homemade bread and rhubarb jam.

'I thought you might need some refreshments.'

The men put down their tools and Ina began filling the glasses, which Effie handed out. Hugh stood to one side, unsure of what to do.

'Toni, tell everyone to take a slice,' said Effie.

Martha couldn't help noticing the casual, friendly way that her daughter addressed the Italian who, she had spotted, was wearing some of Duncan's clothes.

'I wondered why there was a dripping prisoner of war uniform hanging in my kitchen.'

'He had an accident in the pigsty,' replied Effie, still handing out drinks. 'Father said I had to clean his uniform so he needed something else to wear.'

Her mother made no further comment, although Effie knew that didn't mean she wasn't thinking about what she had just heard. Their father dominated so much of their lives, but it was their mother who was the quiet observer and, Effie suspected, the one who analysed situations more deeply.

The Italians formed a second line in front of Hugh and each took a piece of bread off the plate, which he was holding up high in front of himself. They made a big show of thanking him – in Italian and English – and one or two saluted, which made Hugh beam with pride. The Home Guard laid his rifle against the earth mound and walked over with Alastair.

'Good morning Mr Lawson, Alastair,' said Martha, as the two men greeted her. 'How is your Dorothy, Mr Lawson? I haven't seen her in quite a while.'

People sat around eating and chatting. Hugh was soon in an animated conversation with a couple of POWs, none of them seeming in the least bothered by the fact that neither side knew what the other was saying. When everyone had been served, Ina and Effie stood together eating their bread and watching the scene.

'I never thought I would see a sight like this on Kirk Farm,' said Ina.

'And it's only the first morning. Goodness knows what the coming weeks will bring.'

'You seem to be getting on rather well with the good-looking one who you got covered in pig manure.'

'Do you think he's good-looking? I hadn't noticed. Anyway, he's the only one who speaks English, so don't go making something out of nothing.'

'Just because he's wearing Duncan's clothes, don't forget what Father said last night; he's the enemy.'

'Toni's not the enemy,' Effie protested. 'He's gentle. There's no harm or malice in him. You can see it in his eyes. He would rather be at home crafting objects out of wood.'

'Just be careful.'

'Williamina! And you go on about my imagination. Shh now, here comes Father and he doesn't look happy.'

Mr Ross had been moving the sheep with Nip and he now came striding across the field expecting to see men hard at work. Instead he saw them sitting around laughing and eating, the potato dresser silent and Bertie standing idle. As he reached the group Ina and Effie rushed up to him.

'Here you are, Father, you must be thirsty,' said Ina, almost forcing a glass of milk into his hand.

'And hungry,' said Effie shoving a slice of bread into the other. 'Why don't you come and sit down while you eat?'

'And we'll gather everything up so that the men can start again.'

They had each taken an arm, as if he was elderly and needed to be steered to a comfortable spot. He knew well what they were up to, but still his irritation dissipated as quickly as it came. How had he ever played a part in creating two such extraordinary young women?

'I think I better sit down,' he said. 'Otherwise the shock of my daughters being so attentive might be too much for me.'

Effie told Toni to get the men back to work and the POWs

returned their glasses to Martha. A couple of the Italians helped the Home Guard to his feet as the cold weather was affecting his bad hip. It was apparent from the morning's good-natured banter that the retired schoolteacher had got to know these particular POWs quite well over the previous months.

'There you are, Mr Lawson,' Toni said as he brought over his rifle.

'Thanks, son. Now you better get the lads going smart-like.'

The men resumed their various tasks and Mr Ross, refreshed and in a happier frame of mind, set off to check on a calf that he was concerned about. Effie, currently helping to clear more earth from the potato pit, decided that she had to tackle a subject, but she was unsure how to approach it with any degree of tact.

'Toni, just so that you know, the dunny is around the back of the house.'

'The ... dunny?'

'Well, if you or your men need ... you know ...'

'I'm sorry. I don't understand.'

Ina, near enough to overhear, stopped work to follow the conversation.

'Go on little sister, I can't wait to hear this explanation.'

'If you have a call of nature,' said Effie, doing her best to ignore Ina's amusement.

'Call of nature?'

'Toni ... I'm talking about ... if you need to ... manure.'

'Manure!' cried Ina. 'Euphemia, you're priceless!'

'Priceless indeed!' Alastair spluttered, joining in with Ina's laughter.

'Alastair,' Effie called, her face burning with embarrassment, 'you should be doing this.'

'Sorry, I can't help ... it's not my business.'

Alastair's comment reduced Ina to near hysterics, which attracted the attention of a growing number of Italians.

'Oh, for goodness sake! Put that down and come with me.'

Effie matched off and after a moment's hesitation Toni laid down the graip and followed. They went around the house and headed towards a small shed, partly hidden by bushes. She stopped a few yards away.

'There ... the dunny! If you're out in the fields then there are plenty of bushes, but if you're near the house and have to do something ... substantial, then you use the dunny.'

Toni looked at the shed, his face a mask of confusion. He raised his hands and shook his head.

'God grant me patience!'

Effie wasn't certain if he was making fun of her or if he wasn't as bright as she had thought. Both possibilities irritated her enormously. She strode over, grabbed the handle and yanked open the door, standing to one side so that he would be able to see the wooden bench with a hole.

'Now do you understand?'

Toni looked into the gloom with an expression of increasing horror.

'Well, whatever you do in Italy it surely can't be *that* different!' said Effie in exasperation, glancing, for the first time, inside.

'There's more than enough of a draught comes under that door without you opening it!' a voice shouted.

'Mother!'

After a moment of frozen inactivity, Effie slammed the door, took hold of Toni's arm and frogmarched him away.

'You didn't see anything.'

'No.'

'Anything you did see, you will forget immediately.'

'Believe me, I'm trying.'

'And ...'

Effie stopped, bent over and put her hands on her knees; for the second time that day she was utterly helpless with laughter. Toni sat down on a nearby rock and put his head in his hands. His twitching limbs indicated that his attempts to control his own laughter were unsuccessful. It wasn't long before Effie joined him, sitting next to him as naturally as she would have done to Ina.

'I'm sorry,' said Effie, wiping away tears. 'That was so embarrassing I don't know what to say. Goodness knows how I'm going to explain that to my mother ...'

Toni looked at her through his own tear-filled eyes. 'I've seen some sights since joining the army' he said, 'but I think that was perhaps the most frightening.'

It was a long while before they could risk returning to the others and the waiting sacks of potatoes.

8

Walter stared for a long while at his reflection in the mirror. Recently, he had found himself increasingly looking back, recalling periods when his life had been real. He was thinking now about his childhood, and the catastrophe that occurred when he was six. Without any warning, at least to him, his parents had split up and his Dutch mother had taken him to Scotland to stay with a cousin who lived just outside Dundee.

The woman was married to a Church of Scotland minister and they both seemed ancient. Walter was told to call them Aunt Iris and Uncle Jack. He was a clever, sporty boy and quickly adapted to the local school, but his new home was dominated by Bible study, Sunday services and remaining quiet during the endless church meetings held in the crumbling, draughty manse.

Then there was the other catastrophe – when he was twelve and his mother died of influenza. Walter was grateful for the kindness of Aunt Iris, who yearned to take on the responsibility for bringing him up, but he secretly felt wretched about his future. In 1925, shortly after his thirteenth birthday, his father had appeared unexpectedly and announced he was taking his son away.

His father spoke excellent English and that evening Walter had listened intently from the top of the stairs to the heated argument in the kitchen between the three adults. The next morning Walter was told to pack a bag, taking only items he wanted and which couldn't be replaced. He had been surprised at feeling so upset to be leaving the aunt and uncle who had become such a large part of his family. It was a sad farewell, without even the opportunity to say goodbye to friends and classmates.

By lunchtime Möller was sitting opposite his son as the train pulled out of Dundee station. It was the beginning of their journey, one not only of distance but of discovery. Walter's memories of this long-absent parent were those of a small child and had become hazy over the passage of time; playing football and games of chess, bedtime stories, a few trips to the countryside.

Möller, for his part, remembered a lively little boy full of fun and curiosity. He studied the older version and was pleased. Here was a good-looking youth who had the makings of a striking, well-built man. His son was quiet, but that was understandable. Möller knew there was plenty of time to mould him into the person he wanted.

It was during their second day of travelling, when they were alone in the corner of a café, that Möller announced they were on their way to his home in Berlin.

'Father, I thought we were going to Holland.'

'What gave you that idea?'

'I heard you tell Aunt Iris and Uncle Jack.'

'No, you didn't.'

'I did!'

Möller held up his hand.

'I can see that you're a good boy, Walter, bright and respectful. But you have to leave your boyhood behind and start thinking like an adult. From now on, listen carefully to everything I say, whether it's to you or someone else. What I said was that you had more relatives in Holland and it would provide a better environment than Scotland in the coming years. Both points are true. I never said we were going to Holland. They assumed that to be the case ... as did you.'

'But why not just tell them you were taking me to Germany?'

'Because I would have encountered a great deal more resistance and I didn't have time to waste arguing,' his father told him. 'If you want to persuade people to believe something and need to create a false perception to achieve that aim, then it's always more effective to do it without telling a lie.'

Walter paused, struggling to take this in. 'And what will I do in Berlin?'

'You will become a German who will make me proud, who will make your country proud,' his father declared. 'Germany will once again be a great nation. The people were betrayed by the authorities at the end of the war. After our huge sacrifices, all the lives lost, we were sold down the river. That will not happen again. The next time there will be a very different outcome and we will gain our rightful place in the world.'

Möller's voice rose as if giving a speech, and as he realised this he stopped suddenly, visibly calming himself, but not before Walter had glimpsed a side to his nature that he suspected was normally carefully hidden. His words

61

showed a passion and vision both frightening and exciting.

'Germany will need strong men to guide it along the path to its rightful destiny,' his father said in a quiet tone. 'For now, you need to finish your tea and we must continue our journey. There is a long road ahead.'

★

With an effort, Walter brought his mind back to the present. He followed the progress of the war from the radio and newspapers in as much detail as possible, yet always analysed the information to try to differentiate propaganda from truth, to see beyond the gloss put on bad news. He knew that the British were good at making disasters appear like successes, or taking a small gain and promoting it as a major victory.

However, there was no denying that the pendulum of fate had swung against Germany and the continued build-up of American soldiers in the UK could only mean that Britain and its Allies were planning to send an army to the continent. Walter knew that to have any hope of success the numbers would have to be colossal, far too many to transport by means other than the Royal Navy. This meant landing men and equipment, and to do that they needed to practise.

Walter had been a keen student of military tactics and now he felt certain that once residents had been moved out of the Tarbat peninsula, the British Army and Navy would use the beach to the west of Portmahomack to practise transferring large numbers of soldiers and machines from ships to land.

Walter thought it extremely unlikely that such an invasion of continental Europe could take place during the winter months, which meant the spring of 1944 would provide the earliest possibility. For the moment, though, the date was unimportant. The big question was where on the French or Belgian coast would the British attempt to land? Without that detail anything Walter had discovered so far was useless. The German high command would be expecting such a move to be made and he couldn't tell them a single thing they didn't already know.

Walter glanced at his watch and realised he would have to get ready. It wouldn't look good to be late for the morning service. Since the start of the war congregations throughout the country had increased steadily and these days most Sunday services were well attended, regardless of the denomination. Conflict, of any sort, brought people together. The news about the eviction four days earlier would have the pews overflowing. At least he didn't have to worry about finding a seat. Walter walked over to the dresser and picked up his clerical collar.

9

'We have endured many hardships over these last few years. So many of our brothers and sons, fathers and nephews have gone to war and some, tragically, will never return. And now we must face another challenge, one that none of us expected.' Walter spoke in a clear, commanding voice; the actor who coached him would have been proud.

'The authorities want our homes and land. We can be sure that this decision is vital to our success against the evil of Nazi Germany. What we do here over the coming weeks will, I know, help those men fighting so far from home.

'Some of the farmers in our community have spoken to me about their unhappiness at working on the Sabbath, as planned from next weekend when the Home Guard has arranged the necessary manpower. But please know that the Lord understands. Without extra effort it will be impossible to process all of the gathered crops. Britain needs that food and God would not expect us to be even hungrier because we have not worked on those few Sundays.

'Italian prisoners of war have been brought over from

the Kildary camp to provide extra manpower. A few of you have expressed unease at this, but let us not forget that these men are the brothers and sons, fathers and nephews of their families back in Italy.

'We should welcome them. In life, we are not always able to show kindness to the ones we love, but we are faced every day with the opportunity to demonstrate it to others. Such acts will not go unnoticed; they are not without consequences. A kind act begets another in turn, just as an evil act perpetuates hate and a desire for revenge. This war has shown us too much of that.'

Walter paused. He knew that the congregation listened to him intently. When he'd first been told that he would train for the Church, Walter had almost laughed, pointing out that he had no religious feelings whatsoever. The reply had been that such sentiments would only distract him from his true purpose.

Yet Walter didn't feel that he was a hypocrite as he stood in the pulpit looking at the sea of faces before him. He spoke his words with truth and he cared about his flock. After all, these were ordinary people who just wanted to go about their lives, working hard and watching their children grow, no different to families in Germany. There were a few men among them that he would even call friends.

But a man can only be loyal to one master and Walter had never wavered in his utter belief in the person who had visited his father's Berlin apartment that evening in 1930. It was a meeting that changed the course of his life. And Walter believed that the lives of people in Britain would be enriched by the guidance of Germany, its culture, its political systems and language. They simply needed to be shown the way.

'Let us pray,' he intoned and everyone bowed their heads.

The Ross family had their own pew, but Ina and Effie sat at the organ near the entrance. Although they would never dare to be openly disrespectful, the sisters always managed to enjoy a great deal of entertainment in their sheltered position. When the minister announced the next hymn, Ina played a few bars while everyone found the correct page. Effie let one verse go by and as the second began she reached over and turned the music upside down.

'Put that back!'

'You don't need it. Following the notes stifles your performance. Just feel the music, Ina!'

'I'll stifle you if you don't turn it the right way around.'

No one could hear the girls above the sound of singing and Effie started to laugh. Ina, still playing flawlessly, only held on to her indignation for a few moments longer before she too started laughing.

When the service ended, the Reverend Smith stood at the kirk door and thanked everyone for attending, shaking the men's hands and patting children on the head.

'Thank you for speaking about farmers working on the Sabbath, reverend,' said Mr Ross when he drew level. 'I don't like it, but it's going to be tight even with the POWs.'

'How are they shaping up?'

'So far I've only had a half day's work out of them, but they seem decent enough lads. However, there's only one who speaks English and if you ask him to fetch a potato graip he's likely to come back with a hay fork and stab himself with it on the way.'

'Don't tell anyone, but I'm not sure I'd do much better!'

Mr Ross moved outside to join Martha and Hugh as they talked to a few neighbours. Their conversation, dominated by the evacuation, was being repeated among every other small group as people caught up with each other.

The minister had gone back inside when Christopher arrived.

'Reverend Smith, I must apologise for missing the service.'

'Captain Armstrong, please don't worry,' he assured him. 'I'm sure you have many urgent matters to attend to. God will always know what's in your heart.'

'Actually, I was hoping we could speak in private.'

'Of course. Let's go to the vestry. I could do with a cup of tea, although I'm afraid it'll be rather weak.'

The two men sat opposite each other in the tiny room. The minister, at thirty-one, was only three years older than the officer and over the previous months they had developed a relationship that remained formal, but which was close enough for them to enjoy the other's company.

Christopher put his mug on top of the floor-standing safe, which he knew was used to hold the kirk documents and communion plate, along with whatever personal papers the current minister might want stored.

'Thank you for your time, reverend.' Christopher paused. 'The thing is ... I'd like to ask Ina to be my wife and I'm not sure of the best way to go about it.'

'Ina Ross? Well, she's a striking girl and has a lovely

nature,' the minister said approvingly. 'Does she feel the same for you?'

'I know she feels strongly – whether it's enough to want to marry me I won't know until I ask her.'

'Goodness. This certainly makes a pleasant change from the usual questions I get asked. You don't need me to tell you that Edward Ross is a man of the old school in every sense.'

'Yes, I've had to tread rather carefully in my attentions towards his daughter.'

'Hah, I'm sure you have. And what does he think of you?'

'His son Duncan is a private in the army, so that helps. I don't think he'd be against me as a son-in-law, although he will probably want us to wait until the war is over.'

'There's a lot to be said for taking that course of action. What will you do once this evacuation has taken place?'

'Well, the new army camp is almost complete and the first men will arrive next week, so my involvement there is nearly over. Once the civilians have left the area I'll be posted elsewhere.'

The minister's mind was racing as he tried to work out a line of questions that might reveal something useful, while avoiding asking something that was too unconnected. The officer was sharp and a strange query might puzzle him, and that would lead to suspicion. He silently cursed himself for his present lack of inspiration.

'I think you need to get her father on your side,' he said eventually. 'Respectfully say that you would like to ask for his daughter's hand in marriage, but you're not expecting this to happen immediately. However, try not to get pinned down to waiting until after the war. If you can get Mr Ross's approval, while keeping the timescale flexible, then I reckon your way is clear. And good luck.' He raised his mug and Christopher returned the gesture. 'I'll say a prayer for you.'

'Thanks.' The two men chinked mugs. 'I might need it.'

10

As the local minister, Walter visited the POW camp on a regular basis. Not all of the Italians were Catholic or even religious and Walter was good at appealing to all sorts of people, regardless of their beliefs. He could be gentle with children and those near the end of their lives, yet he was also a man who could converse and connect with the roughest in the community.

He was always careful to appear even-handed, never spending more time with one POW over another and not to be obviously seeking out the company of anyone in particular. However, for months he had been grooming Mirko, who reminded him so much of Stein... a brute, but a clever brute and one who was fanatically loyal to the cause in which he believed.

Mirko was the only person Walter had hinted to that there was more to him than his role as a minister. Nothing had been said that could not be brushed off as a misunderstanding should the need arise, but Walter was certain that Mirko understood he was something close to being a spy.

The connection with Mirko was a risk and sometimes Walter wondered why he had taken it. After all, what use could an Italian POW ever be? Yet he yearned to have someone who understood something of his real life. Living in Scotland, charged with the task of finding a secret that could be vital to Germany's war effort was ... lonely.

Since entering the Church eight years earlier Walter had never been truly honest with anyone. And, as Christopher's questions had painfully reminded him, he hadn't been able to take the chance of becoming romantically involved, although there had been more than one woman who would have happily walked down the aisle towards him as a future husband, rather than the figure taking the service. And more than one who would have happily just taken him to their bed.

After his tea with Christopher, Walter had cycled straight to Kildary. He soon found himself walking around the inside of the perimeter fence with one of the older POWs, who complained about the cold as if a man of God might have some control over such events. Walter was only half listening. Whenever he visited, this particular Italian always sought him out with something to grumble about.

'Hey, Rizzi! The minister doesn't want to hear you bleating on about the fucking weather.'

Mirko had come up behind them without either man realising. Walter didn't speak Italian, but the sentiment was fairly obvious. Rizzi hurriedly made his excuses and left.

'He's a moaning turd,' said Mirko, switching to almost fluent English. 'Good morning, Reverend Smith.'

They continued to walk. Walter knew the camp well by now. It consisted of eight huts. Four of them were for

71

accommodation, while the others were the mess, guard-room, administration and recreation huts. The brick build-ing contained washing facilities plus the latrines. There was a small, isolated punishment block, which had been used for storage for as long as anyone could remember.

There was a high barbed-wire fence, but security was not particularly tight as no one expected anyone to attempt to escape, for the simple reason that there was nowhere for them to go. All the same, regulations were strictly adhered to and Walter knew there was a roll-call every morning and evening.

'Are you still beating up those who disagree with your views on Mussolini?'

Some of the Italians were walking around the grounds or standing in groups talking, but nobody came near the two men during their stroll.

'It keeps my hand in,' replied Mirko with a shrug of his broad shoulders.

'Yes, but sometimes it's better for a man not to stand out because of his beliefs ... not to reveal his hand until the time is right, if you take my point.'

'A bit like you, Reverend Smith?'

Walter smiled, responding with his own question.

'I understand the men are scattered about the farms within the evacuation zone?'

'Mainly in small groups, although a dozen are helping out at the biggest,' confirmed Mirko.

'They might end up billeted on farms to give them a longer working day,' Walter went on, 'although they'll almost certainly come back to the camp at weekends.'

'So we'll still be able to meet.'

'Yes.' Walter lowered his voice. 'I would like you to keep your ear to the ground.'

'Excuse me?'

'I mean, listen out for anything you think might be of interest, information that you feel I might be keen to hear. You can tell me anything and I will treat it with the utmost discretion. Particularly secrets ...'

'You can rely on me ... reverend.'

Walter stopped walking and looked into Mirko's face. It was a hard face, one that had rarely, if ever, shown compassion. Yet it was the face of a man who understood the meaning of loyalty, who would sacrifice everything for the person who had gained his devotion. Whatever Mirko might be, he would never betray Walter while their cause remained the same.

'There may come a time,' Walter said, 'when we must rely on each other.'

11

After Sunday lunch Martha, Ina and Effie began the job of fetching some of the large store of apples from the loft. They were joined by four women from the local branch of the Women's Voluntary Service, who came to help turn the fruit into jars of apple jam and chutney, filling the house with a sweet, spiced smell in the process.

The kitchen in particular became a frantic hive of chopping, measuring, stirring and chatter, full of activity and steam. Mr Ross said it was no place for a man, and so he took Hugh outside to feed the hens. He watched his young son running around, still unaware that the family's move would be preceded by the disposal of the livestock. Mr Ross knew how terribly upset the boy would be when he learned that his favourite animals – including Jessie – were going to be sold and never seen again. He sighed, thinking how the news would have to be broken soon.

But for now, Mr Ross left Hugh to his innocent fun and instead strolled along the drive, his mind occupied with the idea of the POWs being billeted at Kirk Farm. As the farm was the third drop-off point in the morning a significant amount of time was wasted transporting the Italians to and from the camp. However, the obvious questions of security, food and somewhere to sleep still needed to be answered.

He hadn't walked far when he saw a figure in army uniform coming down the lane. The man spotted him at the same time and then they were both running and shouting, coming together by the gate where they held each other in a fierce embrace.

'Duncan! Lad, you're a sight for sore eyes.' They pulled apart, both grinning fit to burst. 'Your mother is going to be so pleased, everyone will be. Hugh has been driving us mad, asking when you're going to be here.'

'It's good to see you. You look well, Dad.'

'I'll do. Come on, pick up your kit bag and let's go inside. I have to warn you the kitchen is a den of female domination. We're presently overrun by the jam-making branch of the WVS.'

'In that case, perhaps I should turn around now and you can pretend you haven't seen me.'

The great excitement of his arrival was dampened a little later, at least for Duncan, when Mr Ross told him that an army officer was using his bedroom and he would have to sleep in Hugh's room.

'I'm sorry you can't have your own bed,' Mr Ross said as the two men were walking around the farm, 'but Christopher's a good man. I think you'll like him.'

'I don't care where I sleep,' Duncan said. 'It's the fact I'll have to call him "sir" in front of everyone. How's that going to make me look, especially to Hugh?'

Mr Ross conceded this was a valid point; he could see that it rankled, which made what he had to say next even trickier.

'There's something else, son. Christopher and Ina …
they have an understanding.'

'What the hell does that mean?'

'Mind your language. You're at home now, Duncan,
not in the barracks.'

'Sorry, Dad.' Duncan paused, as if making sense of the
news. 'Are you telling me my sister is courting a captain?'

'Yes – and between the two of us I think it's a bit hasty.
Having said that, they do seem extremely fond of each
other and I can't deny they're well suited.'

'Fantastic! So I'll be saluting my future brother-in-law
every time I pass him on the way to the dunny.'

★

That evening Duncan entertained his family with tales
of the amusing characters and bizarre situations he'd
encountered in the course of army life. Hugh sat on his knee
and Mr Ross was pleased at how his eldest son responded
patiently to his little brother's stream of questions.

As he listened, Mr Ross thought that military life was
perhaps not helping Duncan's tendency to be reckless
– despite the strict discipline involved. He was secretly
worried how Duncan might react when he met Christopher
later on, although he hadn't expressed his concerns, not
even to Martha. He knew that his wife had enough troubles
without him adding to them.

The conversation around the table stopped instantly
when the front door opened and Mr Ross wondered if
the others had been harbouring fears similar to his own.
Duncan, who was still wearing his uniform, quickly lifted

Hugh off his knee so that when Christopher entered the kitchen he could stand to attention.

'Sir.'

'I wouldn't expect any man to address me as sir in his own home. Please call me Christopher.'

Duncan stared at the outstretched hand, hesitating. The rest of the family held their breath and even Hugh remained silent. Ina watched with dread, not wanting this first meeting between two people she loved to go badly. Eventually, Duncan shook Christopher's hand, visibly relaxing as he did. He had met many officers during the last two years and there were plenty he had found standoffish and uninspiring. However, he had the immediate impression that Christopher wouldn't ask a soldier to do anything he wouldn't do himself.

'I'm pleased to meet you, Christopher.'

'And you, Duncan. I look forward to speaking with you over the coming days.'

'Are you going to join us?' asked Ina.

'I don't want to interrupt your reunion.'

'Please, take my seat,' said Duncan, who then went to the living room.

If anyone else had made the offer Christopher would have said he had paperwork to attend to upstairs, but he knew it would appear rude to turn down Duncan's offer. After all, it was his homecoming and if he felt comfortable at having an army captain sitting at the table then Christopher was certainly not going to refuse the chance to be close to Ina.

'Christopher's been teaching me how to box,' said Hugh excitedly, once Duncan had returned with a stool and settled himself next to his mother. The boy rushed across the room and threw a flurry of punches, which the officer good-humouredly fended off with his raised hands.

'That's quite enough of that,' said Martha. 'You know my feelings about that sort of activity and now you're just showing off, Hugh. It's not endearing.'

'You box?' asked Duncan, unable to hide his interest despite his mother's disapproval of the sport.

'Christopher represented his university two years in a row,' said Ina, proudly.

'That was a long time ago,' said Christopher, deftly grabbing Hugh and turning him upside down before depositing the giggling boy on Effie's knee.

'Settle down, son,' said Mr Ross, sternly.

However, Hugh was not to relinquish everyone's attention just yet and he put on the glove puppet he'd been playing with earlier. It was the one of the Reverend Smith and did in fact bear a striking resemblance to him. It was a little too large, but that was so Effie could get her own hand inside; Hugh enjoyed watching his sisters perform a drama as much as he did playing with the puppets himself.

'Look what I've got!' he said.

'Wow, your sisters are both extremely clever,' said Christopher, tactfully.

'Fee's going to write a story about the minister,' continued Hugh.

'Well, I've got a better idea,' Effie said and whispered into his ear.

The others kept quiet; even his mother and father were now indulging Hugh as Effie explained the plot to him.

'When?' he asked eagerly, his eyes wide.

'I have to make them first,' Effie told him.

'But you have to do it while Duncan's here. He has to watch as well.'

'I don't think you're going to win this argument, little sister,' said Duncan. 'Whatever you're cooking up, you've only got two weeks before I return to my unit.'

'Speaking of cooking,' said Martha, 'who would like some cheese?'

'As long as it's crowdie, Mum,' said Duncan. 'I couldn't possibly eat anything else.'

Everyone laughed because crowdie was the only cheese Martha made. They laughed because Duncan was home and they were a family again and for that evening at least, they were all safe.

12

On Monday morning Mr Ross obtained permission from Mr Lawson, the Home Guard, to 'borrow' a couple of POWs to help unload the sacks of potatoes at the railway station. Effie was quick to volunteer to drive the other cart and organise the trip.

Once the two horses were hitched the Italians enthusiastically carried the sacks from the storage shed. They waved their arms and cheered when Effie set off down the drive with Toni by her side, almost as if they were a newly married couple going on their honeymoon. Mr Ross followed, one of the other POWs sitting quietly next to him.

Meanwhile Duncan was with Alastair – a man he counted as a good friend after the many years that he'd been employed at Kirk Farm.

'Bloody hell, you'd think those Italians were on their way to a hero's welcome in Rome, not delivering tatties to Fearn station,' said Duncan. 'Do they always get this excited?'

'Going by what I've seen so far, I would say they do,' Alastair replied. 'God only knows why they were fighting alongside Hitler.'

Effie felt strangely elated at having some time alone with

Toni; her father might be watching, but he wouldn't be able to hear what they were saying.

'Well, does this feel like a taste of freedom?' She asked him, as they trotted along in the cart.

Toni didn't look at her as he spoke. 'A man is only free when he can make choices for himself and is not simply obeying someone else's orders.'

'Oh ... I'm sorry. That was tactless of me.'

She turned to him and they looked at each other in silence while the horse followed the lane of its own accord.

'I didn't mean to sound harsh,' he said. 'I'm pleased to be away from everyone and not locked in. But most of all I'm pleased to be with you.'

Effie laughed. 'I bet you say that to all the girls.'

'No, only you.'

'Only me, then. Why don't you tell me about your life and how you ended up here, Toni?'

'There's nothing special about my story,' he said. 'I come from a real Italian family, with two sisters and a brother. We all talk loudly and at the same time! I didn't want anything to do with the war but I was ... forced?'

'Conscripted?'

'Yes, conscripted into the army and after some training I was sent to fight in North Africa, where I was captured after only a short while. I met Mirko at a prisoner of war camp in Egypt.'

'You've mentioned this Mirko before. Is he a friend?'

'Yes.' Toni nodded, thinking for a moment. 'He has an angry temper, but he's looked out for me and I would have been badly off without his protection. Anyway, we were sent with some of the other men to Scotland and, finally, to Kildary.'

'Is it so very horrible?'

'We're treated well and lucky to be out of the fighting. But Italy's change of sides has split the camp. Friends have become enemies and men who have nothing in common except their loyalty to Mussolini are now as close as brothers. That's horrible.'

For a while they rode in silence, both lost deep in their own thoughts. The horse trundled along towards their destination, happy to get there at a sedate pace. People worked in fields in the distance but they didn't pass anyone on the road.

'We don't even know if we're prisoners of war any more,' Toni said, breaking the silence. 'I don't see how we can be. We're not fighting Britain now. But we still have to wear these uniforms with their targets. They make us look like criminals, not men who have fought for their country. Some men feel very bitter about it. And while we live at the camp we have to obey strict curfews and rules.'

'What about you?' Effie asked. 'Do you feel bitter?'

'Me? I just want to go home.'

'To be a cabinetmaker?'

'Yes.'

Effie paused, as if reflecting on something before she spoke again.

'I want to be a writer.'

'I'm sorry?'

'You asked me the other day what I wanted to do, in my heart. You're the only person who has ever put that question in such a way. And so I've never spoken of it before.'

'What will you write?' Toni said.

'If I had the chance I would write stories for children.'

'And I know you would be wonderful at that.' Toni smiled. 'Hugh has been telling me about your puppets and the plays you perform ... behind the sofa.'

'Has he indeed! I'll be having a few words with my little brother. He's not meant to talk about me to ...'

'Strangers?'

'Anyone.'

'Children say what they feel, what they see, and Hugh thinks you are a great inventor of stories. That's good enough for me.'

Effie, infuriated, remained silent.

'I've made you angry,' said Toni. 'Please don't be cross with Hugh. He'll think I've betrayed him.'

'No, you haven't made me angry ... or Hugh,' she said sighing. 'My mother says I always overreact.'

'Effie!' shouted her father from the cart behind them. 'We're not out for an afternoon stroll. Get a move on.'

When they arrived, Mr Ross went to check with the stationmaster which wagon they were to use. He returned a few minutes later and pointed to one in a nearby siding. Effie positioned her cart and jumped down with Toni. When the soldiers on the platform saw a beautiful young woman pick up the end of a heavy sack they almost fell over each other in their desire to help.

With the soldiers galvanised into such astonishingly quick action, the sacks were soon stacked neatly at the back of the wagon. Mr Ross was used to hard work but he quickly replaced Effie's cart with his. With a fair amount of good-natured leg-pulling on both sides, the soldiers moved his sacks as well.

It was soon time to return, but when Toni went to sit next to Effie again, her father announced that he would have Toni with him for the trip back. Effie, deeply disappointed, could hardly argue with his instruction and it was a gloomy return for her with someone who spoke no English. All the way home, she wondered what was being discussed on the cart behind.

Mr Ross knew that having the Italians billeted on the farm was increasingly looking like the only way to process the crops before the deadline. But before he made such a major decision he wanted to understand the people who would not just be working alongside his family, but living among them.

And so he spent the journey grilling Toni as only a concerned parent would and by the time they reached Kirk Farm Mr Ross's mind was made up. He found Duncan and Christopher talking in the barn and, apparently, getting along well.

'You're not the only one considering this,' Christopher said. 'I've heard that several farmers are thinking along the same lines and I understand Major Cooper, who is in charge of the camp, is open to the idea. Once all the work is done, the POWs can simply go back to living at Kildary.'

Mr Ross said that he should, at the very least, speak to his wife. Six extra men living at Kirk Farm would entail significant amounts of additional work. He found Martha in the kitchen, wrapped in her blue apron to protect her blouse and heavy woollen skirt. She was busy, as always;

and on this occasion was making crowdie from surplus milk. He sat in the wicker chair and watched.

The curd had been hanging in a muslin cloth from a hook in the ceiling for several hours so the whey had already drained into the bowl underneath, ready to be given to the pigs along with other kitchen scraps later on. Martha turned the almost dry mixture into a clean bowl, added some salt and began to mix it with her hands to remove any lumps.

'If you can sit there watching me make cheese, Edward Ross, you've either not enough to do or you're about to make an announcement, both of which make me uneasy,' she said, without looking up from her task.

'You know me too well,' he said, smiling.

'You've got until I've done this, then I have to fetch the washing and do a hundred other things.'

As Martha picked up handfuls of cheese and shaped them into oblongs, he explained his idea. When he finished, Martha stopped what she was doing to consider the implications.

'The Italians seem nice enough boys,' she replied eventually. 'I wouldn't entertain the idea if I felt otherwise, not with Ina and Effie here and our Hugh.'

'I wouldn't worry about Hugh – you'd think most of them were his best friends the way he goes on.'

'Hmm.' Martha turned from the neat pile of cheeses to face him. 'I guess they'd be all right sleeping in the barn with the horses?'

'There's plenty of straw. They'd probably be warmer than they are in the huts at the camp. We'd have to feed them too, and provide anything else they need.'

Martha sighed and began to wrap the small blocks she had created, ready for storing in the pantry.

'Very well, Edward. At least give me as much warning as possible.'

★

The Northern Lights were spectacular that evening and after dinner Ina and Christopher put on as many layers of clothing as they could and went out to watch. Mr Ross didn't consider that they needed a chaperone. He was sure that the temperature outside would put a stop to anything improper taking place.

'Come on,' Ina told Christopher, after they had stood by the horse chestnut tree for several minutes. 'I know a place where we'll get a great view of the sky and be sheltered from the wind.'

She led him along the lane for a short while before taking a narrow path that went up the side of a hill and through a small copse. When they emerged on the other side they were facing the sea.

'It's not far,' she said. 'Effie and I used to come here as children and we still do when we get the chance.' They walked for another ten minutes before Ina suddenly stopped and pointed the torch. 'In here.'

It was a small depression on the hillside, perfectly sur-rounded by rocks, which protected them from the elements once they were lying down yet provided an extraordinary view of the sky and the sea.

'This is rather cosy,' said Christopher, trying to manoeuvre his body into a comfortable position.

'I know.' Ina smiled. 'We can't lie here unless I cuddle into you.'

'Get in here then,' he said, unbuttoning his army great-coat so he could wrap one side around her. 'Hey, mind my pistol!'

She snuggled into him and they lay in silence, marvelling at the glorious display of changing colours and movements above their heads.

'I've never known such happiness,' she said.

'Nor me. Perhaps we could just stay here and hide away from the world?'

'We'd get terribly cold.'

'Mmm ... and hungry.'

'You wouldn't like that.'

'I guess not. I do like to be fed now and again. Ina ... I was going to ask your father something very important, but being here with you like this ...'

'What were you going to ask?'

'Well, what's a man likely to say to the father of a woman, who's beautiful, funny and caring, intelligent and so utterly appealing?'

'Oh, Christopher, don't tease me.'

His kissed the top of her head. 'I was going to seek his permission for your hand in marriage.'

She pulled back to look up at his face.

'Don't say such a thing unless you mean it.'

'I've never been more serious in my entire life, Ina. I want to marry you and if you say yes I'll be the happiest man in the world.'

Ina stayed silent for a few long moments, and Christopher held his breath in a mix of fear and excitement.

'I had hoped,' she said. 'I had hoped so much you would say what you just have. But now I've heard it, I can't believe my ears.'

'Ina Ross,' he shouted out into the night, 'I love you and want to marry you.'

'Don't!' she said, horrified yet laughing in sheer surprise. 'What if someone's passing?'

'Who on earth is going to be passing?'

'You never know.'

'Of course, now I've done everything the wrong way around,' he said, pulling her tight into him again. 'I should have spoken to your father first. That's what the Reverend Smith advised.'

'You've spoken to the minister? Who else knows?'

'I did mention something about it in a letter to my mother.'

'Your mother!' She looked up at him with mock shock. 'What did you say to your mother?'

'I can't tell you, not yet. So, if your father says yes, what would your answer be?'

'You have to speak to my father first.'

'But what would it be?'

Ina didn't reply. Instead she reached up and kissed him, a kiss that was answer enough.

13

Martha didn't get as much of a warning as she might have liked. A series of telephone calls the next day between Christopher and several officials, plus farmers in the affected area, resulted in the decision to allow almost all of the POWs to be billeted at the farms where they were working for the next few weeks. Each Saturday afternoon, the men would be returned to the camp to be collected again on a Monday morning.

The Italian POWs were delighted at the idea. Mirko, in particular, thought the solution would please the Reverend Smith. He'd often wondered about the minister and the strange comments and hints that he sometimes wove into their conversations, and he had come to the conclusion that the minister was somehow working for Germany. Mirko had no idea why he should do such a thing, but he wasn't too bothered about solving the mystery. What he wanted to do was work out how to turn the situation to his advantage.

*

That Wednesday morning the POWs were ordered to have their blankets, eating utensils and personal items ready to take with them. And so it was that less than a week after receiving the letter about their forced evacuation, Kirk Farm was disrupted even further when the Italians arrived, each of them carrying an assortment of bags and bundles.

Mr Ross took them to the large barn that contained the horses' stables. There were two spare stables used for storing loose hay, of which there was a great deal more in the loft at the far end.

'The men should be warm enough in here, Toni,' Mr Ross said. 'Make sure they understand that under no circumstances are they to smoke or strike a light inside. The whole place would go up in flames in no time.'

'Yes, sir.'

'You won't be locked in at night,' Mr Ross went on, 'so I'm relying on you all to be honest, decent and honourable. I'm a fair man. If anyone has a problem, you come to me and I will always listen. Now, it's only appropriate that your men have their own dunny, so let's get that built, then we can go back to sorting those potatoes.'

★

People throughout the area had been contacting friends and relatives, with a large number of them having already arranged temporary accommodation. Many local families were going to Tain, which, as the largest nearby town, offered the potential to absorb them into the community.

Mr Ross had heard of a farm on the Black Isle that had an empty cottage; when he spoke to the farmer the man had promised him paid work over the winter. The two-bedroom cottage would be a tight fit for the five of them, but they would manage and he would adjust to being told what to do, at least for their enforced stay.

There was so much to organise that morning that when Christopher asked to speak to him privately, Mr Ross inwardly groaned at yet another distraction. However, the officer did seem rather on edge, so he suggested they talked while walking up to the top field to check on the cattle.

'Thank you for your time,' Christopher began. 'The thing is ... I would like your permission to ask for your daughter's hand in marriage.'

'Marriage?' said Mr Ross, so surprised that he stopped dead, Nip coming to an instant halt by his side.

'Yes, sir. I realise it may appear to be a little quick, yet I am certain in my heart that Ina is the woman I want to marry and I believe she feels the same.'

'Well ... I must admit I hadn't expected that to be the reason for the conversation. Come on, let's continue,' he said, setting off again. 'I like you, Christopher, and I can see that you're well suited, but this is not something to be rushed into. No one knows where you'll be posted and it's anyone's guess when these hostilities will finally be over. I don't want my Ina to be a war widow.'

'I wouldn't do anything to hurt her.'

'I know you wouldn't ... not intentionally.'

It wasn't until they reached the herd of Aberdeen Angus and had been watching them graze for several minutes that the farmer spoke again.

'By lunchtime tomorrow all of these cattle will be taken to the market for sale. I helped to deliver every one and there'll not be a single trace of them left.'

'I'm sorry.'

'Ah, cattle are reared to be sold, but to lose them all in one go breaks any connection with the past and the land.' Mr Ross paused, collecting his thoughts. 'At least we're hanging on to the dairy cows until we leave. They've been bought by a farmer I know near Hilton and he's agreed we can keep them for now. The land around us is changing, just like the world outside. I fear that very little of the life we knew before the war will remain when this madness is finally over. So much has already been lost.'

He fell silent and the officer remained quiet, letting the older man take the lead.

'I dare say people consider that I'm a bit of a stickler, old fashioned perhaps. I courted Martha for more than three years before I approached her father. I don't mind admitting I was quaking in my boots that day. I understand something of what you feel, coming to me now.

'I want my family to stay together, but each of them will move on at some point. That's only natural. I won't insist that the wedding is delayed until the war is over, but I would ask that you wait until we return to Kirk Farm. If she accepts your offer of marriage, I'll be a proud man to call you my son-in-law.'

Mr Ross smiled and held out his hand.

'Thank you, sir.' Christopher clasped the farmer's strong hand. 'I won't let you down ... or Ina.'

★

Hugh was often the catalyst for an evening of entertainment. His enthusiasm was so infectious that it was next to impossible to deny his requests for a play, particularly as his eighth birthday was that coming Sunday. In truth, they all needed to escape for a few hours from life's current pressures.

Mr Ross invited the Reverend Smith plus Alastair, Barbara and their boys. The fire in the living room was blazing when their guests arrived, negotiating the blackout curtains at the front door as best they could. Kirk Farm was so remote and had only paraffin lamps for light, but still it had the heavy material hanging at every window and external door. Regulations were there for a reason – and, as Martha said, it did reduce the draughts.

Effie and Ina had rehearsed the latest drama while lying in bed during the previous few nights and when everyone had settled themselves in armchairs, wooden seats, stools and the floor, the sisters disappeared behind the sofa, where their various props had already been laid out. The drama was based around the arrival of the POWs and built up quickly to a scene where a young Italian was singing a love song to Kirk Farm's sow. The children were soon laughing hysterically and the adults couldn't do anything else but join in.

It was simple entertainment delivered with skill and charm. The minister in particular seemed entranced and clapped his hands in delight during the performance. Effie had a natural talent for writing, for sweeping up an audience and carrying them along in the story. For a short while the minister could ignore the war and the troubles it brought; he could forget the ache of loneliness that was his constant companion.

When the show ended, the performers stood and took their bow. As everyone applauded, the minister looked at the happy people around him. It made him miss his father even more. There had been no contact between them since 1935, his last time in Germany. He longed to be back in his home city, which he feared was being hurt badly by bombing.

Yet it was evident that he was fond of the Ross family, who often invited him for a meal or to join them for a special occasion. He wished them no harm and hoped they survived the war without encountering the grief that had engulfed so many. The complexity of life was one of the reasons why the puppet shows appealed so much.

Christopher interrupted the minister's thoughts as he jumped up from his seat to announce that Ina and he would sort out hot drinks while people remained in the comfort of the living room and its roaring fire.

'Goodness, we're not soldiers on the parade ground,' she said, when the two of them were in the kitchen.

'I'm sorry, it sounded more like an order than I intended, but I have to do this properly and I can't wait any longer.' He got down on one knee and took hold of her hand. 'Ina Ross, will you do me the honour of being my wife?'

'Christopher Armstrong! I have just spent an hour crouching on a freezing dusty floor, the living room is full of guests waiting for a drink and you pick now to propose!'

'Is it a bad time?'

'Well, I could probably think of a few more romantic settings. Of course I'll marry you. Now come here and kiss me.'

'Not yet.'

He fumbled in his pocket for a moment then eventually retrieved what he was trying to pull out.

'This was my grandmother's. When my mother replied to my letter she sent it, saying it might be suitable for our engagement. Do you like it?'

Ina looked at the ring in his trembling hand and felt such a love for this handsome young officer that she could hardly speak.

'Oh, my love, it's beautiful.'

He smiled and slipped it on her finger. Only then did he stand up and take her in his arms.

'Happy?' he asked, finally pulling back to look at her.

'I'm so happy that everything in my life before this point feels as though it was merely passing time.'

When they walked into the living room with their arms around each other, all conversation faded away.

'Mother, Father, we have something to tell you. Christopher has asked me to marry him ... and I've said yes.'

★

With the POWs living on the farm everyone had to adjust to a new routine and one of the first tasks that following morning was to make the men breakfast. Effie and Ina produced fried-egg sandwiches and took them over to the barn along with mugs of tea. Martha, having milked the cows, then cooked for the family.

They ate their meal around the kitchen table in silence, each of them lost in their own thoughts. Even Hugh was quiet. Before leaving for school he went to say farewell to the cattle, which had been brought into the shed the previous afternoon.

The authorities had hired a local haulage company to handle transportation. Once the animals had been collected from all of the affected farms, the vehicles would meet near Tain in order to travel in convoy. There was a rumour that more than one thousand heads of cattle were being moved that day. Because of the secrecy surrounding the evacuation, selected farmers from other parts of Scotland had been invited to attend the auction, with special trains laid on to take purchased stock away.

Everyone stopped work when the vehicles could be seen coming along the lane. The engine driving the conveyor for the potato dressing was turned off and the Italians went to watch Mr Ross, Duncan and Alastair move the Aberdeen Angus. Martha and her daughters stood silently nearby. The reluctant beasts sensed that something was wrong and made a noisy protest as they were forced up the ramp. When the last lorry was eventually loaded the driver set off after the others.

People stood in silence, watching until there was nothing more to see and the sound of lowing had faded into the distance. Mr Ross simply walked away. Nip followed closely, the dog sensing some of his master's distress.

'Effie, you and Ina can clean out the shed,' said Duncan after a moment or two of quiet.

The task obviously needed to be done, but Effie fumed at the way her brother was issuing orders within days of returning.

'All right,' she replied, through gritted teeth.

'Leave one end for the dairy cows.'

'I'd already worked that out.'

'I'm just making it clear.'

'You don't need to!' Effie snapped, her voice low.

Duncan shrugged and set off after Alastair and the Italians, who had headed back to the potato pits.

'I'm glad Hugh wasn't here to see them taken away,' said Martha to her daughters when the three of them were alone.

'What about Father?' said Ina. 'Shall I go to him?'

'No,' said her mother. 'Leave him with Nip and he'll come back in his own time.'

14

On top of everything else, the newly engaged couple announced that they wanted to celebrate with a party that Friday evening. Saturday would have provided a little more time to prepare, but they knew that Mr Ross would insist that all entertainment ceased before midnight and the start of the Sabbath.

Christopher said he would invite a few fellow officers and that they would bring supplies of beer and other drinks. The sisters got in touch with their friends, while Mr Ross spoke to the Reverend Smith and Alastair, although the latter said Barbara would remain at home with the children.

Hugh was beside himself with excitement. His school closed on the day of the party and as it was almost his birthday he decided that this should be a joint event. Ina indulged him in this, but still she stressed that the evening was for adults and if he stayed up he had to be on 'double best behaviour'.

Martha didn't invite anyone. She simply got on with the extra work that such a party created. Preparing food presented significant challenges when so many ingredients were rationed and creating a presentable table took a fair bit of imagination, hard work and help from neighbours, who donated scarce items such as sugar.

Ina and Effie did help in the kitchen, but they also, according to their father, spent a ridiculous amount of time fussing over their outfits. He was even more frustrated on the Friday when they lit the fire during the afternoon so that they could take a bath, which meant they would refuse to do any tasks that were remotely dirty for the rest of the day.

A loud banging on the front door that evening announced the arrival of the first guests. Hugh opened it to be confronted by a giant of a man wearing an officer's uniform and carrying two crates of beer as if the weight was nothing to him.

'Hello,' he said with a beaming smile.

Hugh had never seen anyone so big and the sight made him forget all the detailed instructions he had received earlier about how to welcome visitors. He stood rooted to the spot in amazement, until remembering that he was meant to actually allow people into the house. He stepped to one side and four officers entered, each carrying an assortment of alcohol. Christopher took Ina in an embrace then made the necessary introductions.

'And finally, this is my very dear friend, Chubby Henderson.'

Ina almost gawped in surprise as much as Hugh, when the man took her hand and kissed it as if they were both Hollywood movie stars.

'I can see immediately why my handsome young colleague has fallen so helplessly in love,' he said. 'I am truly enchanted.'

'I have to warn you that Chubby is the most outrageous flirt in the entire army,' Christopher said. 'He once swallowed a vast tome of medieval gallantry and the phrases have a tendency to repeat on him.'

Ina smiled but was, in truth, unsure how to react to the encounter, which felt so out of place in their living room, with its rather worn furniture and home-made rugs. She was saved from further embarrassment when her sister appeared from the kitchen.

'And you must be the lovely Effie,' said the guest, taking hold of and kissing her hand before an introduction could be made. 'If it were not so totally out of character, I would stand here speechless at the vision of elegance before me.'

'Unfortunately,' said Christopher, 'Chubby has never been known to be speechless, even for a short while.'

'I'm pleased to meet you,' said Effie, flashing him a smile that did indeed live up to his praise. 'But I don't believe that's your real name.'

'Ah, you've found me out. I was, indeed, christened Skinny Henderson. It's a complete mystery as to why I have this nickname.'

'Well, you're welcome at Kirk Farm, whatever you're called.'

Ina's face betrayed her irritation at appearing tongue-tied and awkward when her younger sister could respond so effortlessly. After all, it was her party.

'And look at that beauty!' said Chubby, his eyes wide with excitement.

They all turned to see who or what had caught his attention. 'Does it work?'

100

'That's our grandmother's harmonium,' said Effie. 'Do you want to play it?'

Without another word he set off towards the instrument, leaving her with no choice but to follow as he was still holding her hand.

'What an extraordinary person,' said Ina. 'Is he real?'

'Yes he is extraordinary and yes he is real,' said Christopher. 'I know he comes across as a little odd ...'

'A little?'

'Okay, very odd, but I trust him above any other man I know.'

Ina looked at her fiancé intently, however he was obviously serious, which made her realise that she would have to re-evaluate her opinion of the person currently trying to manoeuvre his enormous buttocks on to the sloping wooden stool. She hoped it would survive the onslaught.

What Christopher didn't say, and couldn't even to the woman he loved, was that his friend had the sharpest mind of anyone he knew – a mind that army intelligence put to excellent use. His bulk and banter made people think he was a bumptious, though harmless, fool ... a perception that suited him perfectly well.

The other guests arrived and the living room and kitchen were soon alive with chatter and laughter. Chubby's skilful performance on the harmonium was replaced by music from the wind-up gramophone. He casually made his way around the room, chatting amicably to people until he was standing near the minister and their meeting could be seen as nothing more than the natural interaction of guests.

'Reverend Smith, I presume,' he said, holding out a

hand. 'I'm Chubby Henderson, a friend of the very fortunate groom-to-be. You must be glad to be here.'

'Here?' repeated the minister, uncertain as to his meaning.

'In Scotland, rather than Holland. I understand your parents are Dutch.'

The minister's expression didn't alter, despite the warning bells ringing in his mind. He smiled back, but he sensed that the man before him was not what he made himself out to be.

He's acting a part.

'These are such anxious times,' he said, without a moment's hesitation in his reply. 'When I think of my poor countrymen, the relatives and friends I left behind … I can't tell you of the number of times I have prayed for them, Mr Henderson.'

'Let us hope that they are safe and soon free of the tyranny they presently endure.'

Both men nodded sadly at the horrendous situation in occupied Holland and Walter remained quiet, so as to let the other man steer the conversation.

'Smith … reverend?'

'Ah, it's really Smit, but when I started my new life in Scotland I felt that adding an "h" would make it more acceptable to local ears. I hope you don't think it's too dishonest.'

'Perfectly sensible,' Chubby agreed. 'I've travelled around quite a bit of your country. It really is lovely. What part are you from, reverend?'

The warning bells rang more loudly. But Walter had no difficulty in talking about his past, for he was simply telling the truth.

'I was born in Rotterdam to a mother who was a seamstress, and a father who worked for the government,' he said.

Chubby nodded. 'So how did you come to be a minister, Reverend Smith?'

Walter was now certain that the man worked for a branch of army intelligence. Apart from his nationality, there was absolutely no reason for the officer to be suspicious, yet Walter sensed an interest that wasn't strictly friendly in this man's questions.

Walter recalled the arguments he had had with his father about where to take his theology degree. Hitler had insisted that he followed this profession so there had been no room for debate on that side of things. However, Walter had wanted to remain in Germany. His father had persuaded him to come to Scotland, which was why he had ended up at the divinity faculty of Glasgow University.

As he stood, discussing his life, Walter silently thanked his father for his foresight. If any of the information he gave was checked, it would be found to be exactly as he described: he had trained and been ordained in Glasgow, where he had worked for a while prior to moving to the Highlands. Along with forged documents showing his father to be Dutch, Walter had papers indicating that the year he had secretly lived in Berlin was spent in Holland. Now that Holland was under Nazi rule, Walter was confident it would be impossible for anyone to discover this wasn't true.

★

When the needle on the gramophone reached the end of the record, Chubby left Walter and went over to the harmonium. The huge man had a good voice and there was soon a small group around the instrument, joining in with the singing. Effie stood in the corner of the room, chatting to one of the other guests. The man was educated and quite attractive, but Effie was glad when he went to the kitchen, where bottles of beer were being kept cool in buckets of icy water. Left alone, she looked around at everyone talking, laughing and singing and felt a hard knot form in her stomach. It took her several moments to realise what was wrong. She felt lonely. This was such an alien sensation that it took her completely by surprise.

Why should I feel lonely among all the people I love?

It wasn't that Effie was envious of Ina. Indeed, she was delighted at the news of the engagement. No, it wasn't jealousy. It was something else entirely. There was someone missing from the party and it didn't take Effie long to acknowledge who it was. Without being noticed, she slipped quietly out of the front door.

When she returned a few minutes later, the first person to spot her was Ina, who stood laughing with their parents and Christopher. At the sight of her sister, Ina's laughter suddenly died, and the others turned to follow her gaze. Gradually, all the conversations, singing and music ceased.

Effie stepped just inside the room. In the doorway behind her, the POWs crowded together. Faced with the dramatic change in atmosphere, they hesitated on the threshold and appeared unwilling to move any further. Effie glanced back at Toni, but could tell by his expression that the men weren't going to enter without approval.

Effie looked at her father, who, for the first time in his life, seemed hesitant in taking charge in his own home. Effie watched him share a glance with Christopher, and realised that she had made a drastic mistake. This was Christopher's party and there were many officers there. She didn't know how they felt about the POWs being present, especially since Italy had been the enemy until only a couple of months earlier. Who knew what experiences they might have had fighting the comrades of those now before them.

Effie felt increasingly desperate, standing alone with everyone staring at her in silence. Her gaze rested on Ina, but she stood motionless, although the pleading in Effie's eyes must have been obvious. Effie felt heat in her cheeks and she wished the ground would swallow her up.

Then a small voice broke the spell that they all appeared to have fallen under.

'Here's a beer, Toni.'

It was Hugh, who had been going around all evening offering guests drinks and food. Before anyone could react, he walked over with a single bottle of beer on his tray, which he held up to the Italian.

'I'll be eight years old on Sunday,' Hugh announced. 'Tonight is my birthday party.'

A couple of the Italians looked back towards the front door, as if considering leaving. Hugh's expression betrayed his disappointment at Toni's apparent rejection and when he spoke again his voice sounded sad and hurt.

'Don't you want a beer? It's still cold.'

It was Duncan who came to the rescue of his younger brother, moving forward out of the crowd.

105

'You take that one, Toni, and I'll get bottles for the others,' he said briskly, immediately turning and heading for the kitchen.

'I'll give you a hand,' said Christopher, following quickly.

'Toni,' said Mr Ross loudly. 'For goodness sake, tell the lads to come into the living room and get warmed up. There's food in the kitchen. Let them know they can help themselves.'

Toni picked up the bottle and thanked Hugh, who beamed, the awkwardness of moments ago already forgotten. Toni then spoke quietly to the five men behind him and they all moved hesitantly into the room. Chubby, who had been watching the scene with intense interest, turned back to the keyboard and started playing again. He had never met the POWs, but shouted over his shoulder as if he had known them for years.

'Hey, Toni, come over here with your boys and give us a song. I've never met an Italian yet who didn't have a good voice.'

The POWs stood around the harmonium, initially talking quietly to themselves. After a brief discussion with Toni, the room was once more filled with singing. Some guests listened keenly, while others returned to their conversations. Ina went over to Effie, who remained rooted to the spot, her face a deep shade of red.

'Effie, I nearly died!'

'How do you think I felt?' Effie responded, her eyes wide.

'Whatever possessed you to bring them over?'

'It just didn't seem fair, all of us enjoying ourselves and

106

them in the barn nearby, so far from their homes and families. Are you angry?'

'I was certainly speechless for a moment, but I'm not cross. You were only doing what you thought was right,' said Ina, pulling Effie into a tight hug.

'I was so worried,' whispered Effie. 'I thought I was going to get into awful trouble when I saw everyone's expressions. I've never seen father look so taken aback!'

'To be honest, I wish I had your nerve,' Ina murmured, releasing her sister. 'Come on, let's go to the kitchen and get a drink. I think we both need one.'

★

'Your father and I are off to our bed,' Martha announced to Ina and Effie later on. 'And it's more than time for you to be in yours,' she added, turning to Hugh.

'Not yet!' he replied.

Ina kneeled in front of him and took hold of his hands.

'I've been so proud of your behaviour tonight,' she said. 'You were the one who prevented a potentially awful moment. Thank you for saving the party.' The boy swelled with pride. 'If you go up now you can go straight into our bed. We'll soon be up.'

Hugh knew this was probably the best offer he was likely to get. However, he decided to push his luck a little further and agreed on the condition that he could say goodnight to everyone, which resulted in a large number of handshakes and hugs, much to his delight and the amusement of the guests.

Walter and Alastair used the departure of the farmer

and his wife from the party to quietly slip away also, so only the younger generation remained. It wasn't long before 'Moonlight Serenade' started playing from the gramophone. Christopher and Ina began to dance, moving slowly around the room with eyes only for each other. They were followed by the other officers, who were quick to approach the female guests. Effie deliberately stayed out of the way, and when the Italians were the only men remaining she walked over to Toni.

'Is your dancing as good as your singing?' she asked.

'It's … manure.'

Effie laughed. 'If it's that bad, perhaps I should ask someone else.'

She was only teasing, but Toni's expression turned suddenly serious. 'I would like to dance with you more than anything.'

Effie felt her stomach flutter as their eyes met, but she kept her composure and smiled. 'Put down your beer then.'

Toni gave the bottle to a friend and let Effie take his hand to lead him to the centre of the floor. They looked at each other for a moment, before he took her in a ballroom hold. However, there wasn't sufficient space for anyone to dance properly and they soon ended up simply swaying to the music, holding each other close.

'Are your men all right?' Effie asked after a while.

Toni was quiet for a moment, as if considering his words carefully. 'We're ashamed at having to wear these clothes when everyone else has done their best to be clean and look nice,' he said. 'But we are very grateful to be asked. We could hear the music and that made us more homesick than ever. Thank you for having the courage. I could tell by the reaction that it was your idea.'

'I...' Effie struggled to find the words to reply.

'What?'

'Nothing.'

'Tell me...' Toni lifted Effie's chin so that their eyes met. 'Please.'

'It sounds weak and selfish, particularly when you are all so far from your families,' Effie said. 'But the truth is, I suddenly felt lonely at the party, even though I was surrounded by people I know and love.'

Again, Toni pondered before answering, his eyebrows furrowed. 'Maybe this evening feels like the start of you losing your closest friend.'

'Ina? Well, put that way I suppose you could be right. We've always been so close, always been there for each other.'

'And now she has someone who means more to her – not that she loves you any less, of course, but Christopher represents her future rather than her past.'

'You're very perceptive.'

'So you were lonely? Why did you come for us?'

'I didn't,' Effie replied quietly. 'I came for you.'

'Me?'

'Yes.'

'And now?'

Effie looked into Toni's huge, deep brown eyes. She didn't reply, but after a few moments she moved closer to him so that their bodies were touching. Some of the women had taken the other Italians on to the floor. No one was bothered by what other couples were doing. For a short while they all did their best to forget the war raging in the world outside. They were young, alive and determined to enjoy themselves.

The party ended, as all good evenings eventually must. The guests made their farewells, the three officers giving a lift to those who lived furthest away. Duncan offered to escort some of the others home. The Italians went back to the barn, but Toni stayed to help clear things away and after a while he was the only one remaining, along with Effie, Ina and Christopher.

'Thank you for having us to your party, sir,' Toni said to Christopher. 'It meant a lot to us.'

'We were pleased to have you here,' Christopher replied, holding out his hand.

Surprised, Toni hesitated, before reaching out to shake it. Then he smiled at Ina and headed for the front door. Effie followed, as if merely seeing him out. They both went outside, where they stood side by side gazing at the sky. It was filled with a stunning array of different coloured streams of light, which swirled, merged and altered every few seconds.

'What are those?' asked Toni, unable to disguise his amazement.

'The Northern Lights. They occur at this time of year when the conditions are right. In years gone by they were believed to be the spirits of departed friends and loved ones. Some people call them the Merry Dancers.'

'The Merry Dancers,' Toni repeated, his voice full of awe. 'They're beautiful. We do not have this in Italy.'

'But you do have warmth,' said Effie, shivering. She regretted leaving her coat inside.

'You're cold,' Toni said, ignoring the beauty above to look at the one standing next to him.

'You asked me a question earlier and I didn't answer,' Effie said. 'You wanted to know if I still felt lonely. Well, I don't. You stopped me from feeling lonely.'

'You did answer,' Toni replied, taking her gently in his arms.

He brought his mouth slowly towards her lips. Above them, the Merry Dancers burst into an explosion of intricate colours that entwined, parted and came together again with a renewed vigour, as if heralding the beginnings of a new life.

15

The farmer and his wife rose the next morning as usual, making no concession for anyone who had stayed up late. Ina and Effie heard Martha raking out the ashes from the kitchen range and it seemed to them that she was deliberately making more noise than needed. The sisters lay either side of Hugh, who could sleep through anything and was still snoozing peacefully.

'It can't be that time already,' whispered Effie with a groan.

'Speaking of time, I couldn't believe how long you stayed outside last night,' Ina said pointedly.

'I was watching the Northern Lights.'

'Is that all you were doing?'

'Is mother going to bang that ash pan for ever?'

'Don't change the subject, Effie. You be careful what you're doing with those Italians.'

'Ina! That's awful. You make it sound as though I'm going around with all of them.'

'Well?'

'Toni and I watched the sky together, just like you and Christopher do.'

'That's totally different. He's a British officer and I've known him for ages.'

'A little over three months! And you can't tell me who I can be friends with.'

'There's friends … and then there's *friends*.'

Effie groaned, burying her face in the pillow. 'Stop, Ina. Now you're sounding like Father. Toni makes me happy. There's no harm in that, or in him. He's a lovely, sweet-natured man and we like each other's company.'

'Mmm.'

'Anyway, it's too early to get up yet,' said Effie, cuddling into Hugh, who was still fast asleep.

★

When the sisters eventually went downstairs, the range was lit and their mother was mixing water and milk with the oats that she had just retrieved from the chest in the scullery. Mr Ross had gone out to bring in the milking cows from the field. The weather, although cold, was fortunately also dry and looked set to remain that way for the next few days, which would make a huge difference to the task that had to be started on the farm that morning.

By eight o'clock Christopher had left for the nearby military camp, and Hugh had emerged and demanded his breakfast – sounding a little too much like his older brother, which earned him a chiding from Martha. The Italians had been instructed to wait in the yard, where they were joined by Duncan and Alastair, each leading a horse and cart. One was piled with empty hessian sacks, the farm's large set of weighing scales and a milk churn full of drinking water, along with several tin mugs. The other cart carried an assortment of tools.

A few moments later Mr Ross arrived with Nip. Spotting him through the window, Effie and Ina reluctantly left the warmth of the kitchen and trooped out to join him. Despite the late night, Effie and Ina looked fresh and pretty in their dungarees, and Effie was not oblivious to the appreciative gazes of the Italians. Mr Ross surveyed the group before him, nodded and set off at a brisk pace.

'Where are we going?' Toni asked Effie. They had managed to get together at the back of the group without, Effie hoped, the manoeuvre being too obvious. Neither of them made any reference to their kiss the previous night, yet even when talking about practical matters their eyes conveyed a secret message.

'The first of the wheat fields,' Effie replied. 'We need to separate the grain from the stalks, but to do that we need a threshing machine. Kirk Farm isn't big enough to have its own, so there's a mobile one due any time. It's being brought here by some of the land girls based at Portmahomack.'

'Girls?'

'Women, Toni. That should cheer up your friends. With so many men away fighting we've taken on a great number of roles and one of them is working the land. It's a bit like Ina and I do already, only we don't wear fancy uniforms or get paid.'

They were too close to the others to discuss anything private, and Effie felt frustrated. During the week, after that first journey, they had made many trips to Fearn station to drop off bags of potatoes, which provided an opportunity to talk freely about their families, their likes and dislikes, their hopes for the future ... Effie had come to treasure these precious moments.

The group only had to wait ten minutes before two tractors came along the lane, each one pulling a strange-looking machine. The Italians looked as puzzled by them as they were by the fact that the skilful drivers were female. Effie almost burst out laughing at their astonished expressions. Two figures on bicycles followed a short distance behind. All four of the women were wearing the distinctive dark-green jumpers and fawn-coloured breeches of the Women's Land Army.

'Effie, make sure the Italians keep out of the way while we set up,' Mr Ross instructed. 'Explain to them what's about to happen and make sure they understand the dangers.'

Effie knew her father had been pleased and surprised at how well the POWs had adapted to the labour, and how quickly the family had come to regard them as a normal part of their lives. Mr Ross had also remarked on Toni's extraordinary interest in everything. He had an almost insatiable curiosity about equipment and the workings of the farm.

'Bring the men over here,' Effie said to Toni.

The thresher and baler were unhitched, and one of the land girls immediately drove off with her tractor. In appearance, at least, the three remaining women could hardly have been more different. One was as tall and thin as another was short and stout, while the third, who had a shock of red hair, fitted neatly between. They soon demonstrated that they knew what they were doing.

'The wheat has been cut, tied in sheaves and then

made up into stooks – that is small stacks, with the heads facing south so that they dry as quickly as possible,' Effie explained to Toni, who quickly translated for the others. 'We later take the stooks and create these huge stacks, this time facing the heads into the centre to prevent them getting wet.'

The Italians listened, but their eyes were fixed on the scene before them, as various parts of the threshing mill, which had been positioned between two stacks, were unfolded and opened up. The remaining tractor was turned around and brought close so that a drive belt could be fixed between it and the mill. 'Now we need to separate the grain from the stalks. This means feeding everything into the opening at the top,' Effie said.

'All of this into that?' Toni said incredulously.

'Yes, and when we've finished this field we move on to the next.'

'*Mamma Mia!* The war will be finished long before us.'

Joan, the shorter of the land girls, checked that the various grease points were well lubricated, while Mr Ross positioned people and gave strict instructions. The tall land girl was called Eileen. She started the tractor's engine and the thresher burst into a cacophony of noise and movement. Every part of it seemed to fly back and forth, jig side to side or bang up and down.

A POW climbed to the top of each stack. Once they were comfortable, they began using their forks to throw down sheaves of wheat to the nearest part of the platform, where another would move them close to Alastair, who stood by the opening of the thresher. He deftly cut the binding with his knife and dropped the loose stalks into the heart of the thresher.

There was little time for the other Italians to take in the sight because almost immediately grain began to fall into the sacks placed at one end, while the stalks were spewed out onto another part of the ground. A POW raked them away and fed them into the hopper of the baler, which turned the loose straw into compacted, oblong blocks.

'I have never experienced anything like this!' Toni exclaimed, staring wide-eyed at the scene before him.

'I've watched this every year since I was young and I still find it fascinating,' Effie replied.

They were standing beside the scales that had been set up close to the sacks, which were slowly filling with grain. Mr Ross came over and let some fall into his hands before examining it closely. Satisfied, he dropped it in with the rest and continued his walk around the machine, shouting out instructions, warnings and praise to the men and women.

One of the most unpleasant tasks was raking away the empty husks that fell underneath the main body of the mill in a cloud of dust and minute particles that stung the eyes and clogged the throat. Joan gathered the chaff and the other women put it into bags, which they carried a short distance away before coming back to start again.

'Threshing requires so many hands that it brings communities together, with workers from one or two farms gathering to help out. The favour is always returned later on,' said Effie. 'Mobile mills are being brought into the area from all over Scotland. Of course, everywhere nearby is under the same pressure we are, so there are no spare workers.'

'The Italians are here to save the day!' Toni joked. 'But what are you and I doing?'

'You're just about to find out.'

Mr Ross told two POWs to carry over the first full sack of grain, which they placed on the bed of the scales. Effie checked its weight.

'A hundredweight. That's fine, thanks.'

She beamed at the men, who grinned back like love-struck schoolboys before returning to the next sack, which was already filling up.

'Come on.' Effie turned back to Toni. 'Help me tie the top then move the bag into the bogie. Once the process gets going there'll be no time for wondering what needs doing.'

The group fell into a routine of throwing, cutting, raking, lifting and loading, accompanied by the noise of whirling and clanking machinery and the steady thrub-thrub of the tractor's engine which, rather too often, belched obnoxious fumes into the air.

A little while later Effie climbed up into the cart. 'Toni, get in,' she called down.

'Now?'

'Yes. We can't add any more or it'll be too heavy.'

'For the horse?'

'No, for the bogie. Come on, we'll take it to the farm.'

Effie was trying to avoid giving her father the chance to order someone else to go with her. She flicked the reins and so by the time Mr Ross spotted them, they were at least fifty yards away. He shook his head, muttered under his breath and went back to work.

'We've escaped!' said Effie as they entered the lane.

Toni smiled. 'When we first went to the station with the potatoes, I'll confess it didn't feel like any sort of freedom. Yet today, sitting next to you and with no one else around, I do almost feel free,' he admitted.

'That's ironic.'

Toni frowned. 'Why?'

'You have found freedom while I have been captured,' Effie said, feeling a warmth in her cheeks.

'By what?'

They rode in silence for a while, Bertie happily plodding at his own pace though the landscape he knew so well.

'I've been captured by you, Toni.'

16

Effie and Toni soon reached the storage shed and Effie skilfully made Bertie back the cart into the building. Toni hadn't said anything since her admission and Effie was fretting that he didn't feel anything towards her after all.

They jumped down from the cart and stood looking at each other in silence. Effie reached the point where she couldn't stand the uncertainty any longer. She was just about to turn away and grab the lug of a sack when Toni finally spoke.

'Effie. What you implied ...'

'Toni!'

They turned together to see Hugh pelting towards them so fast that he was in danger of tumbling over. Effie groaned inwardly at the unfortunate timing of her brother's arrival. They would never get rid of him.

'Ciao, Hugh,' said Toni, who had been teaching the boy some Italian.

'Cheeouw,' replied Hugh excitedly, crashing into his sister. He threw his arms around her waist and hugged her tightly. 'Cheeouw Fee. You've got the first of the grain.'

She looked down at the figure that she loved so much and, resisting a strong urge to sigh, ruffled his hair and laid an arm on his shoulder.

'Yes, the first of the wheat harvest is here. Now we've got to stack it in the dry, ready for it to be taken away another day.'

'I can help!' Hugh said eagerly.

'Every one of those sacks weighs significantly more than you do,' she said with a smile, looking over the boy's head at Toni. He gave her such a warm grin in return that an image flashed into her mind – the two of them in the future, older and married, with their own children playing nearby.

'Well, I can still help,' said Hugh seriously, finally detaching himself. 'I'll make sure you do it properly.'

'We have our instructions,' said Toni, reaching over to pull the nearest bag towards him.

Hugh sat on a bale of straw and kept up an almost constant stream of chatter as they worked.

'Hey, Toni, Fee made a puppet that looks exactly like you.'

Effie's head snapped up from her work. 'Hugh! That's meant to be a secret!'

'Well, it can't be a secret when so many people saw your play.'

'I was in a play?' Toni asked. 'What was it about?'

'It was nothing,' Effie said dismissively, glaring at her brother and wishing more than ever that he hadn't spotted them.

Oblivious, Hugh continued enthusiastically, 'It was about when you sang to our sow. Ina had the pig puppet and they chased each other around while Fee sang. It was really funny, though I don't think the Italian was very good.'

'That's quite enough,' Effie said firmly, her face flushing pink in a mixture of embarrassment, guilt and shame. She turned to Toni, afraid to meet his eye. 'I didn't mean to make fun of you.'

Toni turned his back to her and put both hands to his face, as if he was upset.

Effie felt a sick feeling in her stomach. 'I'm sorry, Toni. I didn't intend for you to ever find out.'

'That doesn't make it any better,' he replied, his muffled voice sounding strained. 'It was a hurtful thing to do.'

'Hugh!' Effie whirled around to scold her brother. 'Look what you've done.'

'It's not the boy's fault,' Toni said quietly. 'You have to take responsibility for your own actions.'

How had this all gone so wrong? Effie felt tears pricking at her eyes. Only a short while earlier she had confessed to Toni that he had captured her heart and now he was angry with her! And all because she had cruelly made him into a figure of fun in front of the family, as well as several other people. She knew deep down that she had been wrong to do it. The man she was falling in love with had been made to appear foolish. She felt awful.

'I'm sorry. It was a cruel thing to do. Please forgive me,' she said, walking up to him.

He turned around, his face still covered, and she pulled him towards her, hugging him tightly. It was pure instinct that made her do it. Hugh, for once, was speechless. It was only when Toni managed to raise his head a little, move one of his hands aside and give an enormous wink that the boy realised he was only pretending.

'I would really ... really have liked to hear you try to sing in Italian,' he said. Then, unable to keep the act up any longer, he started to laugh, his body shaking in her arms.

Effie couldn't believe she had been taken in that easily. However, she was so relieved that he hadn't been serious, and it was so lovely to hold him, that she began laughing as well.

★

Sometime later, Martha was walking to the washing line with the latest pile of wet clothes when she saw the young POW rushing out of the storage shed with Hugh over his shoulder and Effie close behind. The three of them were screaming and shouting out to each other.

Martha watched with a mixture of amusement and concern. It was nice to see them enjoying themselves and she liked the Italian, who was very good with Hugh. Yet she feared that there was more to the scene than an innocent moment of fun.

She hadn't missed the way Effie and Toni reacted to each other ... the little smiles and nods, the knowing glances that conveyed something secret. This was more than a passing friendship; Martha worried it would only end in heartache.

Perhaps it was a blessing that in a few weeks the family would move to the Black Isle and the Italians would be sent back to Kildary. Who knew where the Italians might be based by the time everyone was allowed back on to the Tarbat peninsula. Martha hoped that this flirtation of her daughter's didn't reach a point where she would have to mention it to her husband ... or that something even worse would bring it all out into the open.

17

The three Italians who ran the camp kitchen had been kept on and given cleaning and maintenance tasks while their fellow countrymen were billeted elsewhere. By the time the first lorry arrived that Saturday afternoon, the black, pot-bellied stove in each of the accommodation huts was almost glowing red with heat and there was a healthy pile of chopped wood stacked neatly nearby.

Although there were always checks on what POWs brought back, they climbed down from the vehicle carrying an extraordinary array of objects, from jars of homemade rhubarb jam to musical instruments. Several men cradled baskets of eggs, some of which they had collected themselves from gulls' nests, while more than one had hidden alcohol, donated by friendly farmers.

There was no sign of the ever-hostile Private Atkinson and the guards on duty were relaxed. As long as no one had a tool or implement that could be used as a weapon, they let the Italians keep their hoard of presents. Most of the food was taken straight to the kitchen to be put to whatever use the cooks could make of it. However, all the men were eager to make for their beds, where any post that had arrived during their absence would be waiting.

They received parcels from home and the Red Cross, and a hush descended upon the huts as the men began to open whatever had arrived. Not everyone had something and these men hid their disappointment behind copies of the latest *Il Corriere del Prigioniero*, one of two weekly newsletters printed in London by the government for Italian POWs held in Great Britain.

Toni sat on his mattress and opened a small box. Inside was an assortment of items, from woollen socks and gloves to candles and chocolate. Like everyone else, it was the letters that he was the most keen to examine. He lay back and began to read the first one, which no doubt echoed the comments of worried mothers being read all around the camp by their sons.

Toni's mamma sent her love and said that the family was missing him and hoped that he was keeping well and staying out of danger. They prayed for his speedy and safe return. The only concerning piece of news was that nobody had heard from his older brother Luca for several months and his whereabouts were unknown.

Toni scanned the letter to the end, intending to devour it once he had the gist of the others too. The second letter was from his youngest sister, Anna, who was only sixteen. He could see the conflict between the person who was still a child and the one who was maturing into a woman. Innocent, childish questions and anecdotes were interspersed with more serious, mature observations on wartime Italy. The writing style bounced between the two so much that some of the ink got smudged by Toni's tears. He wouldn't be a part of this magical transformation. When he finally returned home he would be faced

126

with an adult – an adult who would be, in many ways, a stranger.

Toni wondered how much he had changed since joining the army, how much any of those in the hut were the same people they had been before the war. Some of the Italians had left home when their children were too young to have any memories of them and Toni knew these men feared returning home to hostility from sons and daughters who did not recognise the unknown person suddenly sleeping in their mother's bed.

Toni was going through a letter from his own father when the door opened and several figures entered, signifying the arrival of another lorry. Mirko walked with a slight limp as he made his way to his own bed, opposite Toni's.

'Have you hurt yourself?' Toni asked, forcing a smile. He wished he'd had more time to himself.

'Me? Hurt?' replied his friend with a grin. 'Not bloody likely, but I'll be glad to get rid of these from under my crotch.' With a wink, Mirko undid his trousers to reveal two silver hipflasks, tied with string to the inside of each thigh. 'We've fallen on our feet at the place we're working at. The farmer's really into brewing his own alcohol and this' – he lifted the first flask clear – 'is fucking nectar.'

'He gave them to you?'

'Loaned, and I won't get any more if they're not returned undamaged. You know, the British might be bastards, but some of these Highland people are almost acceptable. What about you? How have you got on?'

Toni considered telling him about the Ross family and Effie, about the party and the incredible things he had seen and done, but decided it would be more prudent to be vague.

'It's straight farm work. The man in charge is fair and the family are nice.'

Mirko nodded. 'Ah, well, that's good then.'

'Aren't you going to open your parcel?'

Mirko had ignored the item next to him; he seemed more pleased with the alcohol than the parcel he had received from home.

'I guess so,' he said disinterestedly.

★

There was a carnival atmosphere in the mess hall later on, with friends keen to share stories talking over the top of one another in their enthusiasm. The noise around the tables was so great that no one bothered to turn on the radio, which anyone could listen to when they were free of work.

The cooks had outdone themselves in both quality and quantity and created a dish that was the tastiest anyone had eaten in years. Those who had smuggled in alcohol decided to consume it later, when they were out of sight of the guards. There was a limit to how much they could push their luck, even without Atkinson present.

Lights out was at eight o'clock and POWs were expected to be in their own accommodation huts by this point, although they weren't locked in and were able to go to the latrines at any time. The men in Toni's hut gathered around their stove, which was fed regularly from the pile of wood, and Mirko passed around the hip flasks. A small, thin Italian with mischievous eyes underneath his heavy black brows had brought in a large stone jug full of alcohol.

No amount of questioning or threats would get him to reveal how he had smuggled it in. He simply grinned back at them until they gave up asking.

The Italians knew that the electric light bulbs would go out at precisely the specified time, as they always did, so one minute before eight they lit some of their precious candles. The air was soon thick with a haze of cigarette smoke. Faces were illuminated by the flickering candlelight and the intermittent, tiny red glows of cigarette ends, eerie in the gloom.

The laughter and excited chatter of earlier gave way to a more reflective conversation, which eventually swayed towards the discussion of a rebellion. The most fiercely loyal supporters of Mussolini argued that they should use their freedom to cause havoc for the enemy, setting fire to farm buildings or attempting a mass escape in order to tie up the regular troops. It was, after all, their duty. The men talked themselves into and out of several increasingly wild suggestions, many of which were defeated by their own sheer ludicrousness.

Toni glanced over at Mirko. He knew his friend felt a close bond with the Mussolini supporters, yet he was uncharacteristically quiet that evening.

As though sensing Toni's eyes on him, Mirko suddenly spoke, 'If you escape or carry out acts of sabotage then you'll never be given any freedom again. You'll be moved to a much more secure camp and heavily guarded until the end of the war.'

'But what are we doing to fight the enemy?' asked one man, gesticulating wildly. 'We're soldiers and we should do something to get back at them! Living away from the camp gives us opportunities we've never had before.'

'And we'll get them again if we prove that we can be trusted on this occasion,' replied Mirko, calm but firm. 'I believe there'll be opportunities for a greater revenge than setting fire to an old barn or running around the country-side for a day or two freezing our bollocks off. How long would any of us survive in this weather?'

There was a muted agreement on this point, helped partly by the fact that the wind, which had been getting stronger all evening, was now blowing so fiercely that their hut creaked and the windows rattled under the onslaught.

Not for the first time Toni wondered what he was doing surrounded by men who were so loyal to Il Duce. He had no such feelings. It was only because his bed had originally been here and Mirko had wanted him to stay that he hadn't swapped huts, as so many had after Italy's capitulation and the subsequent bad feeling amongst some of the Italians.

Toni always kept quiet when conversations turned to violence, revenge or Mussolini and the others generally left him alone. The camp was divided on Il Duce, and Toni was the only Italian who managed to float successfully between both sides without incurring the wrath of either.

'Christ, pass that jug around!' said Mirko, in an attempt to steer the conversation on to less dangerous ground. 'Giorgio, didn't you say someone gave you a mouth organ? Let's hear some music rather than this bloody storm.'

Giorgio quickly produced the instrument, which a farm worker had given him a few days earlier, and began to play. He was good. The men put the talk of violence to one side, lit more cigarettes and settled down to listen and drink, reflecting on their lives and thinking of loved ones.

Toni thought about the news he had learnt from his recent letters. Yet his mind kept being pulled back to Kirk Farm and the beautiful girl who made him laugh and feel so happy. He would never have believed he could experience such joy when he was so far away from home. For the first time ever, he began to wonder where he would like 'home' to be.

18

Everyone in the local farming community was now working throughout the week and so fewer people attended the Sunday service. The Home Guard had been organised to help maintain levels of productivity and early that morning hundreds of men arrived at farms in the area. They were fit and able, yet exempt from the armed forces because they worked in reserved occupations.

In the church, Walter was struggling to concentrate on his sermon; he couldn't stop fretting about how to find out why the military wanted the beach. He could see no solution and time was running out. The lacklustre singing made him flinch. Effie and Ina had been replaced on the organ by an elderly woman who, if she ever could play, had long since forgotten how.

As soon as the last member of the congregation left he collected his bicycle – a relic of the Great War – from the manse next door and set off for Kildary. The roads were quiet, as not many people had cars and the difficulty of obtaining petrol meant that private vehicles were rarely used. For local people, transport was normally a case of a bicycle, a horse or one's own two feet. Walter, enjoying the exercise and the peaceful lanes, let his mind drift and he was soon recalling those last weeks with his father before he left Germany to begin his degree.

Rolf Möller had sat his son down as he had some news for him. He'd heard through his various government contacts that the couple called Aunt Iris and Uncle Jack had been killed in an accident. In truth, Walter hadn't thought much about them since leaving Dundee, but he was sorry to learn of their deaths. They had been kind to him and his mother. It wasn't until later that the timing of the tragedy struck him as something of a coincidence; now there was no one in Scotland who could reveal that his father wasn't Dutch, but German.

The suspicion had lain dormant until he left university and returned in secret to Germany to begin his training by Hitler's handpicked team. It was then, one night that Walter and his father were drinking brandy together in the living room of the Berlin apartment, that Möller revealed the truth.

'They were elderly,' he said, 'two grains of sand in what will become an entire beach when the war begins ... I fear it will be a beach so vast that it will stretch beyond our ability to see.'

Walter had put his brandy glass down in horror, shocked by the admission that his relatives had been murdered and by the prediction of the scale of massacres yet to come. He noticed that his father appeared sad, morose in a way that he hadn't seen before.

'So many deaths?' said Walter.

Möller had looked at his son, now a strikingly handsome young man to make Germany proud. His greatest fear was that he could so easily become one of those grains of sand and simply be lost forever.

'War is a bloody business,' he said, pulling himself together with an enormous effort of will. 'Learn from the experts who have been assembled to teach you how to stay alive. Keep safe, find the secret and come home.'

★

Lost in his recollections, Walter arrived at the POW camp. The guard opened the gate to the familiar figure before the minister had even stopped his bicycle. As he entered, he sensed immediately the shift that had occurred in the atmosphere. Perhaps this was to do with the men having spent the previous few days living in more ordinary family settings, away from barbed-wire fences, huts and regulations. They had been exposed to a normal life and it had had a profound effect upon their morale.

Walter walked around the grounds, speaking to the men alone or in small groups, asking them where they had been living and what sort of work they had undertaken. He sifted through all the information, but none of it appeared to be of any use to his quest. And so Walter went to the mess hall to give his service. He knew that the local Catholic priest had held Mass there a little earlier, and that some men would attend both services.

This morning, there were about forty in his congregation, as well as a few guards and a rather ancient sergeant who always stood at the back. Walter suspected that each week he reported to Major Cooper about what had been said.

Walter had to contend with the noise and smells coming from the kitchen at the far end of the building, but his strong, deep voice was more than a match for the occasional clank of pans. He talked about forgiveness and making the most of their current situation, how they must work together in harmony with their fellow countrymen even if they held different political views. Even as he spoke, he knew the sermon was uninspiring.

He stayed talking afterwards and was still there when the last of the Italians started coming in for lunch. It wouldn't be the first time the Reverend Smith had been invited for a meal and the smell of cooking had been making his stomach rumble, so he readily accepted Mirko's offer to sit with him.

The building had two long tables with benches either side. Men often took the opportunity to mingle with those from other huts, but inhabitants from hut 3 tended to stick together. No one wanted to join the 'Mussolini men' as they had come to be known.

'This looks like stew,' said Walter, once they had all sat down.

'Tastes bloody excellent,' said Mirko, who had already begun. 'Quite a few rabbits and chickens found their way here yesterday and it looks as if they've all jumped out of their skins and into the cooking pot, which was good of them.'

The meal turned out to be the highlight of that Sunday's visit and the minister was glad when he was cycling back to the manse. Today had unsettled him, because on the third Sunday of the month he would connect his transmitter/ receiver so as to receive any new instructions or information from Germany. It was the one occasion when he exposed himself to the terrible danger of being discovered for what he really was.

★

Around the time that the minister arrived back at the manse, the workers on Kirk Farm were taking a brief rest. Everyone was tired and covered in bits of straw and dust. The land girls' jumpers were coated in chaff, which stuck stubbornly to the coarse wool. Effie, Ina and Duncan stood to one side sharing a tin mug of water out of the nearby milk churn.

'Well, you've certainly caught the attention of Fiona,' said Ina.

'Which one's she?' replied Duncan with a smile.

'The one with the out-of-control red hair that you're all over whenever you get the chance.'

'A man's got to enjoy himself when he can. There aren't any women at the army base. She's game for a laugh so why shouldn't we have some fun.'

'It depends on what you mean by fun,' said Ina. 'She has feelings. Don't hurt them.'

'You worry too much,' he said, brushing off her warning.

'And you worry too little,' replied Ina. 'You always have. Actions have consequences and Fiona's a nice girl. Don't make her believe it's something serious if you intend to forget her the moment you're back at the barracks.'

'Crikey, how old are you? You'll be giving sermons from the pulpit next. Lighten up. Hey little sister, the mug's empty,' said Duncan, holding it out towards Effie.

'You've drank most of it,' she replied. 'What's wrong with your legs?'

Their conversation was interrupted by the arrival of their father.

'Dad, while we've got the use of a tractor why don't we pull out that old tree stump in the middle field?' said

Duncan, still holding the mug out to Effie. 'It's a pain to plough around with the horses and there's not enough space between it and the embankment to easily work the soil that side.'

'You know why,' said Mr Ross. 'We don't have time for the extra work.'

'But we're wasting land. Do you know in England they're letting the grass grow long in cemeteries to provide extra animal feed?'

'What?' said Ina. 'They're using graveyards?'

'I don't suppose the beasts mind and none of the residents have complained. It might make them feel useful.'

'You've never even driven a tractor,' said Effie to her brother.

'Well, if those land girls can manage, then it can't be difficult,' he replied.

'Really! If you're that capable you can get the water,' said Effie.

★

The Reverend Smith struggled even more with the evening service than he had that morning. Fortunately, nobody remained afterwards as everyone was keen to get home to the comfort of their hearths. Walter felt too uptight to eat and was glad of the decent lunch he'd had at the camp. Once back in the manse he threw some extra logs on the fire in his study, then he sat and watched the flames until it was time to get ready for his arranged time at nine o'clock.

On how many occasions had he waited like this, fighting off the disappointment that he had nothing to report, nervous that he might actually be given some new instructions, fearful that it would simply be another month of silence?

He wondered how many others there were like him scattered around Britain, setting up their equipment at the designated hour, just as he was about to do. Had anyone discovered a great secret and been spirited home to a hero's welcome from the Führer? Was it all merely an extraordinary waste of his life, an insane idea from the very beginning? Having experienced a thrill of excitement when he sensed that the reason behind the evacuation was of huge military significance, he was now strangely deflated and felt less hope than ever of achieving his quest.

Walter put the spark guard in position and went to the kitchen, where he had his domestic wireless. This required two very different batteries to operate, and he was obliged to make regular trips to get one of them, the accumulator, charged. He usually travelled every Saturday to the nearby garage; the heavy glass vessel, with its two lead plates immersed in sulphuric acid, fastened securely in the wicker basket at the front of his bicycle.

Walter disconnected the wires and put the accumulator into a battered Gladstone bag. He was often seen going around with it, so no one would think it unusual, yet he still left it in the manse corridor while he took a slow walk around outside. The night was pitch black and freezing cold so the chances of coming across someone were slim, but he never took any risks on this particular evening of the month.

Satisfied, he retrieved the bag then went to the church, locking the door behind him. The darkness was total, but he knew the layout and easily reached the vestry. Once inside he lit the paraffin lamp that was always on his desk, took the large key off his belt and unlocked the safe. He placed the small suitcase he retrieved on his table and produced another key.

The item in front of him was the most significant threat to his entire existence. If discovered, there was no innocent explanation as to why he had in his possession a spy-set manufactured in Germany. When he'd left Berlin the equipment was the most advanced design Hitler's scientists could offer. Now the technology was no doubt out-dated, but it still did the job required.

Walter began putting the equipment together. He attached a special cable to the accumulator's positive and negative terminals. The set incorporated a device that converted some of this low-voltage energy into the form needed for the valves to function, which meant that he didn't need two batteries.

Often, the riskiest part for any secret operator was the long length of wire required as an aerial. More than one spy had been caught because a keen-eyed neighbour or passer-by had spotted a suspicious wire hanging from a tree or post.

Walter had devised a much safer option. He opened the vestry window and attached a wire to the lightning conductor that was fixed to the outside wall. When he'd first arrived in the area he had carefully cut away the bottom few inches so the metal strip was no longer connected to the ground and therefore not earthed. Later that day he had transmitted the agreed phrase that was to be sent each time he began living in a new location.

'Uncle John. Please tell Father that I have arrived safely at my new post. Norman.'

After a few minutes he had received the reply, which confirmed that the makeshift aerial worked.

'That's great news Norman. Your father sends his love and looks forward to hearing from you again. Uncle John.'

Those few words had been the only contact during the four years he had been in the Tarbat peninsula. Walter sighed and inserted one of the three crystals that were in the suitcase. Each crystal caused the set to operate on a different frequency and alternating them every month made transmissions more difficult to intercept.

He remembered that an elderly parishioner, a keen amateur radio enthusiast, had once confided that the authorities had recruited him to listen for Morse code messages. The radio equipment that he'd had confiscated at the start of the war had been returned to him when he agreed to help. Walter never again heard even a whisper of such a clandestine activity, but that one conversation was enough to make him believe that hundreds of enthusiasts around the country monitored the airwaves for the British government.

Walter plugged in the Morse key then moved the dials to the correct positions and placed his pad and pencil next to him. With five minutes to go he sat down and turned on the set's power, checking that everything appeared to be working and the relevant switch was to the left, for 'Receive'.

The headphones had been adapted to have only one earpiece, which enabled him to hear anything going on nearby. There was always the remote possibility that a parishioner could become ill and send someone to fetch him. Finding no answer at the manse they might bang on the vestry window. This was highly unlikely, but he had to be obsessive about precautions.

The only illumination in the room came from the paraffin lamp and a tiny light on the grey metal panel. He sat in the gloom and shivered. Outside, the wind was growing stronger.

When he'd found out about the evacuation Walter had been forced to inform the church authorities in Edinburgh. Yesterday he'd received a letter telling him that he was to arrive on the fourteenth of December at a parish in Aberdeen and help out for a few months. When the residents of the Tarbat peninsula were finally allowed to return home, the congregation would have to appoint a new minister.

Walter never felt as lonely as he did while sitting in silence like this ... hoping ... fearing ... that the headphones would suddenly burst into life with a series of audible dots and dashes. He let ten minutes pass then flicked the switch to 'Transmit'. The key was specially made so that it didn't make any giveaway tapping sounds during operation, something that had been the downfall of agents on both sides. Walter placed his hand on it, paused for a moment then began.

'Uncle John. Please tell Father that I have a new job and will be in touch again when I am settled. Norman.'

Walter moved the switch to 'Receive' and waited. He began to fear that his contact hadn't got the message or, worse still, that there was no contact any more. Had the operation been abandoned? Had Hitler, now fighting on every front, decided that this idea from so many years ago was no longer worth the manpower and cost? Had Walter been forgotten, left to chase a secret that no one was waiting to hear?

When there were only a few minutes remaining of his allotted slot, the earpiece came alive. Walter grabbed the notepad and scribbled frantically.

'Norman. Your father sends his love and looks forward to hearing from you in the near future. Uncle John.'

That was it. Walter stared at the set. It stayed silent and the intensity of the feelings of hopelessness that overwhelmed him took him completely by surprise. He had never experienced such an emotion. Eventually, reluctantly, he removed the headphones and turned off the power, the tiny light fading away to leave only the dull grey metal, cold and innate.

Then the man, whom the Führer had handpicked to help Germany win the war, to be a hero among a nation of heroes, sat in the gloom. The blackout curtain at the window billowed wildly, and Walter Möller wept.

19

The lifeblood of Kirk Farm continued to drain away when a lorry arrived that Monday morning to remove the pigs.

The previous week Hugh had surprised everyone when Mr Ross explained that the animals had to be sold. The family had all expected an outburst of heartbreaking sobbing and protest, but he had accepted the situation with an astonishing maturity.

Now Hugh stood quietly with his mother at the front door while his father and Duncan herded the pigs up the ramp of the lorry. They were the sole witnesses; everyone else was working in the wheat field. Martha had left her kitchen chores to come outside and stand with her son. She put a hand on his shoulder and he reached up to take hold of it, almost as if he was the one doing the comforting.

Martha looked down at him and had to wipe away a tear. Anyone watching might have thought her unusual display of emotion was due to the sad scene occurring in front of them. But in fact her emotion was one of love and pride. Hugh was growing up so fast and she feared her last baby would be a young man before she knew it, taller and stronger and making her feel old. Memories of bedtime hugs and stories, of caring for him and answering his incessant questions would soon be just that, memories.

As the vehicle pulled away, the two men walked over to the house to watch it trundle down the drive and on to the lane. Duncan put an arm around his mother and she put hers about his waist. She thought how her sons were so very different, one slightly wild and impulsive and the other thoughtful and sensitive. She wondered how they would get on when Hugh was an adult. Perhaps the land and farming life would help to bind them.

'Well, that's that,' said Mr Ross, trying to make the comment sound matter-of-fact. No one was fooled. 'Let's get back to the field. There's work to be done.' He walked away briskly, the ever-faithful Nip by his side.

'Go on, son, keep your father company.'

Duncan hurried to catch up with the older man, and Martha and Hugh watched until they disappeared out of sight around the corner of the far shed.

'And you and I had better get our skates on. There's shopping to be done.' She ruffled his hair. For the moment at least, he was still her wee boy. 'And Bertie's there, patient as ever.'

Martha was going to Inver for supplies. The village's two smallest shops had already closed because of the evacuation, but the main store would remain open until the end. The community couldn't manage without it. The premises stocked a huge variety of produce, from bread and medicines to shoes, fruit and vegetables, while it also housed the post office, an ironmonger's and a Christian bookshop.

The farm buildings fell quiet and calm. But in the wheat field the tractor belched fumes, the arm of the baler pumped up and down, and the threshing mill jiggled and jumped as though it was possessed, as if at any moment it might hurtle off by itself into the distance.

Alastair had been overseeing the work while Mr Ross and Duncan dealt with the lorry, but in reality everyone knew what they were responsible for and had fallen into a steady routine as soon as they started that morning. The Italians worked well alongside the land girls, and various easy friendships had formed.

Duncan could often be seen helping Fiona, and they always chatted privately together during breaks. The three land girls cycled home every evening to their lodgings in Portmahomack, and a couple of times Duncan had gone over there to take Fiona to the local pub.

Likewise, Effie and Toni spent as much time as they could together, either working side by side or transporting sacks of grain to the storage shed. As Martha had wanted Bertie for her journey, one of the other horses was being used that morning and when Effie judged that the load was sufficient she told Toni to get into the bogie with her. The noise of the tractor and petrol engine of the baler faded as they left the field and moved cautiously along the track.

'On Wednesday, when they take away the sheep, my father is going in one of the lorries to Dingwall,' Effie said. 'It's near to where we'll be living until we return so he's going to meet the farmer and view the cottage to check everything's in order.'

'The days go by so fast,' said Toni sadly. 'I can't believe how much has happened in little over a week ... how much I've altered.'

They rode in silence for a while before Effie replied.

'Ten days ago I wouldn't have believed it possible that I could feel so differently about my life in such a short time. You've turned everything upside down.'

They were out of sight of the field and the farm. She tugged on the reins and the horse stopped.

'For the last few days … and nights … I've thought of little else except that moment we spent under the Northern Lights,' she said.

'Nor have I.'

He leaned across and gently kissed her on the lips. When he moved away she reached over to pull him back, then gave him a kiss that revealed the passion smouldering inside her. She knew immediately that he felt the same. When they eventually parted, they were both flushed and breathless.

'We mustn't,' she said.

'I'm sorry.'

'Don't be. But we must be careful. My mother misses nothing and I daren't get home looking so excited when all I'm meant to be doing is driving the bogie.'

Effie flicked the reins and the horse began to walk again. However, when they arrived home, she remembered her mother was going to Inver.

'So the house is empty?' said Toni.

'Yes … why do you ask?'

'You'll think me silly.'

'It's a bit late to be worrying about that. Why do you ask if anyone's around?'

'I would love to see your puppets.'

'My puppets!' she said, punching him on the arm. 'Here am I concerned that you wanted to … yes, well, never mind.

146

And it's toys made out of wool and cloth that you want to see. Come on, we can't take too long and we'll have to work double quick to unload the sacks. And then I'm going to return to the field red in the face and breathless when all I've been doing is moving grain.'

They jumped down and went inside. When Effie paused in the hallway he feared she might have changed her mind.

'We'll get into terrible trouble if you're found upstairs,' she said.

'Perhaps we shouldn't?'

'No, I suppose not. Come on. I'll race you.'

They ran up the stairs, holding and pulling at each other so that they were both laughing by the time they reached the top.

'You cheated!' she said.

'So did you. It would have been quicker to take the steps normally.'

'Yes, but it wouldn't have been so much fun. They're in here,' she said, leading him towards a door further along the corridor. 'This is Hugh's room. We'll have to be careful to replace everything exactly because he has a phenomenal memory for detail and will notice if something's been moved.'

Toni looked in wonder at the puppets. Some were knitted out of wool, while others were made out of fabric, but there were several on wooden sticks with painted papier-mâché heads or bodies.

'These are amazing,' he said, looking around and carefully picking up examples to examine them more closely. 'They don't all go over your hand?'

'Only about half of them. There are some on strings. Look.'

Effie picked up a figure dressed like the local postman. By manipulating the cross bars she made it walk across the bed, holding out a tiny envelope as if delivering post. Toni was delighted, particularly when he discovered that this could be removed from the raised hand.

'There's a message inside that says *Time to go to sleep*, which always makes Hugh laugh,' explained Effie. 'It was more difficult trying to write the words small enough than it was making the entire thing.'

On the top shelf there was a row of figures representing the family, with Martha in her blue apron and Mr Ross in his overalls, a lamb under one arm.

'Hugh loves this,' said Effie, putting on a glove puppet that looked like Ina and fitting a miniature puppet over its hand. 'There. A world of make-believe within a world of make-believe.'

'That's marvellous,' said Toni, but then his face grew more serious when he spotted the POW. Almost hesitating, he turned it around to reveal the red target disc on the back of the jacket. 'Is this what you think of me?'

'No ... this is what I think.'

And she kissed him, again leaving no doubt as to her feelings.

'We have to go,' said Effie as she drew away from him. 'We've pushed our luck enough as it is. But I'm so happy that you wanted to see my creations.'

'Thank you for showing me.'

'Here,' she said and took the POW to put it back in its place before checking that everything else was as it should be. 'Come on, we'd better start unloading or people will wonder where we are.'

They had just reached the top of the stairs when they heard the front door open followed by the familiar sound of Mr Ross's heavy shoes.

'Father!' whispered Effie in horror. 'In here, quick.' She opened the nearest door, gestured at Toni to remain quiet and pushed him into the room.

'Hello, Father, I wasn't expecting you,' she said, arriving at the bottom of the stairs as casual as could be.

'The engine for the baler has run out of petrol. It's my fault. With everything else going on I forgot to keep it topped up, so I'm just on my way with a full can. What were you doing upstairs?'

'I just needed something.'

'What?'

'There are things a young woman needs at times.'

'Oh ... sorry. But where's Toni? The sacks are still in the bogie.'

'Urgent call of nature. But we're about to start unloading. We'll be in the wheat field again before you know it.'

'Mmm ... well, as I had to come back I thought I would get some tobacco. My pouch is empty.'

★

Toni stood completely still, looking around with interest at the unfamiliar surroundings. It was immediately apparent that this was Captain Armstrong's bedroom. Toni could hear muffled voices, but there was no sign of anyone coming upstairs. After a while, he took a tentative step,

149

checking that the floorboards didn't creak. They were solidly fixed and he gained more confidence as he walked slowly around, his natural curiosity piqued as he examined the various objects laid out in military precision.

When he reached the wardrobe he cautiously pulled forward the door and was soon marvelling at the quality of the clothes hanging from the rail. At the bottom of one corner there was a leather briefcase. He picked up the case to admire the workmanship then he put his nose close, inhaled deeply and smiled. This wasn't merely a smell; it was a sensation that was closely connected with happy childhood memories.

The catches were locked, however he couldn't help but start to search, being careful not to disturb anything. There weren't many places to look and he soon ended up in front of the wardrobe once more, prepared to admit defeat. Then he considered where he would hide a key when there was an inquisitive small boy in the house.

Toni reached up and put his hand on it immediately. The briefcase parted to reveal a thin sheaf of papers and a folder. Now he was treading on dangerous ground. He knew he should return everything straight away, yet he felt compelled to remove the folder to glance at the contents, convincing himself it would only be for a few seconds, with no harm done.

But across the top sheet in bold letters were the words 'Top Secret'. Toni had never known something that was 'top secret' and his heart beat faster in excitement. This was a fantastic game, a wonderful puzzle. For a moment he focused on the sounds in the house. There were faint noises coming from the kitchen, which meant that Effie was with her father and no doubt still trying to get rid of him.

When he read the heading on the next page, Toni paused, a wave of guilt washing over him. He ignored the feelings and began to read.

20

Walter had never known himself to be so on edge. Sleep was increasingly elusive and he was too easily irritated by people coming to him with problems or seeking advice. It wasn't a good situation or mental state to be in and he reckoned that being away for a few hours would do no harm.

And so, after breakfast that Wednesday, he set off on his bicycle towards the coast on the west. He didn't expect the journey to reveal any useful information, but he felt that he should at least look at the beach he believed the military intended to use and the exercise might stop him feeling so jumpy.

It had been nearly two weeks since local residents had received their forms of requisition and the area already felt different. Soon after the announcement, a lot of single people moved to cities such as Glasgow and Aberdeen, where they could easily find employment. In addition, some families had wasted no time in leaving their houses, with the keys in the front door as instructed by the authorities.

The Tarbat peninsula had always been sparsely populated and as Walter travelled along, passing empty properties and fields, he felt that it now had a sense of desolation.

The sheep were due to be removed that morning and farms that had existed with livestock alone would become sad places indeed. Only those that grew crops were busy and noisy, a contrast to the silence that was creeping over the land like the shadow of a slow-moving storm cloud.

★

Mr Ross climbed into the cab of the last lorry to be loaded with his sheep and a few moments later it set off. He would make his own way back once he had visited their temporary accommodation. One good thing about wartime was that people could be certain of a lift and so he had no concerns about getting home.

Duncan would be in charge for the day, as Alastair had left earlier to ride over to meet the farmer he was going to work for when he left with his family. His employment with the Ross family would end that coming Sunday, the twenty-eighth of November.

Even Martha and Hugh would be away as she wanted to visit an elderly neighbour who was in poor health. She secretly feared that they might never see each other again once everyone had moved. Martha had prepared lunch as much as possible before leaving with her youngest son, who was not too happy at the prospect of the walk or the visit.

Everyone had quickly fallen into their usual rhythm that morning, although with two men short there was even more work to do. Effie and Toni took the sacks to the storage shed when there were sufficient on the cart and people had become used to seeing the couple going around together.

Bertie was once again in the harness, as three of the Clydesdales had been sold. Prices at the Dingwall auction for the cattle and pigs had been depressed, as the start of winter was a bad time to sell livestock, which meant that Mr Ross hadn't been able to turn down a good offer for the horses.

Duncan enjoyed being in charge and instructed three Italians to clear away the chaff and put it into bags, while he gave the land girls slightly more pleasant jobs. They were now on the last stack in that field, after which they would move the machinery into the adjoining one. The previous day a lorry had taken away the sacks of grain, which provided space for the cartloads yet to come. When Effie and Toni made their first journey that morning they found the house and buildings deserted.

'So, the house is empty again?' said Toni.

'I don't care if there is no one left in the entire Highlands, we're not repeating what we did on Monday! You wouldn't believe the nightmares I've had about my father finding you in Christopher's room. Bad enough to be caught upstairs, but going into his sanctuary is a sin of unimaginable seriousness. It's a good job you were standing exactly where I'd left you when I came back in.'

'You did look rather flushed when you opened the door.'

'Flushed is about right. And, now that you mention it, I do seem to spend a lot of my time these days with a red face ... It's lucky it wasn't my mother who came home. She would have sniffed you out quicker than Nip.'

All the same, there was a glorious freedom about having the place to themselves. Moving the grain was interspersed with the hugs, kisses and caresses of young people in love.

'Whatever happens ... we will be together after the war,' said Toni, when they had completed their task. 'But, you know, we Italians ... we like to make lots of babies!'

'Well, I might have something to say about that.'

He took her in his arms.

'What would you say?'

'That having your children would be the greatest gift I could imagine.'

'I love you, Effie.'

'I know.'

She reached up and kissed him and by the time they pulled part she was red in the face, again.

★

Walter entered the village of Inver to be greeted by the sight of three army ambulances lined up outside two houses. He stopped a little distance away to watch and when an elderly man came by he asked what was happening. Walter found that his clerical collar always opened doors in many different ways. In this instance, when the stranger saw the collar he appeared even keener to explain the odd scene.

'It's a protest, minister,' said the man, almost with glee. 'Two families have refused to leave, saying they're all down with a bad dose of the flu. Well, there have been a couple of elderly folk with it and they've been taken to hospital, but the doctor reckons these are severe doses of ... shyness. The army have played them at their own game. They've sent in ambulances to carry them away whether they're willing or not.'

'I suppose if they suddenly have the strength to resist

then they've proved the case against themselves,' said Walter, trying to sound interested, as the man seemed to expect this.

'That about sums it up. You'll be visiting someone in the village?'

Walter wasn't about to get embroiled in any sort of explanation about why he was there, so he made a big show of glancing at his watch.

'Goodness, I have to be going.' He put his foot on the pedal and started to move away. 'It's been nice meeting you.'

A few moments later, he left his bicycle outside the village and began to stroll along the path that ran parallel to the beach, which formed the south side of Inver Bay. The authorities had placed coils of barbed wire at intervals, yet it was easy enough to negotiate these. He relied on his clerical collar to get him out of any potential awkwardness if he was challenged. However, there was no one in sight and he walked onto the beach to stand at the water's edge.

He studied the shore opposite and the surrounding area, giving the appearance of someone merely enjoying the landscape. After walking for about ten minutes the land opposite came to an abrupt end and the water became a much larger expanse, signifying that he was now on the edge of the Dornoch Firth.

The Arboll burn ran into the sea a little further on and he used the slippery stepping-stones to cross it, then continued until he was standing a short distance away from a house which marked the small hamlet of Balnabruach. Portmahomack was only a few minutes further on, but he couldn't think of any benefit in going there.

The sea was choppy, with white breakers flicking across the surface, while the wind blowing against his face was icy. It was no surprise that the area was deserted. The bleakness of the weather echoed his own feeling of loneliness. There was nothing for him here. Was there anything for him anywhere? He turned around and headed back to Inver, calculating that if he went straight to Kirk Farm he should arrive at lunchtime. At least there would be some decent company and a bowl of something tasty to eat.

★

There was no one to bring food to the field and so Duncan announced that everyone could eat in the kitchen, a suggestion that appealed to all concerned. When Ina decided it was time for her and Effie to get to the house they set off in the cart, arriving just as the minister was cycling into the yard.

'Reverend Smith, you've missed our parents,' said Ina. 'They're both away. However, you're welcome to stay for lunch. We're just about to get things ready.'

'That's very kind of you,' he said. 'I don't want to impose.'

'How are you at cutting bread?' asked Effie.

'Fairly handy.'

'Come on then, that's payment enough.'

The three of them went inside and set about their tasks in amicable silence. Ina moved the huge pan of thick soup that her mother had made earlier on to the range then went about setting the table, while Walter sorted out the bread and Effie fetched cheese and butter from the pantry.

It wasn't long before they spotted the POWs through the window. The men began moving the sacks into the shed, while Joan and Eileen unhitched Bertie and led him to the stables.

'I wonder where our brother and Fiona are,' said Effie, seeing that there was no sign of them outside.

'Is there a ... friendship?' asked Walter, curious but not wanting to be over-familiar.

'That's debatable,' said Ina. 'I think she may be easily led and I worry Duncan might not behave as properly as he should.'

'I see. But they are adults and the war does make men and women behave with a little less caution than they might do otherwise.'

'I think you're being rather tactful, Reverend Smith,' said Effie.

'Ah, but that's the nature of my vocation.'

They could hear workers using the outside tap to wash before they entered in ones and twos, all happily squeezing around the table as more came in. When everyone had been served and grace said, they tucked into the food.

'Did anyone see what happened to Duncan?' said Effie.

'He was talking with Fiona when we left,' replied Toni. 'It didn't look as though they would be following very soon.'

'I suppose we should leave them something,' said Ina.

'It would serve him right if we didn't,' said Effie, only partly in jest.

They ate in a relaxed atmosphere, brought together by the bond formed by working hard alongside each other in challenging circumstances. No one appeared in any rush and there was a great deal of good-natured amusement when an Italian tried out some English phrases on Eileen.

'Toni,' said Ina, 'ask Biagino where he learned that sentence.'

Toni spoke to his friend and then confirmed that her brother had indeed taught the man the rather inappropriate comment.

'I thought so,' said Ina. 'I'll be having a few words with him about that.'

'Please explain what it means,' said Effie, 'and tell him not to say it again.'

Toni spoke at length and there was a moment of stunned silence before the Italians burst out laughing and the victim of the joke offered his profound, gracious apologies to Eileen. She patted him on the arm and smiled to show no harm had been done. 'Not to worry,' she said. 'You should hear some of the abuse us land girls experience.'

'Reverend Smith, will you have some cheese?' asked Ina, wanting to change the subject.

'That sounds like an —'

The front door banged open, cutting him short, and a few seconds later Fiona burst into the room, her pretty face a mask of tears and misery.

'Whatever's happened?' cried Effie.

She stood in front of them all, too distressed to speak, crying and gasping for breath.

'Shh now, tell us what's happened,' said Walter, standing up.

'I didn't want to do it! I didn't want to do it.'

'What?' Ina cried. 'What is it?'

'He kept on at me about it … then when there was just the two of us, I couldn't stop him.'

The room suddenly filled with a sense of such foreboding that Ina and Effie stood up slowly, holding their breath in dread.

'We took the tractor to the middle field,' Fiona gasped, trying to settle herself. 'He wanted to pull out the old tree stump to surprise Mr Ross. I told him to let me drive it, but he wouldn't listen. Then, then … I don't really know. Somehow the chain came free … he couldn't stop the tractor.'

'How badly is he hurt?' asked Ina, knowing by Fiona's terrible distress that her brother had been injured.

'I thought he might be all right,' she went on, desperately fighting to control her sobbing. 'I saw him thrown clear, but when I ran to see …'

'Tell us,' said Walter.

'The tractor had rolled over and landed on top of him.'

Fiona burst into fresh tears and could say no more.

Toni jumped up and so did the other Italians, even though they didn't fully understand what had occurred. One man steered the distraught woman into his chair.

'Duncan!' cried Effie, making a dash for the door, followed by Ina and Toni.

'WAIT!'

The authority of the voice froze everyone to the spot. For all of the times they had heard him preach, for all the conversations they had enjoyed, no one had ever experienced such a show of power from the minister.

'Nobody moves until I say. Fiona, tell us exactly how they are each positioned.'

'He ... he's trapped face down at the bottom of the embankment. The top of the tractor is across the lower half of his back.'

'It's upside down?' queried Walter.

'Yes. You'll have to lift the whole thing to free him.'

Walter's questions triggered a series of images that flashed through his mind ... the fortnight he spent living in the wild with an engineer from the German army ... building bridges, making rafts, lifting heavy weights ... fulcrums ... pivots ... rope and tackle. The memories were so rapid that no one looking at him was aware of anything other than a moment's hesitation. Then, he was suddenly a whirlwind of questions and instructions.

'Ina, what horses are there on the farm?'

'Only Bertie.'

'You and Effie fix a harness to him, get a length of stout rope and ride out. Where's your medical box?'

'In the scullery.'

Next, Walter turned to Joan.

'Get the box and a blanket, something we can carry Duncan in. I don't care if you have to rip it off a bed. But first get the operator to put you through to Doctor Gray and explain what's happened. Toni, take three men and bring two of the big timbers from the storage shed. Everyone else with me. GO!'

21

Figures rushed out of the house and scattered in different directions across the yard. Walter led his group to the workshop, where he grabbed spades, picks and crowbars and thrust them into the hands of the Italians before sprinting in the direction of the middle field.

Walter didn't carry anything himself; he wanted to reach the scene first so that he could assess the situation in more detail. However, he was still half a field away when Effie and Ina came thundering by, urging Bertie on with frenzied shouts and kicks. When they arrived, Effie was the first to dismount. Upon reaching her brother she curled up on the ground and pressed her face close to his.

'It's all right, darling,' she whispered, wiping away his tears. 'Ina and I are here to look after you. Everyone's coming to help. We'll soon have you home and in bed. It looks as though you'll be staying with us for a bit longer before returning to your unit.'

Duncan couldn't speak and his breathing was laboured. Ina stood by holding the coiled rope and watching, helpless. Beside her, Walter tried to work out how best to lift the weight. This was no way for anyone to die. Those carrying the tools arrived next and in the distance Toni and his men could be seen struggling to carry the heavy timbers that were meant for an extension yet to be built.

Walter snapped into action. 'Ina, take Bertie up the embankment. Tie the rope to the harness and throw me the other end. Get it over the top of the tree stump. We'll use it as the apex for the lift. You men start digging out the earth here and here,' said Walter, gesturing at the ground before them.

Effie remained with her brother, whispering to him and stroking his hair. Everyone else was frantic with activity. When the end of the rope suddenly dropped over the slope, Walter tied it securely to the part of the tractor where he thought the stump would provide the greatest leverage. Fiona might have been almost hysterical, but she had been correct in saying they would have to lift the entire tractor. Walter guessed it weighed at least two tons.

Toni and his men almost collapsed when they arrived. Walter let them catch their breath and instructed the others to insert the timbers beneath the frame, although it took several minutes of cursing and manoeuvring to position them the way he wanted.

Over the last four years the minister had watched the Ross sisters grow from girls into women. He knew them well and he understood their natures, which was why he wanted Effie with Bertie. The horse would kill itself attempting to do her bidding. He kneeled down beside Effie and spoke as reassuringly as he could.

'Effie, I need you to replace Ina and tell her to come down here. Quickly now, there's no time to lose.'

Effie grimaced but obeyed. Moments later Ina appeared

163

by Walter's side. He led her a short distance away from the others.

'I want you and Eileen to get a firm hold of Duncan, under his armpits. As soon as he's free of the tractor, you have to pull him clear.' Ina nodded and was about to move when Walter put a hand on her shoulder. 'Ina... he'll scream. He'll break your heart begging you to stop, but you have to pull him clear in one go. I don't think we'll be able to hold the tractor off him for more than a few seconds.'

Ina's eyes were wet with tears, but she remained composed. 'I understand.'

'Good.'

Walter positioned the men around the tractor, and Ina and Eileen kneeled either side of Duncan. In the distance Joan could be spotted rushing towards them with a box and blanket. The space they had to work in was so cramped that they were getting in each other's way, but no one complained.

'Effie,' shouted Walter, 'take the strain.'

Effie took hold of Bertie's bridle and made the horse walk forward until it stopped with a jerk and a snort when the rope tightened.

'On three!' Walter commanded. 'One... two... three!'

The men were transformed into grunting, struggling, gasping figures with faces so contorted by effort that they were almost unrecognisable. Effie was yanking with such force on the leather bridle that she feared it might snap.

'Pull, Bertie. Pull, my love. PULL!'

Walter could feel the ligaments and muscles in his back stretching and straining. One of the tractor's wheels had embedded itself in the embankment and he realised he should have had the men dig away some of the earth.

'Lift, you fucking bastard.'

Walter was no longer the gentle minister, laying a caring hand on the forehead of a dying parishioner. He was no longer the handsome, soft-spoken man, the slightly odd bachelor chasing wildlife around the countryside. He was bursting with a fury and strength that no one had seen in him before.

Ina and Eileen looked at each other across the body between them with utter dread. Duncan's moans were becoming feebler. On the higher ground Effie had lost all sense of reason. She screamed at Bertie. The horse was wild-eyed, every sinew, tendon and muscle heaving against the rope with an effort that was beyond anything that could be sensibly expected from an animal. Then, almost without warning, Bertie took a tiny step... and another.

Walter's mind had disappeared into an unknown, dark place. It was as if the years of living a lie had been like a dripping tap, steadily eroding his sanity until he suddenly found himself mad. It was the scream that brought him back to reality. A single, high-pitched cry of agony that made him realise the tractor had lifted.

'He's clear!' shouted Ina.

Men threw themselves from under the timbers and the horse was dragged backwards several paces. It stood, trembling and sweating, froth spraying from its mouth. Effie stared at her empty hands, as though she couldn't quite believe they had succeeded. Eileen was on all fours retching, as was one of the Italians, while several others were crossing themselves. Ina, kneeling on the ground, had covered her face with her hands.

Walter stared down at the mangled body and shuddered with revulsion. The grotesque angle of the legs made him think of Effie's puppet of the postman, when she made the limbs stick out in a way that was impossible for a real person.

'Dear God,' whispered Effie. Walter turned to find her standing beside him. He took in her pale face and thought for a moment that she was going to be sick. She seemed to have lost all her strength and stood as motionless as the remains of the old sycamore.

Walter desperately tried to prevent another series of images flashing through his mind, but they pushed their way in, no matter how hard he tried ... the sights he had seen while spending time with a doctor at a hospital in Berlin. The man had been traumatised by his experiences during the First World War and Walter had questioned his sanity. The old man had made him study hideously injured people and watch gruesome operations. Walter had suffered from nightmares for months after.

In the evenings the doctor would sit drinking whatever spirits were to hand and recount in detail how he triaged soldiers brought to him from the trenches. There simply hadn't been the capacity to try to save them all, he said, and he would have to condemn a man to death with no more than a quick glance. The stretcher-bearers would wait for his signal and then move off – certain death to the left, a slim chance of life to the right. For some reason, the doctor had wanted to pass on this skill to Walter.

The minister forced himself to take in the horror of the

scene. Duncan had soiled himself, yet there was no sign of blood. However, the internal bleeding would no doubt be extensive. It was doubtful that the farmer's son would even survive the journey back to the house.

'Toni,' Walter said quietly. 'We need to turn him on to his back.'

Toni nodded. It was clear from the sombre expression on his face that he understood. A man should die looking up at the sky and at those he loved, not with his face stuck in the dirt. Toni spoke to his comrades and they moved forward slowly, waiting for further instructions. Walter took the blanket off the sobbing Joan and spread it out on the ground nearby.

'We'll do this as gently as we can, but we have to do it,' he said to the men. 'Don't hesitate halfway. Ina, take his head. Ina.'

Ina wiped her eyes and nodded. Carefully, they lifted the farmer's son and laid him tenderly on the blanket. The scream that followed didn't come from him. He was already too weak for that. It came from Martha, who was rushing across the field towards them, her thick woollen skirt lifted high as she ran, faster than anyone would have thought possible.

Walter quickly covered the bottom half of Duncan's body with the remaining part of the blanket, while the men moved away to make room. Effie went to Toni. He held her tightly.

Martha reached the group, her breath coming in great gasps as she kneeled down beside her son, taking hold of one of his hands and doing her best to soothe him.

Ina stood up, grief and despair etched so deeply into

her beautiful face that she was unrecognisable from the cheerful, smiling person who had served them turnip and potato soup only a short while earlier. She glanced around her, and Walter realised she was looking for Christopher, who wasn't there. Walter moved towards her and she collapsed into his arms, weeping uncontrollably.

It was Toni who saw the small figure in overalls running across the stubble.

'Reverend Smith.'

Walter looked up and followed the Italian's gaze. He had to take charge of the situation quickly.

He squeezed Ina's shoulder and spoke quietly but firmly. 'Ina, you've got to dry your eyes now. Hugh's coming. This is no sight for a boy. Take him home.'

Ina raised her head from Walter's chest and saw that her younger brother was going to reach them at any moment. She took a long, deep breath, glanced at her mother, and then set off to stop him. Walter watched. Hugh was a big lad for his age and he worried that Ina would not be able to get him back to the house if he refused to go. There was only one person he could send.

'Toni, you've got to help her. Take the boy to the cottage to stay with Alastair's family tonight. Tell Ina she'll probably have to go with him. Get them there before we return.'

Toni let go of Effie, giving her a quick kiss on the forehead before running after her sister, who was struggling to hold on to the wildly squirming Hugh, his cries of protest clearly audible. When the Italian reached them he bent over as if to speak, then in one fluid movement scooped Hugh up, put him firmly over his shoulder and strode away. Ina followed close behind, failing in her attempts to stop the small fists beating against Toni's back.

Walter turned towards the tragic scene a few feet away. Martha was stroking Duncan's hair. 'We'll get you back to your bed soon,' she murmured to her son. 'Doctor Gray is on his way.'

'Effie,' said Walter, 'your mother is going to need you.'

Effie looked over at the two people on the ground. It took her a few moments to comprehend exactly what the minister meant.

'You have to be strong,' Walter said.

Effie nodded and they both went over; Effie put an arm around her mother and Walter placed a hand on Duncan's head, just above the staring, unseeing eyes. He hesitated for a few seconds then closed them.

'He's not suffering any more, Martha. Duncan's at peace with God.'

'No!' Martha gasped. 'He can't be. I was just talking to him.'

'Mother, we need to let the Reverend Smith attend to this. We'll carry Duncan back and lay him on his bed, just as you promised.'

'How could this have happened?' cried Martha. 'He was only meant to be helping with the crops.'

Effie tenderly pulled her mother to her feet, while Walter and the remaining men carefully lifted the body of Edward Ross's eldest son, the one who had been destined to take over Kirk Farm, and began a journey that none of them would ever forget.

22

The men carried Duncan up the stairs and laid him gently on Hugh's bed. Effie sat her shivering mother at the kitchen table and stoked up the fire in the range. The two land girls, Joan and Eileen, had followed the group back from the field and discreetly removed Fiona to one of the outbuildings before breaking the news. Eileen left her crying in the arms of Joan and went back to rescue Bertie.

Their grim task over, the Italians filed solemnly out of the front door and went to the barn. Walter was the last down. He came into the kitchen and sat silently at the table, looking as if he was haunted by some fearful memory. He had aged unbelievably over the last hour.

There was no sign of Ina, Hugh or Toni and the unnatural stillness of the house was broken only by Martha's weeping and the ticking of the grandfather clock. Ten minutes later, the front door opened and Doctor Gray entered. He could tell immediately by their expressions that he was too late.

'I'll take you upstairs,' said Effie flatly, her only acknowledgement of his arrival.

The doctor looked at Effie with concern, but didn't say anything. He followed her to the tiny bedroom where

Duncan was lying wrapped in the blanket. Effie stayed in the doorway while the doctor confirmed the identity of the body and that he was dead. It didn't take much skill to do either. Effie couldn't watch, but as she turned away something caught her eye … a tiny man dressed in a postman's uniform, with a smiling face and a letter in his hand.

Time to go to sleep.

'No!'

Effie rushed to the shelf, grabbed the figure and hurled it away. It bounced off the doorframe and flew back towards her.

'You're obscene! You're obscene!' she shouted, kicking the puppet so that bits of it broke off and flew across the floor.

The doctor put his arms around her, restraining her. Effie struggled against him. She was filled with a desire to destroy all the puppets. Their grinning expressions seemed to taunt her from the shelves.

'It's all right,' the doctor soothed, holding her tight. 'Let it out. Let it all out.'

Effie began trembling and a great sob escaped her lips. 'You're obscene,' she repeated feebly to the scattered arms and legs. The doctor released his hold so that he could turn her around to face him. Effie buried her face in his chest and cried and cried until there were no tears left.

Just then, Toni appeared in the doorway, his face a mask of concern. 'Effie,' he said quietly.

'Toni!' Effie rushed to him, and he held her tenderly.

'Ina and Hugh are safely with Alastair's family,' he said. 'Reverend Smith is with your mother and I'm here now to look after you.'

'I ... I don't want the puppets in this room.'

'That's all right. Why don't we move them to your bedroom instead?'

'Will you help?'

'Of course.'

'I can't do it alone.'

'You don't have to. I'll stay for as long as you need me.'

Effie clung to Toni without even glancing up at him. Her sobbing had ceased, and she felt weak with grief.

The doctor cleared his throat. 'I'll go and see to your mother, Effie, and leave you both to carry out your task. I'll only be downstairs.'

He squeezed past the couple, putting a reassuring hand on Effie's shoulder as he went by. Effie and Toni continued to hold each other for several minutes until Effie finally pulled away.

'I'm all right for now. Will you please pick up those pieces and put them in the corridor. They can go on the fire sometime.'

Together they transferred the puppets to the sisters' bedroom, quickly filling the space on the dresser and on top of the wardrobe. Several ended up on the windowsill and a few had to make do with a corner of the floor. Neither of them spoke and when the job was done they stood near the shelves in Hugh's room, which were empty, apart from one object.

'You've left Hugh's teddy bear,' Toni said.

Effie picked it up.

'This was given to Duncan by our grandmother Kirsty when he wasn't much more than a baby,' she said, looking fondly at the toy. 'This one can stay.' She replaced it, then looked at the figure on the bed, which she had been unable to acknowledge. 'He could be so infuriating at times.'

'Brothers are meant to be like that,' said Toni.

'But he could be such fun, too, particularly when we were little. He was the older brother that Ina and I adored, the one who always got away with that little bit extra, pushing his luck and taking chances that no one else would. Mother often said I was more like Duncan than I would ever admit. I did love him.'

Toni reached for her hand. 'I'm sure he knew and that he loved you as well.'

Effie moved to sit on the edge of the mattress. At least Duncan's expression of agony had gone; he looked at peace. She took out her hanky and spat on it.

'Look at you,' she said gently to her brother, wiping away some of the soil on his cheek. 'We can't have you lying there with a dirty face. You'll have to be a smart boy for Mother. She'll be coming to see you later ... when she's feeling better.'

Effie smoothed down Duncan's hair as best she could then laid his arms across his chest and neatly arranged the blanket so that only his head was visible. As she stood up, two figures appeared at the door.

'Ina!'

Ina stood with Martha, and both women had an air of determination about them.

'Alastair's returned,' said Ina. 'We explained to him what happened while Hugh was sitting on the settee with his boys, so that they all heard together. Afterwards I asked Hugh if he would stay and let me come home to help. I've never been more proud of him. He's going to remain at the cottage, but he asked if you would go later to see him.'

'Yes,' said Effie, barely aware that tears were streaming down her face, as they were on her sister's.

'I will not have my son lying in filthy clothes,' said Martha. She had become the practical farmer's wife once more and was carrying a bowl of hot water with soap and towels. She turned to Toni. 'I'm grateful to you for your kindness to my daughter. Please thank your men for their aid. I'll ask you to leave us now so that we can see to Duncan.'

'Of course, Mrs Ross.'

★

Toni stuck his head into the kitchen on his way out. There was no sign of the doctor, but the minister was sitting with a mug of tea. He looked ashen and for an instant Toni had the impression that the other man was frightened. Walter caught Toni's movement out of the corner of his eye and sat up straighter, as if composing himself.

'Come in,' he called to Toni. 'Here, I made a pot of tea. I'll get you a mug.'

Toni stood by the table, which was still laid out with the remnants of the meal they had all been eating when Fiona burst into the room.

'Shall we tidy this?' he asked.

Walter looked surprised at the mess, as if seeing it for the first time. 'Yes, I suppose we could at least do some of it.'

As quietly as they could the two men cleared away the plates and cutlery. Then they stood by the range and finished their now lukewarm tea.

'What will happen about telling Mr Ross?' asked Toni.

Walter signed, his expression sombre. 'I'll wait at the gate, so that I can speak to him in private.'

'I can stay as well, if you like, but I'll leave when we see him coming along the lane. I know he's a proud man and it would be best that he is alone with his minister when he learns of such tragic news.'

Walter nodded stiffly. 'Thanks, Toni. Let's hope he's here soon.'

★

While the men were clearing away, Martha and her daughters carefully removed Duncan's clothes. They worked methodically, tenderly washing and drying his body. No one spoke. Occasionally, one of the women would lean down and kiss his forehead or gently stroke his cheek. Together, they put clean linen on the mattress then dressed him in the family's best pyjamas, the ones normally only worn if Doctor Gray was visiting. Martha combed Duncan's hair, and when they had finished he looked as though he was merely sleeping.

23

The Reverend Smith and the undertaker arrived the next morning and arrangements were made for the funeral to take place that coming Saturday. There would be no work on the farm that day, so the Italians would return to their camp on the Friday afternoon.

The community came together, as they always did in times of need. A local farmer arrived with a tractor and his men. With help from the Italians the upturned vehicle was brought back into use, driving the threshing mill once more. Joan, Eileen and Fiona continued to cycle over from Portmahomack, as they had done since bringing the machinery. Like the others, they carried on with a grim determination to get the job completed.

Mr Ross oversaw the activity in the wheat field as usual. He looked pale and withdrawn, but got on with the task in hand. Ina stayed in the house to help her mother, who insisted on preparing meals. Being busy brought a comfort of sorts, albeit a temporary, superficial one.

Effie didn't speak as she drove the cart to the storage shed. Next to her, Toni also remained silent. She appreciated his understanding that, for the moment, she wanted to be left with her thoughts.

By chance she had been looking out of the kitchen window the previous afternoon when her father had returned home and was met at the gate by the Reverend Smith. She had seen her father sway so severely that the minister had been forced to take a firm hold of his arm and guide him safely indoors. Effie didn't like to think about the scene that followed, when the man who had always been her strong protector was half-carried into the room, a sobbing wreck with no resemblance to the person she loved and admired. The memory was too raw and she tried to push it away from her mind.

Instead, she thought about how she had kneeled with Hugh the night before to join him in his prayers. Alastair's sons were a similar age and the three boys were good friends, which helped enormously in making Hugh feel safe. Effie had tucked him up with Duncan's old teddy bear, telling him that if he cuddled the toy it was, in a way, like comforting Duncan.

Effie turned to Toni yet remained silent. Although they hadn't spoken that morning, Effie felt closer to Toni than ever before. There was an intimacy in their silence that she hadn't known – even with Ina. Here was the man she would marry and spend the rest of her life with. In her heart there was no doubt of their future.

★

During the day the family visited Duncan individually, when they felt it was the right time for them. Some sat quietly. Others chattered as if they had bumped into an old friend. Everyone had their own way of coping. There

177

were many hugs and tears between the women and they all made sure they visited Hugh. Mr Ross did not. After his initial burst of grief he had hidden his emotions behind a façade of stoicism that everyone suspected would crumble at some point.

After lunch on the Friday he went to the cottage to deliver Hugh's best clothes and bring him back for a brief visit. As they walked to the house he explained what was going to happen at the funeral service. His young son, hugging the teddy bear, appeared to accept this quite readily.

As they went up the stairs together, the farmer hoped that he could find the right balance between letting Hugh say farewell in his own way, in private, while remaining nearby in case he became frightened or upset. The window had been left slightly open and the bedroom was very cold. Mr Ross and Hugh stood by the bed without speaking or moving for several minutes, the mist of their breath the only sign of life in the room.

'He can't hurt you,' Mr Ross said.

'I know that. He never hurt me,' Hugh replied, turning his attention to the figure on the bed. 'Hello, Duncan. I've brought your teddy bear. I don't need it now I'm eight.' Hugh tucked the bear under the blanket so that it nestled against the body, then he reached over and kissed Duncan on the forehead. 'Thank you for being a good brother. I'll never forget the fun times we had.'

With that, he straightened up and faced his father.

'Duncan and I have said goodbye, Father. Can I please see Effie now and have a scone?'

Mr Ross couldn't answer. He simply nodded and moved to one side to let the boy pass. He listened to Hugh hurry

178

down the stairs and into the kitchen, where his sisters and mother made a great fuss.

Dear God above, Mr Ross thought. *Grant me the strength that innocence gives to children.*

★

For the men billeted at Kirk Farm, returning early to the camp was a bizarre experience. Toni's hut felt colder than it did outside, so he lit the stove before unpacking any of his belongings. Still shivering, he left for the mess hall, which he knew would be warm and where he could use his camp tokens to obtain more toothpaste and writing paper.

The POWs sat together for their meal that evening. The cooks were eager to hear news of what they had been doing, but the new arrivals were subdued and not in the mood for excited chatter. Toni was the only person in a hut by himself, but he turned down the offer to join the others once they had eaten.

Instead, he collected his toiletries and went to the wash block. It was strange for there to be no one at the sinks – no part-naked bodies queuing for the showers, no singing or chatter. The silence was total and the building felt desolate, like him.

Once back on his bed he reread his most recent letters, stopping a few minutes before eight o'clock to light a couple of candles. He had wished so often to have some privacy and peace, but being alone was unnerving. He had grown used to hearing men snore and move about, and it was a comfort now. Ironically, sleep looked likely to evade him that night.

He took a couple of blankets and made himself as comfortable as possible in a chair near the stove, positioning the candles to hold some of the surrounding blackness at bay. Toni and Mirko were two of the few POWs who didn't smoke and it was odd not to see a grey haze drifting in the dim light.

Toni went over the events of the week, right up to leaving the farm that afternoon. He pictured the look of misery on Effie's face as he was driven away. The family would have to endure the funeral service in the morning and he wondered how they would all cope.

How were he and the woman he loved going to get together once the war was over? Would it be possible for him to remain in Scotland? If he was forced to return to Italy, could he come back? Surely the British authorities couldn't forbid people from returning, not forever. Perhaps Effie could come to Termoli ... Whatever happened, he knew that their love would never fade and in that knowledge lay hope.

24

The coffin was outside the front door, on top of a wooden bier. A group of men dressed in their Sunday suits had already gathered around it, with Christopher the sole person in uniform. At a funeral, only the deceased's immediate female relatives were allowed in the house along with any children. Barbara and her boys, considered part of the family, had arrived earlier with Hugh.

Soon, more men appeared, neighbours and friends, all of the various cousins, second cousins and those so far removed that the lineage connecting them had been lost long ago. It didn't matter. They came. Those with no links whatsoever came, because this was how it was done. People were practical about such matters and no one considered it strange for a man to turn up and show his respects to someone he had never met.

Martha stood in the doorway with Hugh and her daughters. When it seemed that nobody else was coming, the Reverend Smith began the service.

First there was a reading from Scripture. Then there was the singing of a psalm, a few more readings from Scripture, two prayers and they ended with a psalm. That was it. He said very little about Duncan the person, who he had been or what he had done.

Now there was work to be done, protocol to be adhered to. Death was simply a part of the cycle of life and grief was something to be kept for the privacy of one's own home … of one's own heart.

Mr Ross, Alastair and Christopher were among the eight men who took hold of the handles along each side of the bier. There were no last minute embraces or gestures of support to the women they loved standing so close by. In the Highlands, even a mother did not go to her son's graveside when he was buried. Christopher had to force himself not to glance in Ina's direction.

The minister walked at the front and the others followed in silence behind the coffin. It was too far to carry all the way to the cemetery at Portmahomack and a neighbour was waiting with a horse-drawn cart further along the lane.

The family watched from the doorway as the group walked slowly along the drive and out through the gate. Effie wished that Toni was there to hold her. They hadn't spoken much during the last few days, but still his presence had been the greatest comfort she could imagine. As the Italians had left the previous afternoon she had felt a terrible loneliness descend upon her.

It was difficult to imagine how life could be borne without him. Kirk Farm and the people on it were being torn apart.

Effie glanced at Ina and saw her own misery reflected in her sister's face. At least Ina had a secure future ahead with Christopher, a man any woman would be pleased to call her husband. Christopher was considerate and handsome,

182

and Effie had always thought her sister beautiful. There was a refinement about her that went beyond her physical grace.

She reflected, too, how handsome Duncan had been. Many a local girl would have snapped him up if he hadn't been so flighty. Now he was leaving Kirk Farm for the last time, his body in a wooden box because of a stupid attempt to remove a tree stump that had been in the field for years.

The utter foolishness and waste of it all had washed over the family in waves of anger and guilt. Her father had been beside himself with blame because he had been away that day with Alastair. If either one had been present, Duncan would never have taken the tractor. Effie knew there was a great deal more anguish to come. But for now there were jobs to be done, which would occupy their hands at least.

The distance to Portmahomack meant that no one was expected back at Kirk Farm for at least a couple of hours. It was the custom for close male relatives or friends to return to the deceased's house for refreshments after a burial. Everyone else would go back to their own homes. Barbara didn't wait for Alastair and took her sons to the cottage, where she still had much to do in preparation for the family leaving the following day.

Together, Ina and Effie organised Hugh's room and made up the bed, then Ina went downstairs to join her mother, leaving Effie and Hugh to replace the puppets. A gap was left on the shelf where the teddy bear used to sit. Somehow it seemed the right thing to do. However, Hugh noticed that there was one other item missing.

'Fee, where's Mister Postman?'

Effie kneeled in front of him.

'I'm sorry, I threw him out.'

'Why?'

'He upset me.'

Hugh considered this for several moments.

'I never knew Mister Postman was like that.'

Effie put a hand to her mouth, but still a sound that could either have been a laugh or a sob escaped. Instinctively, Hugh wiped away a tear that was rolling slowly down her cheek.

'If he was nasty, then I'm glad he's gone.'

It was too much. She held him tightly and started to cry. Hugh rubbed her back tenderly.

'Don't be upset, Fee. It was only a puppet.'

★

That Saturday morning felt more unreal to Toni than the previous evening, as the sight of the empty camp in daylight made it even more desolate. The POWs had little work to do so they played cards, repaired their clothes and listened to the radio in the mess hall. The news was dominated by accounts of huge sea battles between the American and Japanese navies, and the extensive bombing raids that were devastating cities throughout Germany. The men listened for news of the position of Italians held by the Allies in POW camps, but there was nothing.

By mid afternoon trucks started to arrive and during the next hour the camp was transformed into a noisy, bustling place, full of shouting, gesticulating groups of Italians. Mirko found Toni lying on his bed, reading a book in English that Effie had lent him.

'You look like you've been here for ages,' he said, putting down a bag.

'I have.'

'Then why so gloomy?' asked Mirko, removing the first of the hidden hip flasks from beneath his trousers.

Toni looked at the other man for a while, still unsure how much to tell him of his troubles. However, he needed to talk to someone and Mirko, in his own odd way, had always had a sort of wisdom about him.

'It's a long story, so you need to sit down.' Toni glanced about them. There were other men in the hut, but no one was close enough to overhear. 'It's also very private. If anyone comes near, I'll stop.'

'All right,' said Mirko, sitting on his bed opposite. 'You better have a shot of this.'

Toni's eyes watered as the liquid burned his throat.

'Good stuff, eh?' said Mirko, as he took a swig himself.

Once Toni began it was as though a floodgate had been opened. He told Mirko about Kirk Farm and the Ross family, how he'd fallen in love with Effie and how they wanted to marry, about Duncan being killed under the tractor. Mirko listened patiently, occasionally taking a drink from the flask, but never interrupting. At last Toni paused for a long moment and Mirko thought his friend had finished.

However, Toni still had a story to tell, but for now he remained undecided even after sharing so many of his intimate feelings. The story was about a secret... a top secret. He knew Mirko would be pleased to hear it and Toni believed it could do no harm. He took a deep breath then recounted how he had gone upstairs with Effie to see

185

the puppets – he protested when Mirko raised an eyebrow – and then how the unexpected arrival of Mr Ross had forced him to hide in the room of the British officer.

He confessed that he'd looked in the wardrobe, unlocked the briefcase and removed the folder to read the documents. Then he began to tell Mirko about the contents. Toni didn't spot the shift in Mirko's expression or his absolute stillness, apart from his beefy hands that gripped the flask with such force that the sides bent inwards. If Toni had looked more carefully at the older man he would have seen his eyes flash with excitement and noticed his breathing become ragged.

'Who have you spoken to about the document?' Mirko said at last.

'No one.'

'Not even that girl you love?'

'Definitely not. Effie would be horrified at what I did. I'm horrified.'

Mirko leaned over and placed a hand on Toni's knee. It was only then that Toni noticed the strange expression on his face.

'Listen carefully,' Mirko said in a low voice. 'You don't tell anyone, not your priest at confession, not your mother ... no one. Don't even hint at its existence. Do you understand?'

'Yes, and for the love of God, stop crushing my leg!'

Mirko looked down and relaxed, forcing himself to smile before removing his hand.

'Why would I tell anyone? I'm ashamed of what I did. I wouldn't have told you if I knew you were going to hurt me.'

186

'Here, have another swig and let's get to the mess hall early. Tomorrow's Sunday, which means we get a lie in.'

★

Ina and Effie clung to each other in bed that night while they talked through the events of the day: the service, the men returning and standing around the living-room fire, afterwards when there was only the immediate family. Christopher said he had to return to the new military base, but Ina knew this was an excuse to let the five of them have that one night alone in the house. She wished he was there, just along the corridor; he would be a comfort to her, even though they wouldn't be together physically.

'I'm worried about Father,' Ina whispered.

'I know, me too. After that initial shock, when it was all too much for him to hide his true feelings, he's been holding everything inside.'

'He's trying to be strong for us, but I wish he would just cry and wail like we do.'

'And what Hugh makes of it all is a mystery,' admitted Effie. 'This afternoon, the Reverend Smith told me not to force the issue and let him bring it up if he wants to talk about it.'

They were silent for a while, listening to the wind moaning outside.

'When ... it all happened,' said Effie.

'What?'

'The Reverend Smith ... he seemed like a different person.'

'We would have been in trouble without him.'

'Yes, but did you see the way he took control? He could have been Christopher.'

'Christopher?'

'He was like an army officer, someone trained to command men in situations of stress or danger. I thought the gentle minister we know had been replaced by a completely different man. For a while, I could see nothing of the preacher in the pulpit. He even looked like a stranger.'

Any comment Ina might have wanted to make was lost when the door slowly opened, then closed a few seconds later. A small figure climbed under the blankets and over the top of Effie to get between the sisters.

'Baby, you're freezing,' said Ina, putting a hand on Hugh's bare feet.

Hugh clung to Effie. It was always the same when the three of them lay together at night. Ina didn't mind, not too much anyway. Her sister connected with their brother in a way she didn't, which was partly down to them being closer in age and partly because she was Effie. That night, with their older brother in his grave, Ina felt her heart would burst with how much she loved them both. As they settled down to sleep, Ina thought how she wouldn't change them for the world, not one tiny bit.

25

After the service that Sunday morning Mr Ross took his family to visit Duncan's grave. Bertie pulled the small cart, which Alastair had cleaned, and Ina had draped blankets over the seats to protect their best clothes further. They rode in silence along empty roads, passing deserted fields and houses.

Ironically, the fishing village of Portmahomack was bustling, as many residents from the evacuation area had moved to live with relatives there, even though they'd be cut off for most of each day once the military implemented the travel restrictions.

The farmer led his wife by the arm, with his young son, his only remaining son, holding the hands of his sisters as they walked slowly through the cemetery. There were other visitors, too, some tidying the areas around graves, others simply standing in silence, reflecting. Martha had brought a small spray of cotoneaster, the small red berries stark against the dark green leaves. She kneeled down and placed them on the freshly dug soil then remained there with a hand on the earth so as to create a physical closeness to the body buried beneath.

'You'll be with your grandfather Gordon and grandmother Kirsty now,' she said. 'They'll take good care of you, Duncan. We've all come today ... Effie and Ina and Hugh, and your father. Of course, he was here yesterday with the other men, including the Reverend Smith and Christopher. Christopher told me he would have been proud to be your brother-in-law and ...'

Martha couldn't continue. Mr Ross laid a hand on her shoulder as she wept. He was the only one not crying, yet grief and despair seemed to be etched into his face all the more deeply because of the lack of tears.

'Well, son,' he said. 'We all wanted to pay our respects. You'll understand that we need to return to the farm shortly. We've left Alastair with the Home Guard and the land girls. But you know he has to leave today, so it's only right that I take over and free him.'

'We'll come back,' said Ina, 'before we leave Kirk Farm. I promise. And if we don't visit in the months to come it's only because we're not allowed into the area.'

'I'll come, Duncan,' said Hugh. 'I'll tell you how I'm getting on at the new school.'

Only Effie didn't speak. For once, she could find no words ... at least none that she felt were worth saying.

The family remained for a while longer, then Mr Ross helped Martha to her feet and led them to the graveside of his own parents.

'Mother ... Father ... I know you'll help to look after our Duncan, who's joined you too soon. I don't yet understand the Lord's reasons for taking him away from us. He's still just a lad and will need your wise guidance ...'

Despite his determination and strength, the farmer

could manage no more. A great sob burst from his mouth, his shoulders slumped as he bent over and cried uncontrollable tears.

★

'Hey, Rizzi! What do you think you're doing?'

The Italian was standing by the gate and turned around as he heard Mirko's unmistakable growl. He remained silent until the leader of the 'Mussolini men' reached him.

'I was about to speak to the minister,' he replied, indicating the distinctive figure currently approaching the camp on his bicycle.

'No, you weren't. Piss off!'

Mirko grinned when, for an instant, it looked as if Rizzi was actually about to disagree, but after a brief hesitation he walked away without any further comment. The guard had already opened the gate and the new arrival dismounted and entered.

'Reverend Smith.'

'Mirko.'

'I would appreciate a private word if you have the time.'

The two men looked around. There was no one nearby.

'Why don't we take a walk about the perimeter?' said Walter.

'Yes, that would make a nice change.' They strolled at their usual slow pace in an effort to make the route feel longer than it really was. 'I had a long chat with Toni yesterday about the unfortunate event that occurred at the farm.'

'It was awful. It's been one of the most disturbing weeks I've ever known,' said Walter truthfully. 'No one should die like that.'

'Toni told me a great deal about the family. He's fallen in love with one of the farmer's daughters.'

'Yes, I hadn't realised until the accident. I guess it was a day of raw honesty and neither of them tried to hide their feelings. None of us could hide our feelings that afternoon.'

'A pretty girl?'

'Quite beautiful in a fresh, country sort of way.'

Walter couldn't help but wonder where on earth the conversation was going; he hoped the Italian wasn't going to ask him to arrange a 'liaison' with a local woman.

'Toni has been shaken by the incident. He felt the need to talk about it ... and other things.'

They fell silent as they passed a group of POWs standing around, cigarettes in hand.

'Other things?'

'Toni did something that he's ashamed of.'

'It's difficult to believe anything too shameful of such a likeable lad.'

'Yes, but he has this uncontrollable curiosity. I'm surprised it's not got him into trouble before. Anyway ...'

And so Mirko spun out the story about how Toni had ended up hiding in the bedroom of Captain Armstrong. He reeled in the minister with a description of the briefcase, the document and the top secret reason behind the enforced evacuation. By this point they had stopped walking and were facing each other.

Mirko could see the desperation in the other man's eyes,

the fanaticism as it bubbled to the surface like some spell in a witches' cauldron.

'I knew it was the beach they wanted! Did he discover where the British intend to land?'

'Oh yes. I know.'

'Where? For God's sake, tell me where!'

Walter was almost shouting by now, and in his intensity he'd grabbed on tight to one of Mirko's huge arms.

'Let go of me. We don't want anyone getting the wrong idea,' Mirko said, marvelling at how this man had kept this side of his nature hidden for so long. 'You see, reverend … I could tell you, but what's in it for me?'

The minister released his hold on Mirko so fiercely that the Italian flinched at the loathing in his eyes, the sense that he might strike him.

'I need this secret,' he hissed. 'Tell me and I'll take you to Germany with me.'

'U-boat?'

Walter nodded.

'Then what happens?'

'Anything you desire. I'll have my life back and you'll have a new one. You could be set up in a quiet part of the country, a rich man with no worries. Or you can return to Italy, with a promotion in the army and fight again if that's what you want. Jesus Christ, you can have fucking dinner with Mussolini, but tell me!'

'And how do I know this will happen?'

'I give you my word. I swear that the Führer himself will welcome you as a hero. I swear it, Mirko.'

'All right, keep your voice down. Let's move on. We're attracting attention.'

They continued walking, Walter shaking as he tried to regain control.

'What about Toni?' said Mirko.

'What about him?'

'He can't be left behind. He knows too much.'

'Then sort it! I'm sure you're quite capable.'

'No! Toni doesn't get hurt.'

Walter struggled not to lash out in anger as frustration threatened to consume him. The young Italian was meaningless compared to the prize almost within his grasp. However, he would have to tread carefully.

'Do you trust him?' he asked.

'He'll do what I say, which is good enough. Toni has to come with us. He's the one who saw the document and can describe it to the experts in Germany, explain how it was laid out, whether there were diagrams or images. Let's face it. Hitler will be keener to have Toni than either of us.'

Walter silently acknowledged the point.

A brute, but a clever brute.

'All right, the three of us leave together, but we'll have to act quickly,' said Walter. 'I'll make contact tonight.'

'Radio?'

'That's my business.'

'Fair enough.'

'But none of this happens unless you tell me where the British intend to land.'

Mirko could see that the minister was serious; there was no option for him other than to reveal the information. All pretence had been blown away during the last fifteen minutes and now they were both set upon a course that was moving beyond their control.

'All right, reverend. I'll put you out of your misery. When the British and their Allies invade the continent ... which everyone knows has to happen if they hope to win the war ... they'll land on the beaches of Normandy.'

26

Ingrid Bauer was one of three women, all fanatically loyal to the Nazi party, handpicked by Hitler to be operators of their powerful receiver/transmitter. Weeks, months and now years had gone by since they had set out on this mission, never imagining in the heady excitement of those early days that it would dominate their lives for so long.

Uncle John. Great news. Agnes is pregnant. Please tell Father. I look forward to seeing him soon. Norman.

'Agnes is pregnant,' she said to the empty room, repeating the agreed phrase. 'After all this time one of them has successfully discovered a secret that is worth bringing them home for.'

Bauer sat quietly, reflecting on the message that had come in. She didn't feel the great thrill or rush of emotion she had expected when this moment came. Instead, she stayed at her seat by the equipment and thought about the people caught up in this shadowy world of espionage.

Since the German occupation of Norway her team had worked from a large, secluded house near the coastal village of Egersund. Everyone wore civilian clothing and kept a low profile, but still there were three male guards. Their orders, signed by the Führer himself, ensured they were left alone and that they had significant power when it came to commandeering supplies.

The women were responsible for maintaining contact with eight agents in Scotland. Two of them had not been heard from for more than a year. The potential reasons for this were many, including the very real risk of them having been killed in a bombing raid ... just as Rolf Möller had been ten months earlier.

Along with the influential guests who were with him when his Berlin apartment had taken a direct hit, Möller had been so obliterated that it had been impossible to tell what body part belonged to which person. Bauer thought that someone should tell the son his father was dead, but there were strict rules about passing on such information and she would never disobey her instructions.

Bauer switched her equipment to 'Transmit' and sent a message to Berlin.

*

Walter had been in a state of enormous turmoil since Mirko revealed the details of the document that morning. The listening post was in constant operation so that agents were able to make instantaneous contact, but he had waited until the cover of darkness before assembling the spy-set and sending his message. Since then he had sat in the cold and gloom of the vestry, waiting for a reply. Walter didn't want to admit it, but he had been losing hope and had begun to doubt that those three words would ever be sent ... *Agnes is pregnant.*

He stood up and paced around. He was confident that

Germany would react quickly; however, whether that was a matter of a few days or longer was impossible to know. They would have to be picked up by the eleventh of December, a date that was less than two weeks away. Walter realised that, ironically, the area's much-reduced population would work to their advantage as there would be much less chance of the U-boat being spotted.

When the receiver suddenly burst into life, Walter dived for the headset and began writing in his notepad.

Hello Norman. That is excellent news. Your father is travel-ling, but will be in touch on Tuesday evening around eight. Congratulations. Uncle John.

Walter checked over what he had written. The code stipulated some simple guidelines as regards dates and times and so he added a day and an hour to those specified. That meant he had to be ready to receive a message on Wednesday at nine o'clock.

Walter knew that until he was rescued, the risk of being discovered would be greater than it had ever been in the thirteen years since he had set off as a young man to begin this bizarre, unnatural existence. Throughout all that time, he had maintained a tight control over every aspect of his life. This control was now slipping away rapidly, leaving him exposed to danger like never before.

27

Terrible sorrow cast a deep shadow over Kirk Farm and it seemed that the sun would never again shine on the land. Shortly after the Ross family returned from the cemetery, Alastair, Barbara and their sons left in the van that had been hired to transport them and their belongings to their new home. It seemed that sadness was being heaped upon grief like hay thrown casually onto a stack.

Even when the Italians returned on the Monday morning, there was no banter or laughter. The sadness cast a pall over them all and they worked even harder as they tried to find relief in physical exhaustion. When there was a sufficient load of grain in the cart Effie got in the seat and Toni climbed in next to her.

'How are you?' he asked, once they were alone on the track.

'I don't know. We visited the grave yesterday and spoke to Duncan, as if he was actually standing there listening. Even Hugh said something.'

'But you didn't?'

She shook her head.

'Sometimes, when we can't find the right words to

express what's in our hearts, it's best not to speak,' said Toni. 'I'm sure your brother will always know what you feel inside.'

Effie stopped the cart, tears pouring down her face. He took her in his arms and she clung to him. It was a long while before she gathered her composure.

'We've lost Duncan and who knows what else may happen before this war is over,' she said. 'I don't want to lose you.'

'You won't, my love.' He took her hand in his. 'I think Kirk Farm is the answer.'

'What do you mean?'

'You're being moved off the land and we'll be sent back to Kildary, then who knows where to, but the farm will remain like a beacon. Even if I'm forced to return to Italy and we're apart for years, I'll be able to find you if you're here.'

'Yes. We mustn't give up hope. I'll always be waiting. I promise.'

'And I promise that I'll write as soon as I can, then we'll make plans. I know that what we face is going to be hard, but we're still young and have our whole lives ahead.'

'Plenty of time for those babies,' she said, managing to smile.

Toni reached over and kissed her tenderly.

'Come on, I think we need to get to the farm and unload these sacks,' he said.

As they arrived at the storage shed, they saw members of the Women's Volunteer Service walking up the drive. They had come to help Martha turn more of the apples into jam and chutney. Effie was glad that they would once again fill the kitchen with steam and the entire house with a sweet, homely smell.

★

There was no such activity on the Tuesday as Martha took a rare break and went to have lunch with a friend who was leaving the following day and did not plan to return. She wouldn't listen to Hugh's protests that he wanted to stay with the Italians; and so her son accompanied her.

At lunchtime, when Effie and Toni unloaded the latest delivery of grain, they unhitched the horse and led it into the stable to join Bertie, who already had his head in a bag of oats. The horses couldn't be worked for at least an hour and a half after they'd eaten, which afforded Effie and Toni the luxury of some privacy. They stood for a while, just the other side of the stable door.

'It's quiet, with no one around and hardly any animals,' said Toni.

'Yes,' replied Effie.

'Are you all right? You've been on edge all morning.'

'I want ...'

'What?'

'I want you to come with me.'

And with that, she took his hand and led him to the far end of the stables. When she started to climb the ladder up to the loft, he hesitated for a moment then followed.

'What are we doing here?' he asked, once they were standing amid piled-up loose straw and the Italians' few possessions.

Effie's heart was beating so loudly she thought it was

201

about to explode from her chest. You couldn't grow up on a farm and have two brothers without understanding something about the facts of life, but she had never even kissed a boy before Toni. What she was about to do went against everything she had been taught by her parents and the kirk, by her school and the community she'd been a part of all her life.

Toni had stirred feelings in her, wilder and deeper than she'd ever imagined possible, but it was something much stronger than lust that drove her down this path. She wanted this moment of intimacy, needed it. If they were going to survive a separation, then she had to have this memory of togetherness to cling to.

'I want us to lie together ... as a man and woman do.'

'Oh Effie, I have dreamed of this ever since I met you. I want it so much, but I can't do something that might hurt you, that would endanger your future. What if your parents found out?'

'I can take that risk. What I can't risk is that we never see each other again ...'

'We will,' he said, interrupting her, but she put a finger over his lips.

'Duncan's death, here on the farm he grew up on, has made me realise we can't take anything for granted. I won't spend the rest of my life regretting that we didn't take this opportunity. Toni, please ... make love to me.'

★

The atmosphere had been extremely subdued since the accident, but that Tuesday evening Ina sensed her sister was beset by emotions other than the grief they all felt. In bed, Effie clung to her the way she used to as a child when she'd had a nightmare.

'What's wrong?' asked Ina after they had been lying without speaking for several minutes.

Effie wanted to say that nothing was wrong, but she was racked with such a conflict of feelings that it had been almost impossible to sit still at the kitchen table even while their father said grace. Her head was spinning with a whirl of images of their nakedness in the straw, of how they'd touched each other, their bodies intertwined, the sensations and noises, the expressions of anguish and of joy.

'There's something I want to talk about,' Effie said at last, 'but I have to know that you'll never reveal what I say … not to Christopher, Mother or Father or the minister. Not to anyone, ever.'

'Goodness, what on earth is it?'

'You have to promise me, Ina.'

'If it means that much, I promise you can speak to me and I will keep your secret. We're sisters and that's what sisters do for each other.'

Ina stroked the hair resting against her shoulder and waited for the explanation, imagining it was connected to Duncan, some past event or comment made in anger that Effie was perhaps struggling to cope with in her remorse and guilt.

'Earlier on, Toni and I were alone with the horses when everyone else was in the fields having lunch. We went up to the hay loft … then we lay together … as a husband and wife do.'

The confession was so utterly unexpected, the subject so

alien to the lives they led that it took Ina several moments to accept what she had just been told.

'Effie! What have you done? I don't believe I'm hearing this. Have you gone mad? What if Father finds out? You've only known him for a couple of weeks. And he's Italian. It's shameful. More than shameful ... it's disgusting.'

Ina blurted her words out so rapidly that there was no chance to interrupt. Effie pulled away in response, breaking the connection between them. In the pitch black they couldn't see each other.

'It wasn't disgusting. It was the most beautiful experience I've ever known. I love Toni and ... and I wanted to be with him in that way.'

As the implications sunk in, Ina could hardly get her words out.

'How could you!' she spat in anger and resentment. 'Only days after we've buried our brother you're disgracing yourself with a foreigner.'

'It's because of Duncan that I did it. None of us can be certain of our futures. Toni and I might never get the chance again.'

'How dare you use his death as an excuse to give in to base cravings. How dare you!'

'Don't you want to with Christopher?'

'No! How could you imply such a thing? We won't until we marry. I know how to behave decently and not rush about like a sow in heat.'

'If you love him you should take him to your bed,' Effie declared, straining to keep her voice low so that they weren't overheard.

'Don't you ever question my feelings for Christopher.

He's an honourable man, something your Italian lover obviously doesn't appreciate, otherwise he would never put your reputation at such risk. Did you even consider that you might fall pregnant?'

'Yes, and if I do then I'll have his baby and be proud of it.'

'You stupid, selfish fool. There's no pride in having a baby out of wedlock. There's only shame and sorrow – for you and the child. Don't you think our family have suffered enough?'

Just then the door opened and they heard the familiar sound of little footsteps entering the room.

'Not now, Hugh!' said Effie harshly. 'Go back to your room.'

Even in the darkness and silence they sensed the boy's shock as he took in the meaning of this rejection from the person he worshipped more than anyone. The door closed, shutting out the sound of him bursting into tears.

'That was cruel and uncalled for. Don't take out your guilt on Hugh.'

'I'm sorry. I'll make it up to him.'

'You can't make up for what you've done today. I'm more shocked and disappointed by your confession than anything I've ever heard in my life. I thought I knew you, Effie. I believed you had standards and principles, that you had some respect for the teaching of the kirk.'

Effie reached out across the bed. When Ina felt her sister's fingers touch her arm she knocked them away.

'Please don't be angry,' Effie begged. 'Toni and I want to be married.'

'Married,' said Ina, spitting out the word. 'You'll never

be married to him and if anyone finds out what you've done it's unlikely you'll ever be married to any man. I hope you think your beautiful experience was worth it.'

The sisters fell silent. The only sounds were Effie's sobs and Ina's ragged breaths.

'I'll fetch Hugh,' said Effie, suddenly desperate to hug the small body that would love her unconditionally, whatever her crime in the eyes of society or God.

'No, you can stay here. I'll sleep in his bed tonight.' Ina got up and put on her dressing gown. 'I'll keep your dirty secret, but not because I've promised. I'll keep it because I won't be the one to cause Mother and Father more pain. You can remain here alone and consider the appalling shame you've brought on yourself. While you're at it, pray to the good Lord that you don't destroy the whole family with what you've done.'

28

Martha was too wrapped up in her own grief to notice the strange tension between her daughters that Wednesday morning, while she attributed their red eyes and odd expressions to the tragic accident of the previous week. She also assumed this was why Hugh was being unusually clingy. He followed her wherever she went and demanded to be constantly hugged. In a way, Martha didn't mind; cuddles with her young son provided some small comfort to the ache she felt inside.

As before, Effie and Toni drove and unloaded the carts. He kept quiet until they were alone.

'You're hurting inside,' he said. 'Do you regret what we have done?'

She pulled on the reins and the horse stopped.

'It's not that I regret what we did. I don't, not for a moment,' she said, looking at his concerned face. 'The truth is, I needed to confide in someone and told Ina when we were in bed last night.'

'And she reacted badly?'

'More than that. I've never known her to be so angry.'

'Will your sister give us away?'

'No. But now there's a huge gulf between us, one that

I would never have believed possible. I can't understand why her reaction was so severe.'

'I'm sorry to have come between you and Ina.'

'It's not your fault. It was my decision to tell her. I wish I hadn't, but what's done is done.'

They sat in silence, Bertie waiting patiently.

'I'll never forget yesterday for as long as I live,' he said, taking her hand and pressing it to his lips.

'Nor me. We have to keep our hope alive.'

'Until the day I die I will always be yours and yours alone.'

'I know. And, Toni, I will never love anyone the way I love you.'

★

Hugh was playing by the fire. When he heard gentle tapping he looked towards the source and discovered the puppet that resembled Effie peering around the door. The tiny figure in overalls was already on his hand and he turned it away to face the flames. Effie entered the living room, walking slowly over with her puppet 'crying' on her shoulder, then she kneeled down and moved her hand towards her brother's.

However, no matter how much she tried to seek forgiveness, the puppet of the boy stubbornly, and skilfully, refused to acknowledge the newcomer. Effie had hurt Hugh by sending him away so harshly the night before and he had avoided her throughout the day. Now his rejection was making an awful day even worse.

Neither of them spoke. This was his world of make-believe and he moved seamlessly between it and reality as though they were the same thing. Effie knew that what she was about to do was unfair. She moved her puppet to the floor, paused for a moment then started banging its head against the wood. Hugh flinched, as if his sister really was hurting herself. He flung himself into her arms.

'No! Stop!'

It was Effie who burst into tears.

'I'm sorry, darling. I'm sorry.'

'You sent me away.'

'I know. I needed to speak to Ina alone. She was very cross with me.'

'Why? Had you been naughty?'

'Well ... she thought so. I was trying to make up with her when you came in. It was bad timing, that's all.'

Hugh nestled into Effie, the toys lying abandoned around them.

'It's all right,' he said, thoughtfully. 'That time, you needed Ina more than I needed to be hugged.'

An enormous sob escaped from Effie.

'Oh, Hugh. How can you be so wise? I was never like that at your age.'

'Maybe you were and you've forgotten. Adults can have really bad memories'

'You're right we do.' Effie hugged her little brother close. 'But never forget that I love you so very much.'

'I know ... so, will you make me another puppet?'

★

Walter sat in the gloom of the vestry, looking at the spy-set that he had once more assembled. He'd spent much of the day walking around the countryside trying to avoid people, which was at least becoming easier to do as more families left the area.

He was exhausted from lack of sleep yet exhilarated and on edge. This evening he would receive the details about where and when the U-boat would pick him up. He glanced at his watch, but it was still too early to switch on the power. It was crucial to remain cautious in everything.

Two things stopped him from sending the details he had discovered about the Normandy landings. The first was the chance that the transmission might be intercepted by a nearby listening post and the second, perhaps the real reason, was that he couldn't bear for his quest to simply come to an end with a radio signal. The importance and purpose of his very existence would be reduced to dust by a few audible dots and dashes. And then he would never be picked up and returned home.

Walter would not let that happen. After all these years he had the great secret in his grasp. With German intelligence knowing this information and the British unaware they knew, the Führer would be able to deliver a massive blow to the enemy. The Allied forces would be slaughtered like fish in a barrel as they disembarked from their landing craft. They would become the grains of sand that his father had predicted so long ago: '*a beach so enormous it will stretch beyond our ability to see*'.

Walter realised he was breathing hard and trembling at the thought of so many deaths.

By his actions he would be responsible for the deaths of all those brothers and sons, fathers and nephews, husbands and lovers. With a great effort of will he forced himself to steady his breath and focus on the task ahead.

'That's war,' he said quietly, before switching on the power and preparing the set to receive his instructions.

29

The service that Sunday morning was Walter's last in the kirk. What little congregation there was stayed behind to say goodbye and wish him luck. As they shook his hand and kept him engaged in small talk, he struggled to hide his frustration at the delay.

At last he managed to get away and start his journey to the camp. On the way he had to cycle between soldiers setting up a roadblock and the closeness of the encounter made him twitchy. Travel restrictions wouldn't be put in place until the following weekend, but still barriers were being constructed across the two roads that ran though the evacuation zone to Portmahomack.

Mirko was waiting just inside the gates, trying to give the impression of being out for a casual stroll around. As soon as the minister entered they walked away to a secluded spot.

'It's set for this Thursday evening. I wish it was sooner.'

'Keep your nerve, reverend. It's good timing. Some men have returned to the camp permanently because their work on the farms is completed. I should be here from Tuesday and everyone will have to be back by Thursday, which means Toni will be with me.'

'Are you concerned about him?'

'He's like a bloody love-sick puppy, but he'll be all right if we're together.'

'When we part, I'll shake your hand as if we're saying goodbye for the last time. I'll pass you a folded map of where to get to. About half a mile past Kirk Farm there's a ruin of an old barn. Toni should be able to get you there easily. Be there by ten-thirty.'

'What happens if you don't turn up?'

The idea of the Italians escaping without him filled Walter with horror. However, the secret had to be delivered.

'All right. If I'm not there make your way down to the beach. There's a fisherman's bothy.'

'What the fuck's that?'

'A hut. You can't miss it. The U-boat will be waiting in the Moray Firth in line with it. They'll send a dinghy ashore. Can you steal a torch?'

'Yes.'

'The signal is three quick flashes and two long. Wait about twenty seconds then repeat the sequence until you get a reply. Don't underestimate how long it will take you to reach the area from here. I would allow two hours and that assumes you don't get held up trying to avoid patrols.'

Mirko thought for a moment, then, nodded as if he had made a decision.

'Roll-call is at five o'clock. We'll be ready to leave when the lights go out at eight. Men are always hurrying around just before then. The guards are sloppy. They simply don't believe that anyone would ever try to escape.'

They looked at each other in silence, as alike and yet as different as it was possible to be.

'If you're not at the barn by ten-thirty, I'll leave by myself.'

'We'll be there. Nothing will stop me getting out of this shit-hole.'

'Until Thursday then,' said Walter, holding out his hand.

★

'No! I won't go!'

As the men in hut 3 started to leave for lunch in the mess hall, Mirko kept Toni behind until there was only the two of them. The younger man's face turned ashen when he heard the plan.

'It's not up for debate. This is what we're doing and you'd better get used to the idea.'

'You can't make me go.'

'I can actually, but I don't want to. I'd rather you came willingly. You owe me. You owe me a lot and this is payback. On Thursday we'll break out of the camp and you'll take us to the place marked on this map and we'll meet my contact there.'

'Who's this German spy – your *contact*?'

'Keep your fucking voice down. It's best you don't know for now. Take my word for it, we can trust him. After this, you can return to your family, away from the war. Learn to be a cabinetmaker and be happy.'

'I won't leave Effie. It doesn't matter how much I owe you. Your plan is insane.'

'You'll be moved back to the camp by Thursday, so this makes no difference to your chances of seeing her again.

I'm not ruining my plans for a girl. If you mean that much to each other then she'll be waiting for you after the war.'

Toni had to concede that what Mirko said was true. By the end of the week, everyone would have left the Tarbat peninsula and the painful reality of it was that there was no chance of being together with Effie until hostilities had ceased.

'Look, I can see that you love her,' Mirko said, attempting to sound conciliatory. 'She sounds like a woman worth waiting for. But we have other duties. We're still Italian soldiers no matter what else has happened. If we do this thing we'll be wealthy men, we'll have power. Imagine how much you could help your parents and then afterwards, whoever wins the war, it's got to be better to be rich than poor. Just think, you'll be able to return to Scotland. Otherwise it could take years to raise the cash needed to travel so far.'

Toni, his face full of sorrow, sat down heavily. Mirko moved to be beside him, glad that Toni now appeared to be backing down. He didn't want to have been forced to use threats ... or worse.

'I know it's not what you want,' he said, putting his arm around Toni's shoulder, 'but I promise that next week we'll be sitting together as free men, drinking good Italian wine and all of this wet fucking weather and shitty camp will be a distant memory.'

Toni looked at the other man and knew in his heart that he had no choice.

'Let me see that map again.'

30

By late Monday morning the last of the wheat had been processed on Kirk Farm and everyone returned to the farmhouse for a last meal of soup and bread. Effie drove the cart back, but she let the men unload the grain while she took Bertie to the stables to be fed. Toni managed to slip away unnoticed to join her.

'You know, when we're finally allowed back there'll be nothing here,' said Effie, brushing the horse's coat. 'There'll be no crops to harvest, no livestock and probably even fewer birds in the trees and hedgerows. The army's heavy tanks will crush the land and destroy the fences and drainage systems. Generations of hard work to create good, fertile fields will be undone. Kirk Farm will never be as it used to ... and neither will those living here.'

'I'm sorry,' said Toni, not sure what to say and saddened to see Effie so gloomy. He quickly changed the subject. 'How are you and Ina?'

Effie sighed. 'Not good. For the last five nights we've kept as far apart as possible in bed, both of us shivering in the dark and hardly sleeping. It's been horrible. She's so angry with me that it's no use trying to explain any further.'

'She's not spoken to me either, but it's a lot easier for us to avoid each other.'

'Do you know what day it is?' Effie asked.

Toni frowned. 'Monday.'

'It's my eighteenth birthday.'

'I didn't know.'

Toni watched Effie as she brushed Bertie with increasing vigour. 'I'm glad people have forgotten. How could anyone wish me a happy birthday when our lives are being torn to shreds?' She suddenly stopped and rested her head against the horse's side. 'I'm sorry. I shouldn't be like this when I've found more happiness than I could have imagined.'

She put down the brush and went over to him, sliding her arms around him and pulling him close. They held each other in silence for several minutes, neither of them caring if anyone entered the building.

'Come on,' Effie said eventually. 'We should join the others to say goodbye.'

★

There were plenty of tears when the land girls said farewell. The women each gave Mr Ross a huge hug. The reserved elder of the kirk was a little surprised at such forward behaviour, but they had all been through so much pain that he hugged them back for a long time, particularly Fiona. It was as if he thought there was a tiny part of Duncan inside her and he needed to hold on.

Finally, Joan climbed into the tractor. Her bicycle had already been tied to the back. She started the engine and headed off down the lane and out of sight, the other two

217

women following behind on their bicycles. Despite the many promises of keeping in touch, no one expected to see them again. The war thrust strangers together for short bursts of intense activity and emotion, and then separated them again just as quickly, just as completely.

Mr Ross took the Italians to the potato field where there was still some work to do. On the way, Toni asked him if he could use the workshop and have any scraps of wood that were lying around when he had a bit of spare time. The farmer could see no harm in it and readily agreed.

Ina, Effie and Martha went inside to continue sorting out what they were going to take to their temporary accommodation and what could be left in the loft. Mr Ross had decided not to take the authorities up on their offer to store furniture outside the evacuation zone. Instead, large objects would be covered with old sheets and he would trust in people's good natures that no damage would be caused deliberately.

Items such as pots and pans were scarce commodities and were added to the list of items to be taken with them, which included all of their clothes, bedding, food and personal effects. The sisters were forced to work together to carry objects like the gramophone up the ladder, but they spoke only when they had to and the atmosphere between them continued to be strained and uncomfortable.

On Tuesday, Mr Ross took the two dairy cows to the farmer in Hilton who had bought them. It had been a generous offer on the other man's part to let the animals remain on Kirk Farm until the last few days. Martha had been unable to prevent the tears streaming down her face when she had milked them earlier that morning. Everyone

218

said goodbye, even the Italians, and Hugh buried his face in Effie's side as their father and Nip walked the beasts down the drive.

The dressing of the potatoes was eventually completed that afternoon and the last load was brought back to the storage shed. On the Wednesday morning a lorry arrived and the sacks of potatoes and grain were soon transferred and taken away. The Italians were given various tasks around the farm – clearing up and cleaning equipment, and storing whatever needed to be put away for the coming months securely in a barn or shed.

Effie rode Bertie over to the farmer near Tain who had agreed to look after him while they were away. On her way over, she was amazed at the stillness and quiet of the countryside. The lack of noise was unnerving. Bertie seemed agitated by it too; the horse's movements were jittery and skittish.

'It's all right,' she said, patting his neck to reassure him. 'You sense it as well, don't you? The emptiness, as though we're the only creatures left on the planet. Bit by bit we're being split up and sent away. Tomorrow it will be Toni's turn … Oh, Bertie, what am I going to do without him?'

Bertie snorted and shook his head. Effie sighed and patted his neck again.

'I'll miss you too, my faithful old friend. They had better look after you at this place, or they'll have me to answer to.'

31

The authorities had arranged for a lorry to collect the Italians early Thursday afternoon. Once they were gone, the Ross family intended to make another trip to Duncan's grave. They were due to leave the farm on Saturday and after that it would be impossible to visit the cemetery until the military had left the area, because anyone travelling through the restricted zone needed a special pass.

Toni had been busy in the workshop since early morning, initially working by the light of a paraffin lamp. Effie tracked him down there when she and Ina went over to the barn with breakfast for the Italians. She stood watching him bent over the bench, his back towards her. He was unaware that someone had entered.

'I've brought your breakfast,' she said after a moment.

He turned around and smiled, the same beautiful smile he had given her the first time they met. It felt like a lifetime ago.

'Hello,' he said, putting down the chisel he was working with.

'You've got two boiled eggs, a slice of bread and a mug of tea,' Effie said, bringing the plate over to him. 'What are you making? Oh! That's incredible.'

Toni had made a wooden dog, the limbs and head threaded with thin wire, which ran up to crossbars. While he removed an eggshell, Effie skilfully made the puppet walk around the bench top, dropping its head occasionally as if it was sniffing. Then she brought it over to his mug and lifted one of the back legs. They both laughed. It was a good act. In truth, their hearts were breaking.

'It's meant to be Nip,' Toni explained. 'But I couldn't actually make it look like him.'

'Just tell Hugh that it's Nip and he'll be even more delighted. Thank you so much. It's very kind of you,' Effie said, putting the puppet carefully on the bench. An awkward silence fell between them, and Toni struggled to find something to say.

'The egg is good,' he ventured.

'It's still warm?'

'Yes, it's lovely.'

'I tried to find you as quickly as I could, so that it would still be warm.'

'It's perfect.'

'A cousin of ours is coming over today to take away the remaining hens. There aren't that many left.'

'They've been tasty.'

They fell silent again. Toni drank some of his tea, and then cleared his throat. 'I've made something for you, but it's not quite finished, so you can't have it just yet,' he said.

'What is it?'

'Well, it's not a puppet.'

Effie smiled, but her lip started to tremble and a huge tear ran down one cheek.

'Toni!' she cried, flinging herself into his arms. 'What

221

am I going to do without you near? I'm going to be so lonely. And I'm frightened.'

'What are you scared of?'

'I can't fight off a feeling that something awful is going to happen.'

He knew exactly what she meant, although his fears were based on the knowledge that he was going to try and break out of a POW camp that evening. He would have to avoid being shot by an army patrol while hurrying through the dark to meet up with a German spy, before getting into a U-boat and facing the hazards of the sea. He was terrified at the utter madness of it all. But, as he stood holding Effie, next to a boiled egg and a wooden puppet of a dog called Nip, thoughts of the night ahead could so easily be dismissed as no more than a dreadful nightmare.

'Nothing bad is going to happen,' he said, trying to reassure himself as much as her. 'We just have to be brave and face the coming weeks and months as best we can.'

Effie sniffed. 'I don't even have a photograph of you.'

She pulled back and gazed up at him.

'I'll keep the image of that beautiful smile of yours in my head forever,' she said, stroking his cheek and smiling.

'Well, that's as good as any photograph.'

Effie nodded. 'Now, I should let you get your breakfast otherwise you won't be able to finish my present.'

And with that, she turned and left.

★

Walter woke early that Thursday and began his final preparations for the night's events. First, he went to the vestry and removed the small suitcase from the safe. The latter now contained nothing more than a few church documents, the communion plate and the collection from the last Sunday service. Walter added what money he had, as it was no longer of use to him, then locked the safe and hung the key from a hook on the wall nearby.

Once in the kitchen, he dismantled the receiver/transmitter, breaking it down into the smallest components possible, which he laid neatly on the table.

Walter often chopped wood in the back garden, using a heavy axe loaned by Mr Ross. Selecting one of the set's crystals, he went outside and placed it on the chopping block. He took up position, pausing to adjust his stance, before bringing the flat end of the metal head sweeping down. The impact reduced the glass to powder, leaving only a few splinters.

Satisfied, he went inside to fetch the remaining parts and battered them until they were completely unrecognisable. The broken parts were thrown on the midden and the tangled metal left by the garden gate, where it would eventually be taken away by the travelling folk. When he had finished, there were only a few dozen screws left so he added these to the old toolbox under the stairs.

Walter chose dark, warm clothing for the evening, including two thick woollen jumpers; he wouldn't be wearing a jacket or coat. The open suitcase held one more object, fixed to the inside of the lid. Walter pulled off the tape that held it in place and took the object in his hand.

He stared at it for a moment, then took hold of the handle and pulled the smooth blade from its leather sheath. It was a killer's knife. Walter thought back to the numerous lessons he had endured with Stein, who had taken great delight in showing him how to murder someone quickly and quietly.

Stein had been disappointed that he had to demonstrate using a dummy and had suggested that he be given a few long-term inmates from the local prison. No one would notice they had gone, he argued. Fortunately, his request had been denied. Walter shuddered at the memory and slid the blade back, before tucking it under a pair of thick trousers.

He packed the empty suitcase with personal belongings. The manse had a shallow loft and he had already placed most of his possessions at the far end, where there was a convenient alcove that made them hard to spot from a cursory glance around the otherwise empty space.

The previous day he had sent a letter to the parish in Aberdeen, explaining that there had been a sudden illness in the family and his arrival would be delayed. He apologised for the inconvenience and trusted that the congregation would understand.

Such correspondence should really have gone to the assembly council in Edinburgh, but Walter was sowing confusion. He guessed that it would be quite some time before the kirk elders in Aberdeen finally queried his lack of appearance. After all, no one wanted to get a minister into trouble. The church authorities would then be faced with the problem of how to find out where he was. They would not be able to rule out the possibility that he had been hurt or even killed in a bombing raid. It should prove to be extremely difficult to determine whether he had actually 'disappeared'.

Walter had spread the rumour that he was leaving the next day, Friday, although most people had already left the area and the actual date of his departure was of little interest to anyone. The elders of the kirk had already gone, apart from Mr Ross. Walter decided to cycle over to Kirk Farm to see him.

As he rode into the yard, the eerie feel of the place struck him. The only people around were a couple of Italians sweeping up, but they looked as though they were just filling time. Mr Ross had obviously spotted him through a window because he came out of the house while Walter was still propping up his bicycle.

'Reverend Smith. There was no need to bring that back,' Mr Ross said, gesturing towards the axe that Walter had rested casually across his shoulder.

'It's only right and proper that this is returned to its owner,' Walter replied, handing it over.

'We'll store it in the workshop. Then perhaps you'll join us for a hot drink?'

When they entered the workshop, they found Toni busy at the bench. The minister was eager to find out how the Italian reacted to his presence, but Toni greeted him respectfully as usual, giving no indication that he knew who Walter really was.

'That's a beautiful item,' Walter said, admiring the craftsmanship of the small box Toni was working on. It was simple but elegant, and the lid had been inlaid with a different wood.

'Some young lady back in Italy is going to get a lovely present one day,' Mr Ross said, picking it up to examine more closely.

Walter realised with surprise that Mr Ross had no idea that this was a gift for one of his daughters. He did recall that on the day of Duncan's accident the farmer hadn't been present during the very public display of affection between Effie and the Italian. Yet he still found it quite extraordinary how often those closest to someone were the last to find out about a situation that was obvious to everyone else.

It was strange to sit around the kitchen table with the Ross family for the last time. They were all subdued, apart from Hugh, who perched on Effie's knee and played enthusiastically with a couple of puppets. Looking around at the familiar faces, Walter acknowledged that he would miss them. During the last four years, he had grown close to the family.

★

Walter started his farewells with hugs and handshakes at the front door before cycling off down the drive, waving and calling out best wishes and blessings until he was out of hearing. Standing just outside the front door, Effie put an arm around her father's waist and he put one around her shoulder as they watched the figure pass the gate and go out on to the lane.

'You'll miss him, Father,' Effie said when Walter had disappeared from sight.

'Yes, he's been a good friend and an excellent minister.'

Silence settled between them for a while. Effie rested her head against her father's chest, surveying the quiet yard. Then her father spoke again. 'This bloody war ...'

The bitterness in his voice surprised Effie, but she knew it was Duncan he was thinking about, so she made no comment and instead hugged him more tightly. Both her parents had looked ill since that tragic day, but her father appeared more vulnerable. His usual stoicism seemed to have deserted him. A shared concern for his health had helped to build a bridge between the sisters, who had discussed the situation the previous night in the privacy of their room.

Afterwards, Effie had moved hesitantly across the bed until their bodies were almost touching. There had been a tense, dreadful pause before Ina had finally lifted her arm and allowed Effie to cuddle up against her, as they had done since they were small. Neither of them spoke, yet Effie could tell that Ina was silently weeping … as she was herself.

32

Leaving her father back at the house, Effie hurried over to the workshop, where she found Toni tidying up. It was almost lunchtime, and she knew this would be their last chance of some privacy.

'Toni!' she sobbed, running into his arms.

'I know,' he said, his voice cracking with emotion as he stroked her hair. 'But we have to stay positive. It will be temporary.'

'But what are we going to do while we're apart?'

'Live life to the full. We're lucky. We'll survive the war. There have been too many who have had that chance taken away. In memory of those who've died we shouldn't waste a single second of the years ahead.'

'I wish I had your strength.'

'You're strong, Effie,' Toni said quietly. 'You're the strongest person I know. Whatever fate throws in your direction, you'll come through well in the end. I know it.'

They pulled apart to look at each other. He tenderly wiped away her tears and she did the same to him, her hand cupping his face.

'You're the only girl there'll ever be for me, Effie Ross.'

Effie smiled sadly. 'I might not be a girl by the time we meet again.'

'Then I look forward to meeting the beautiful woman that I know you will become. Here,' Toni said, moving to the workbench. He lifted a cloth to reveal the finished wooden box. 'This is for you.'

Effie studied the skilfully made item from every angle. 'It's lovely,' she said, trying to lift the lid.

Toni quickly placed his hand over hers. 'No, you must promise that you won't open it until tomorrow.'

Effie frowned. 'Why?'

'I can't explain.' Effie was struck by the seriousness of his expression. He gripped her hand tightly. 'Please, Effie, you have to accept that this is what I want.'

Effie realised there must be something inside. Perhaps it was a letter.

'All right, I'll wait.'

Toni visibly relaxed. 'Thank you.'

Effie studied his face. 'Toni ... is there something you're not telling me?'

He took her in his arms. Effie felt strongly that he was holding something back, but all he said was, 'You must trust me that everything I do is for the best.' His voice should have been reassuring, but it had the opposite effect on Effie, who could sense the effort going into his attempt to appear calm.

'Now you're frightening me, Toni.'

'Do you love me?'

'You know I do. And I always will, in here,' she replied, putting a hand over her heart.

'And you will ...'

229

'Fee!'

Hugh's voice from the doorway stopped their conversation in its tracks. 'There you are. I've been looking all over. Lunch is ready and everyone else is waiting in the kitchen and I'm really hungry.'

Effie and Toni still had their arms around each other, but Hugh didn't react. It was clearly far more important to him that he got something to eat.

'I guess this is goodbye,' Toni said.

'Yes,' Effie replied.

As they separated, she slipped the box into a pocket in her dungarees. Hugh rushed over and took his sister's hand. Effie tried to wipe away any trace of tears. She thought her heart would break, but she took a deep breath to calm herself and let Hugh lead her back to the house.

★

The first thing Walter did upon returning to the manse was put a match to the rolled-up newspaper in the grate and make sure the kindling had caught alight. Then, he went over to the church to tidy up as best he could. He closed the main door, leaving the key in the lock behind him, just as people in the evacuation zone had been advised to do with their houses.

He had kept sufficient food for one decent meal, although it proved to be a challenge to eat. His emotions were all over the place, swinging between an overwhelming sense of apprehension, which bordered on panic, to an unnatural calmness, brought on by the knowledge that he was near the end of his false life. He washed up and cleaned the kitchen, then returned to the study and carefully went through the bookcase and dresser, burning anything that could appear remotely suspicious.

Finally, Walter took off his clerical collar and threw it into the fire then added the spares, one by one. It was fascinating to watch them being consumed by the flames, which flared up brightly for the briefest of moments. He was no longer a minister of the church.

Although there were still several hours to go, Walter went upstairs and changed into the clothes he had laid out. He placed the ones he had been wearing in the Gladstone bag and made his last trip to the loft.

Now, there was little for him to do except wait until it was time to leave. He found himself daydreaming about the reunion he was going to have with his father once he was back in the Fatherland.

'*You've made me the proudest man in Germany.*'

Walter smiled. He was going to be fêted by the Führer once the extent of his great sacrifice and success could be told publically. He couldn't wait to see his father's face when he returned, victorious. He felt a bubble of excitement, which he squashed down. First, he needed to get through the night ahead. On the small table beside him, his knife was lying alongside a torch and his spare jumper. But there was one other item to deal with. Walter was surprised at his reluctance to destroy it. He flicked through its familiar pages one last time.

The Bible had been a gift from the retiring minister he had succeeded in Glasgow. There was an inscription to Walter, written in the old minister's neat handwriting on the first page. That's what made it dangerous. Walter had intended to simply burn the Bible, the final tie to his former existence. However, the Bible had been by his side for years and had become a companion of sorts, despite his initial horror at the career he was forced to take. He recalled some of his more memorable sermons, the special events in the religious calendar, the funerals and weddings he had taken. It hadn't been a totally unfulfilled life.

'For better or worse,' he said to the empty room.

He carefully removed the page with the hand-written note and threw it on to the fire. Then he went to the bookcase and returned the Bible to a shelf.

33

Mirko took to one side the men who shared his bunk and that of Toni's, and revealed to them that he and Toni planned to escape that night. They listened quietly.

'You can rely on us,' said one of the Italians, when Mirko had finished speaking. 'Just tell us what we have to do.'

Mirko nodded. 'Everything has to appear normal. We'll leave at lights out. When you go to bed, make up ours to look as though there's someone in them. That's all.'

'What about roll-call in the morning?'

'Make up our beds when you do yours then everyone plead ignorance. We were there in the evening and no one heard or saw us leaving during the night. They won't be able to prove anything.'

'But what if you get caught quickly?' the other man asked. 'They'll know we're lying if we say you were present until we all went to bed.'

'Improvise,' said Mirko, slapping him on the arm a little too hard and smiling widely. 'Don't worry, they won't find us.'

Toni was so nervous that he couldn't eat his meal in the mess hall, but Mirko hissed at him across the table that he would attract attention, so he forced down small mouthfuls even though they made him feel sick. As eight o'clock approached, they put on extra layers of clothing under their POW uniforms. Their coats were too cumbersome to wear. They needed to be agile and fast.

The guards didn't patrol with dogs and there were no watchtowers, only static lights placed at set intervals around the perimeter. Mirko had identified an area nearby where they could crawl under the fence if they cut the bottom two wires. He had smuggled in a pair of pliers, taken from the farm he had been working at, along with two short strips of barbed wire, which had been significantly more painful to bring in undetected.

When they went outside that evening, they were just two more figures among the crowd making a final trip to the wash block. Casually, they made their way to the far side of the building, then hid in the shadows. The two guards always started their patrol from the gate, taking ten minutes to make one circuit of the camp.

Mirko had calculated that it would take a minute for the soldiers to move away far enough from the spot he had identified to no longer pose a risk, and that he and Toni would have to be gone at least one minute before they came back around from the other direction. He already had the pliers in his hand as the soldiers sauntered past, gossiping about a local barmaid and paying little attention to their surroundings. As they passed by, Mirko began counting. When he was satisfied, he tapped Toni's leg and they set off, keeping low and quiet.

It didn't take long to reach the other side of the fence, and once there they worked quickly. After they had finished, only a close inspection would reveal the damage.

Mirko led the way across a small, grassy patch of open ground and into the nearby wood, where they stopped.

'Not bad, eh?' Mirko whispered excitedly. 'I reckon we were through and away in less than six minutes.'

Toni didn't reply. He was panting, adrenaline coursing through him. There was a full moon, and the Northern Lights cast a multitude of colours in the distance. Mirko dropped the pliers into a hollow, where they lay out of sight to anyone passing.

'It's a great night for an escape. A great night to gain our freedom,' he said, squeezing Toni's shoulder. 'Come on. Let's get some distance between us and the camp.'

Mirko set a fast, yet cautious, pace. They didn't encounter any patrols and the roads were almost deserted, so they risked using them for long sections of their journey, always straining their ears and eyes for potential danger. At one point, they heard the grinding engine of a solitary lorry, struggling with a heavy load. It was some way off, so they were hiding in the bushes long before the vehicle reached them. It was shortly after this that Mirko stopped. The two men automatically crouched down before Mirko spoke.

'You have to take the lead from here,' he instructed. 'But don't slacken the pace. We don't know what delays there might be ahead.' He reached forward and put a hand on the side of Toni's head. 'All right?'

'I'm all right.'

He didn't sound convincing.

'We'll soon be drinking that good Italian wine,' Mirko said softly, patting him with uncharacteristic gentleness. 'Just keep your nerve. I'll be right behind you.'

34

Ina and Christopher went outside to watch the Northern Lights, which had been unusually active. The rest of the family stayed around the roaring fire in the living room, Hugh playing on the floor with a couple of puppets. His other toys had been packed away. Effie was touched that he had kept out a puppet that represented her.

She studied him, so completely lost in his own world of make-believe that he was oblivious to anything else. The 'writer' in Effie was fascinated by his imagination. She would play with her brother for hours, trying to understand the process behind the creation of his imaginary worlds. But she had found that getting inside his head was a great deal more difficult than she had expected.

You could never really know what was in another person's mind. Trying not to be obvious, Effie shifted her gaze to her father, puffing away on his pipe while reading the local newspaper. Paper shortages had resulted in them becoming increasingly thin as the war had progressed. This edition was dominated by an article that compared the evacuation to the Highland clearances of the eighteenth and nineteenth centuries.

Her father had changed since Duncan's death. They all

had, of course, but it was most obvious in her father, who had tried to maintain a semblance of normality in their lives, to pretend that things hadn't changed so irrevocably. Effie thought it was a coping mechanism and a way of trying to support everyone else. She guessed that they were all probably doing the same, in their own way. The pressure caused by the impending move at least provided something else to focus on and kept them all frantically busy.

Her mother sat on the other side of the fire, knitting. Her eyes were red and swollen, and her face was drawn. Like mothers the world over, she was the glue that held the family together in a thousand different ways, both visible and invisible. She had a quiet strength that Effie drew on whenever she felt that her grief might overwhelm her.

Effie's thoughts drifted to the events of earlier in the day ... visiting Duncan's grave, her last few moments with Toni, her heart breaking as she watched him being driven away on the lorry. From the moment she had been dragged out of the workshop by Hugh, she had been forced to treat Toni no differently to the rest of the Italians. Kildary might only be a few miles away, but that evening, it felt as though it was on the other side of the world.

Effie had knitting on her lap, but she had been ignoring it ever since sitting down. She simply couldn't settle, so she took a paraffin lamp and went upstairs. She removed Toni's gift from its hiding place and sat with it on the bed.

He had been adamant that the box wasn't to be opened until the following day but, although she had agreed, Effie felt that there was something wrong. Her emotions were so shredded that her instincts had been swamped recently, yet now that she thought about it, Toni's insistence wasn't natural. There was obviously a specific reason for it, and the more Effie considered what this could be, the more she was filled with unease. No, it wasn't unease. It was fear.

I'm sorry, Toni.

Gently, she lifted the snugly fitting lid. Inside was a tightly folded piece of paper. Effie opened it with shaking hands and as she read the small, neat handwriting, she felt her heart begin to beat faster. She was right to have looked ... she was right to have been afraid.

'Oh, no! Toni, what have you done?'

Effie's footsteps pounded down the stairs. As she ran along the hall she could hear her father shouting, but she ignored him and her coat in the porch before disappearing off into the night.

PART TWO

35

The escaped Italians made their way steadily along the edge of Kirk Farm's top field and continued heading for the landmark indicated on the minister's map.

'There,' said Toni, crouching down to speak about fifteen minutes later. 'Just along that path is the building where we're supposed to meet.'

'All right. Well done. I'll take the lead from here,' said Mirko, moving forward cautiously.

They stopped again when they were close to the ruined barn and remained hidden as they scanned the area, looking for any signs of life.

'I don't see anyone,' whispered Toni.

'Nor me. I guess we've beaten him. Let's go inside to wait.'

'There's no need,' said Walter, stepping out from the shadows only a few yards away.

'Fuck!' cried Mirko, leaping up in surprise. 'What are you doing there?'

'I was making sure you hadn't been followed.'

'Followed! No chance.'

'Well, you made enough noise. I take it you had no trouble getting out of the camp?'

'It was ridiculously easy.'

Toni stared at the minister as if seeing a ghost. Walter smiled, but there was no warmth in his expression, or the remotest hint of the man who a few hours earlier had cycled down the farm's drive, waving fondly and shouting blessings.

'Surprised to see me.'

'You! Reverend Smith ... you're the spy?'

'You can call me Walter. The Reverend Smith no longer exists. Now let's go,' he said, exerting his authority over the other men.

★

Ina lay snuggled into Christopher, protected from the cold wind by his coat, part of which he had wrapped around her. They were watching the swirl of coloured lights in the sky from their secret hideaway, the place she'd have once only ever occupied with Effie. Ina still felt a deep sorrow that she had fallen out with her sister, but she felt too that she'd been in the right to be shocked to the core by Effie's sinfulness.

'What are you thinking?' asked Christopher.

'Oh, just how so much has changed.'

'Duncan?'

'Yes ... and Effie.'

'Effie?'

'It's sister talk. Now we're all leaving and you'll be posted elsewhere. Where will we be when this war is finally over?'

'You and I will be married. Whether the war is over or not, after your family have returned home that's the point at which we will walk down the aisle. Herr Hitler won't determine our wedding date.'

'Until then, you have to keep safe,' she said, reaching up to kiss him on the cheek.

'How safe?'

She smiled then kissed him properly. They lay back, silent and content, while bands of brilliant green shimmered in the distance.

'It's strange,' he said after a while. 'I can almost hear the wind calling your name ... Ina ... Ina.'

'Quiet,' she said, straining to hear. 'That's not the wind. Someone is calling my name!'

They scrambled to their feet and hurried back along the path, where they met Effie, too out of breath to speak.

'What is it?' asked Ina. 'Has there been an accident?'

'Something awful is going to happen. Toni didn't mean any harm. That's not his nature.'

'What are you talking about?' Christopher asked.

'Toni made a small box, as a gift. He gave it to me earlier, making me promise not to open it until tomorrow. But I did and inside was a letter.'

'What could be so important about a letter from a prisoner of war that you have to rush out here?' asked Ina, her tone conveying just what she thought of her sister's relationship.

'A couple of weeks ago we were alone on the farm. We didn't mean to do anything wrong. Then Father came home unexpectedly and I had to hide Toni in the nearest room ... it was yours,' she said, looking at the officer and pausing. 'While I was downstairs trying to get rid of Father, Toni found a briefcase in the wardrobe. He ... he read some papers.'

243

'What papers?' asked Christopher, his voice clipped with tension.

'Not all his letter made sense … something about … Operation Overlord.'

'Tell me the rest. Now!'

'There's a prisoner of war called Mirko. The two of them are escaping from the camp this evening. Toni doesn't want to go. He's being forced.'

'Why?' said Christopher, puzzled. 'What good will it do them to break out from Kildary? They'll be caught by the morning.'

'There's a German spy, too; he's been living in the area. Mirko has made contact. The three of them are leaving together.'

'Jesus Christ,' he said, grabbing Effie by the shoulders as he realised the significance of her words. 'You stupid girl! You don't know what you've done!'

Both of the women cried out in alarm at his sudden anger.

'You're hurting me!'

'Christopher, what is it? Why are you in such a state?'

He let go and started to pace around.

'You've put the lives of thousands of our troops in danger. If Germany finds out about Overlord it will drag out the war for months.'

'Oh no,' cried Ina. 'What have you done?'

'All I did was to love someone.'

'Shut up! Both of you! I need to think.' He was frantic, walking around in a tight circle, talking to himself as he analysed the possibilities. 'They can only escape via a U-boat and if the Italians are involved it can't pick them

244

up too far from the camp. They'll have to make their way to somewhere on the peninsula. Not the west coast, it's too busy. It has to be the Moray Firth. The Seaboard villages aren't affected by the evacuation so it needs to be a place north of there, away from people ... a quiet place. There are only two paths down to the shore along that stretch.'

Christopher stopped pacing, removed his coat and threw it at Effie, who was now shivering after her rush up the hill.

'What are you doing?' asked Ina, horrified. 'You can't go after them by yourself.'

He went up to her, calmer now that his decision was made, and took hold of her hand.

'After tonight, we don't wait to get married. We do it as soon as possible. Promise me.'

'Yes ... yes I promise,' replied Ina, her voice shaky with tears.

'I have to go after them, my love. There's no choice. But you have to do something for me and it's vitally important.'

'Anything.'

'Run home as fast as you can and get the operator to put you through to the camp. You have to speak to Major Cooper. For God's sake, don't sound hysterical or you'll never get beyond the guard on duty. Tell him that Captain Armstrong says there's been a breakout and a German spy has discovered the real reason behind the evacuation. Say that I believe a U-boat is going to pick up the men between Hilton and Rockfield.'

'What will he do?'

'He'll have the whole bloody army out, but only if you make him believe you.'

'I won't let you down. I love you, my darling.'

'I love you more than I can say.' He took her face in his hands, kissed her, then stepped away and took out his service pistol.

'Keep safe,' said Ina.

He smiled and a few moments later had gone. Ina set off as speedily as she could on the rough ground, with Effie close behind. They stumbled, ran, fell and scrambled in their manic race home. It was when they were some way down the path that led to the lane just beyond the gates to the farm that Effie stopped. Ina continued a few more yards before realising that she was no longer there.

'What are you doing?' she gasped, turning around to see what had happened.

Effie stood for a few seconds, as if considering something, then she started to remove the greatcoat.

'There's no time to waste,' said Ina.

Effie walked over to her.

'I'm going back. It doesn't take both of us to alert the authorities. I have to find Toni.'

Despite the urgency, Ina didn't answer immediately.

'I'll never forgive you if anything happens to Christopher.'

'I know. That's the other reason I have to go. I can't wear this,' she said, laying the garment on a nearby rock. 'It's too heavy. Raise the alarm. All our lives depend on it. Whatever happens I'll always love you, Ina.'

Her sister opened her mouth to answer, but in a sudden, swift movement she turned about and set off once more.

36

Walter stopped. They were following a path that ran along the cliff edge and which eventually joined a track leading to the long stretch of grassy land that ran parallel to the stony beach.

'See that,' he said, pointing out a small wooden structure in the distance. 'That's the fisherman's bothy. The U-boat should surface in line with it. Once we're closer, I'll signal. The way down is further along. We'll have to pass the hut and come back along the shore.'

They were about to move off when Mirko spoke. The urgency in his quiet voice froze them instantly.

'Wait! I thought I saw something, over there.'

The three of them stared in the direction he was indicating, but saw nothing unusual for several moments. Suddenly the outline of a man could be seen as he moved over a rise in the ground.

'Shit,' said Mirko. 'For once, I hoped I was wrong.' They watched for a while longer in silence. 'He looks like he's by himself. If our escape had been discovered, the place would be swarming with soldiers.'

Toni was gripped by a dreadful fear that he knew exactly who the man was, which meant that Effie had already read his letter. How much more damage would his foolishness cause?

'He's on the track that we're going to join,' said Walter. 'If he continues we'll run straight into each other. You two have to sort this out. I can't be delayed. Kill him if you have to, but be quick then meet me at the hut.'

'You better not leave without us,' said Mirko.

'Be there on time and I won't. Look, cut across this way. There's a sharp bend on the route he's taking. You should get there before he does and there are plenty of places to hide. The pair of you should be able to surprise him easily enough.'

'All right, we'll see you later. Toni, I hope you know what side you're on.'

Walter watched the two Italians hurry though the gorse, which provided them with cover. He also wondered if the figure was Captain Armstrong, though why the officer should be out on this particular night was a mystery.

★

Christopher had been travelling as fast as he dared over the uneven, treacherous ground. He knew he was dangerously outnumbered and was trying to balance stealth against speed. And Toni was an unknown factor. The friendly Italian wouldn't be able to sit on the fence any more.

The officer's awareness that he'd made a grave error in removing those particular documents from the military base made him feel sick to his stomach. He had broken a strict regulation, but Kirk Farm had seemed so peaceful and he had fallen so in love with Ina that it had felt nothing bad would ever happen there. He had been lulled into a false sense of security.

If he survived the next few hours he would be in serious trouble with his superiors. One way or another, he would pay a high price for his error of judgement.

★

Walter didn't slacken his pace once he was alone and soon reached a spot where he could not be seen by anyone on the land behind him. He was still on the cliff edge, but near enough to the bothy below to be in line with the U-boat if it was in the correct position out in the firth. He unclipped the torch from the chain on his belt and began to signal.

★

Christopher had just gone around a bend when something that felt like an enraged bull charged into him. His pistol flew into the bushes as he went down. But his senses were on a knife edge and his reflexes fast as a whip. He rolled with the impact and used the other man's momentum and his own strength to lift and throw the figure that instinct told him was trying to land on top of him.

It was an astonished Mirko who found himself flying through the air when he'd expected to crush the other man sufficiently so that he could easily knock him out. Instead, he hit the ground hard, his right knee banging against a tree stump. He was on his feet again almost immediately, but then a vicious right hook caught him on the side of the face and a powerful left jab sent him backwards, arms

249

flailing in the air. He was only saved because his opponent tripped too and also went sprawling.

They were both quick to get up and eyed each other warily, far enough apart not to be rushed and taken by surprise. Christopher glanced around, yet there was no sign of anyone else.

'It's just you and me, pup,' said the Italian, weighing up the officer. The man was strong and tall; he certainly knew how to hit and had the benefit of a greater reach. In other circumstances Mirko would have enjoyed the challenge, but right now he cursed his luck at encountering someone who could actually fight.

Christopher was doing the same. In the brief contact between their bodies he had felt the Italian's immense power and knew the risk of letting him get too close. It was to his advantage to cause as much of a delay as possible, although it would never be long enough for help to arrive. This fight would be brutal and short.

The track opened up around the bend and the surrounding ground was wide enough for them to circle each other as they sought a handy stone or hefty branch to use as a weapon. But there was nothing and Mirko decided to take the initiative.

He moved forward and made a big show of intending to lash out with his right fist. As Christopher went to block the punch Mirko brought up his left arm with incredible speed. However, the officer had fought many talented boxers in the ring and had seen the feint for what it was.

He leaned backwards and as the fist passed harmlessly by he stepped in with a flurry of punches that the Italian was hard pressed to fend off. It was almost by bad luck that

Christopher took a hard blow that sent him reeling. They were both panting now, reassessing the dangers facing them.

'You can fight, I'll hand you that,' Mirko said. 'It's a pity you're not Italian.'

'It's a pity you're not where you belong ... in a prisoner of war camp.'

'I'll not be going there again, pup.'

'We'll see.'

Then Mirko called out, 'Toni! Where the fuck are you? We don't have time to waste. Find something to hit the bastard with.'

'Toni!' Christopher shouted in alarm. 'Follow what's in your heart. This is not your fight.'

'Of course it's his fight.'

'Italians are now Britain's allies.'

'Not all of us.'

Toni watched from the shadows, remaining hidden and silent, paralysed by indecision and the sheer horror of it all. He knew that this was his fault, that someone was about to die because of his curiosity. Yet he simply didn't know what his part in this awful drama should be.

'Looks like I'll have to finish you off by myself,' said Mirko.

'Thought you'd already tried that.'

This time Mirko charged at the officer for real and managed to grab hold of him, trying to manoeuvre him into position. They grappled roughly then Mirko suddenly pulled back his head. The movement was slight and fast, but an image flashed through Christopher's mind: a Scottish sergeant, tough as old leather, who once taught him unarmed combat.

251

'Remember, sir, if you're fighting a bugger that simply won't go down, give him a Glasgow kiss.'

Christopher bent his knees, making his whole body drop several inches at the exact moment Mirko head-butted him. Their foreheads came together in a clash of blinding white pain that sent them staggering away from each other and falling to their knees. The Italian recovered first and moments later they were rolling on the ground. This was no longer a fight of any skill. It was a wild scrap of gouging eyes, grabbing throats, desperate punches and kicks.

'Help me, Toni!' cried out Christopher, in fear of his life.

'Get me a fucking rock!' shouted Mirko in fury.

Toni moved out of the shadows and as he did so his foot struck something, almost as if it had been planted there, waiting for him. He bent down and used both hands to lift the object, then he walked over to the men, still rolling around, each trying to gain an edge.

Toni lifted his arms and howled in dismay. He had got this far in the war without even firing a rifle. Now, he was about to kill another human being in a violent, despicably intimate way. He knew he would never be that cheeky young lad from Termoli again. He brought down the rock with all his strength. When it hit the back of the skull there was a dull thud, the most sickening sound Toni had ever heard.

37

Walter fixed his concentration entirely on the stretch of water ahead. In the distance, the Northern Lights were dimming. He continued to send the signal, three quick flashes and two long, but so far there had been no reply.

It was after eleven and he was worried that something had gone wrong. The sea had become an increasingly dangerous place for Germany's U-boats and he feared that the vessel might not even have reached the Moray Firth. And with every minute that passed the chance of the guards discovering the escape from the camp increased.

There was no 'plan B'. Walter had risked everything on this one throw of the dice. If they weren't rescued that night, the Italians would soon be captured and it would only be a matter of time before he was discovered, hiding away in a dirty lodging house in some strange town or city.

Then he saw it, a long black shape emerging from the water, the moonlight making the spray look like hundreds of tiny electric sparks. The U-boat was further out into the firth than he'd expected and Walter assumed this was because the water was too shallow closer to the land. He guessed that the captain would have a dinghy launched before ordering his vessel to dive once more to the greater safety of periscope height.

Walter attached the torch to his belt and got to his feet, wondering if the Italians had dealt with the figure on the hill.

★

Toni was on all fours, retching and sobbing. Christopher lay on his back, too out of breath to shift the huge weight that now lay across him. Eventually, he regained enough strength to push Mirko's body over and get himself on to his knees. Even in his early days in the boxing ring when the pace and power of other men had outflanked him, he had never experienced such a beating.

'You did the right thing.'

Toni was too distraught to answer and when at last the officer managed to get to his feet he walked shakily over and put a hand on the young man's shoulder.

'Don't worry. Your actions will go well for you. I'll speak up in your defence. Come, stand up. I still need your help. We must find my gun. I can't take on someone else with just my fists tonight.'

They rummaged around, searching the undergrowth near the original attack. It was difficult to identity a small, dark object, but finally Toni's hand brushed against the cold metal of the barrel.

'Here,' he said, holding it out.

'Thanks,' said the officer, checking the pistol. 'You better stay nearby and try to keep out of any more trouble.

254

One day we'll be married to those Ross sisters and you and I will be brothers-in-law.'

'You know?'

'Good God, man, it's so obvious that you and Effie are both besotted.' Christopher held out his hand. 'You saved my life.'

Toni shook it and seconds later the other man set off for the shore.

Left alone, the young Italian had never felt such overwhelming wretchedness. He went over to Mirko's body and stood beside it. Sightless eyes stared up at the sky.

Toni kneeled down, knowing that if he did not do this he would regret it for ever. Gently, he laid his hand on the man's forehead and prayed, asking for Mirko's forgiveness and for God to take this soul, however violent and misguided, into his keeping.

Toni thought how it was not Mirko's fault that there was a war. Men all over had been driven to behaviour they would otherwise have kept in check. When Toni had made his peace as best he could, he closed Mirko's eyes. As he did so, he jumped to his feet, repeating a sudden thought aloud in alarm.

'Christopher doesn't know the identity of the spy!'

38

It took Walter longer than he'd expected to reach the path that led to the shore. Gathering clouds occasionally obscured the moonlight, making his progress erratic. On this new stretch there were sections where the ground fell away steeply and he knew he would have to tread carefully. The prospect of causing himself an injury at this stage was too ironic to contemplate.

'Don't move another inch or I'll shoot.'

With those words, Christopher stepped out from a hiding place that Walter had just passed.

'Captain Armstrong!' he cried, reverting instantly to the role that had been a part of his life for so long. 'Thank the Lord I've found you.'

'Reverend Smith! What on earth are you doing here?'

'Old Mrs MacDonald at Rockfield,' Walter said, turning around. 'I swear I've never met someone with such a severe case of intermittent dying syndrome. This is the third time in the last two months that I've been called out in the night to attend to her because she had only a few more hours to live.'

Christopher lowered his gun as the minister walked towards him. 'But why are you here,' he asked, 'so far out of the way?'

'Well, it was a very strange thing. As I was cycling home I saw a man sneaking about in the shadows. It looked so suspicious that I decided to follow on foot, although goodness knows what I would have done if I had actually caught him.'

'Did you recognise him?'

'No, he was always too far away. But it was certainly a man and a pretty agile one. From the direction he was heading, I reckon he's making for the bothy.'

'That makes sense. Thanks for the tip, reverend. I suggest you get away now, but I would appreciate it if you could find an army patrol and let them know what's happened.'

Walter was now near enough to see that the officer had been beaten severely.

'Your face! Captain Armstrong, are you all right?' The man's obvious injuries gave him an excuse to move even closer.

'I'll live, but I think Ina will be in for a fright.'

Christopher realised there was something wrong, although he couldn't immediately grasp what. He could see that the Reverend Smith appeared concerned and had reached out an arm ... Christopher followed it slowly with his eyes until he got to the fingers that were clenched around the handle of a knife. To his horror, he saw that the blade was buried so deep in his stomach that none of it was visible.

As the minster yanked this viciously out, his world exploded in an unbelievable agony. The gun slipped from his grasp as his legs buckled. Walter threw down his weapon and in a gesture of bizarre tenderness he caught the officer and lowered him gently.

257

'Why did you have to come here tonight? I didn't want this. You're a good man who I would have been proud to call my friend.'

'You!' he said, in total disbelief and almost paralysed by the intensity of the pain.

'I'm sorry. Believe me, I would rather that you and Ina had found your happiness.'

'Damn you to hell.'

'Hell will be an overcrowded place by the time this war is over.'

As they spoke, Walter reached again for the knife. He couldn't risk leaving the officer alive, and bleeding to death alone in the dark was a poor way to die. Better to make it instant. Walter put a hand on Christopher's forehead, as he had so often done with people who were ill, but this time he was steadying the officer's head as he slowly brought the unseen blade under his chin. One thrust up into the brain would be the kindest act.

'I'm sorry —'

Walter's sentence was left unfinished as someone slammed into him with such force that he was carried over the nearby edge, where he rolled down the bank before hitting his shoulder against a boulder. The impetus of the assault had also taken the other man over and they rose to their feet, both too dazed to react straight away.

'You bloody stupid traitor,' Walter shouted.

'I'm no traitor,' said Toni, defiant. 'I'm fighting for the cause I believe in.'

'You're a fool. You would have been a hero in all of Germany.'

'But I'm not German.'

'No matter, you'll soon be dead wherever you're from.'

Walter still had hold of the knife. His right arm felt slightly numb, but he was sure he had little to fear from his light and inexperienced opponent.

The first Walter knew of the danger was the agony of his nose cracking with the impact of a stone Toni had hurled at his face. He cried out in shock and pain as Toni moved in and threw a couple of hard punches before grabbing the wrist of the hand holding the knife.

Walter grabbed Toni's other wrist so that they were locked together, struggling and cursing. The German's greater strength began to tell and the Italian was forced down until he was on his back and the blade edged steadily and surely to a position above his heart.

This wasn't going to be messy. It would be a clean, killing stroke. The precision and relative ease with which the man was lining up the weapon was almost obscene. Toni knew he couldn't stop him and cried out in terror as he felt the sharpened tip being manipulated so that it would slip unhindered between the ribs. He closed his eyes and muttered.

'Your prayers won't help you now,' snarled Walter.

His death was so near, yet even in this state of finality he sensed something odd, a shift in the surroundings that made no sense. When he opened his eyes he saw Effie, heaving with all her might on his attacker's arm, pushing him with her legs to topple him over. Moments later, the three of them were a mass of tangled limbs and shouts of alarm as they slipped further down the bank.

Walter fell awkwardly, his left arm and Toni's right trapped underneath his body as the lovers landed on top, driving the air from his lungs and winding him badly. All focus was on the six inches of steel which hovered, trembling, just above Walter. Effie had both of her hands wrapped tightly around his, but she was too light to force it towards him using only her weight.

She suddenly snatched hold of the torch that was still fastened to his belt and pulled. Here was someone who had spent years carrying bales of hay and working in the fields. The knife began to move and the person known to everyone as the Reverend Smith realised that he couldn't prevent what was about to happen. In one last act of desperation he twisted his wrist, still gripped fiercely by Toni, so that the blade would enter just below the ribcage and be angled towards his abdomen.

'No ... don't,' he said, in a voice unnaturally high with fear.

The tip pierced his skin and seemed to hesitate, as though reluctant to be used against its owner.

'Stop. I'm your minister.'

But in truth the knife was designed to make taking another's life easy. As if its decision was made, the finely honed edge sliced smoothly through the outer layer of fat.

'I beg you! Don't. Think of your father.'

Effie couldn't bear the pleading and screamed to drown out his words.

'Shut up! Shut up! Shut up!'

Even the hardened muscles of Walter's abdomen presented little resistance to the blade as it continued its journey, narrowly missing his liver.

'Nein! Nein!'

Then it pierced his gut and he faltered.

'Vater ...'

'Stop, Effie. Stop.'

She was crying almost hysterically and it took a long while for her to realise it was Toni speaking as he tried to prise open her fingers.

'Let go. Let go, my love. It's over.'

Only then did she realise that the man lying beneath her was still and silent.

'It's over,' said Toni gently.

39

Christopher had never known such cold. He tried to convince himself this was because of lying still for so long on the freezing ground. However, he was too weak to get up, so he knew in his heart that it was because of loss of blood. After someone had charged into the minister, sending both of them plunging down the nearby slope, he had heard raised, angry voices.

Then, unless he had been hallucinating, Effie had appeared briefly by his side, her beautiful face tight with fear. He had pointed in the direction that the men had fallen and in the next instant she was gone. Perhaps it had just been his imagination. But ... no, there she was again, climbing up over the ledge.

'Christopher!' she cried, stumbling towards him and falling on her knees at his side.

'The spy ...' he whispered.

Toni appeared beside her and laid a hand gently on Christopher's shoulder.

'He's dead, sir. You don't have to worry about him.'

He felt Effie pulling at his clothing, trying to examine his injuries. Pain shot through him, and he realised he was moaning. Effie pulled her hand away, her expression frightened.

'We've got to stop the bleeding,' she said.

He put a trembling hand on her arm.

'Too late, Effie.'

'Don't think for one moment that you're dying on me, Christopher Armstrong. I absolutely forbid it! Just imagine what Ina would say.'

At the thought of Ina, Christopher managed to smile. He turned his head slowly towards the Italian.

'You ... you saved me a second time.'

'I'd rather it didn't become a habit, sir.'

'Toni, you've got to go for help,' Effie cried. 'There must be patrols in the area. Please find one of them, my love, as quickly as possible.'

Toni nodded, springing into action. 'I promise I'll be back soon,' he said, before running up the path and out of sight.

When he had gone, Effie turned her attention back to Christopher. She smiled down at him, but the worry in her face was unmistakable. 'Let's get you more comfortable,' she said gently.

Reaching her hands under his shoulders, she managed to manoeuvre him into a position that enabled her to cradle him in her arms. He lay back against her, feeling the heat of her body.

'Effie,' he managed to say. 'Tell Ina ... I love her.'

He felt Effie tense against him, and when she spoke, her voice was thick with emotion. 'You can tell her yourself. And for goodness sake, get married as soon as you're well again, then all of our lives will be more bearable.'

'And you ... and Toni.'

'Yes ... yes, that's exactly what we'll do,' she said, hugging him close.

★

He felt as if he was drowning, his chest on fire with the desperate need for air, but when Walter gasped, he couldn't believe the agony it caused him. He remained motionless, taking rapid, shallow breaths while trying to make sense of what was happening. There were people speaking somewhere nearby, yet it didn't appear that anyone was next to him. Effie and Toni must have gone to attend to Christopher. That meant they had left him, probably assuming he was dead.

Not dead yet.

He raised his head slightly, and tried to study the angle, position and depth of the knife, grimacing as he did so. It had obviously missed any vital organs or he wouldn't be lying there calculating the damage. The desire to pull out the blade in the hope that this would reduce the pain was almost overpowering.

However, he remembered Stein once saying that if you were knifed then it was safer to leave the blade in place, otherwise you ran a greater risk of bleeding to death. Walter felt carefully around the stab wound, trying not to cry out in pain. Although his jumpers were wet, they didn't appear to be soaked in blood.

The bothy was about five minutes away. If he could slide down the bank just a few yards away, he could pick up the path again. The way to the rendezvous site would be clear.

The dinghy would surely be close to the shore by now. He needed to keep going for perhaps just a half an hour to make it to the U-boat, where there would be medical help.

With tiny, agonising movements, Walter rolled over and rose to his knees. He swayed, fearing he was about to faint again. However, the feeling passed and he was eventually able to get to his feet, wobbling unsteadily.

★

Private Atkinson's hostility towards the Italians at the Kildary camp had not gone unnoticed by Major Cooper, and so Atkinson had increasingly been sent on patrols rather than being used on guard duty. Wherever he went, he was usually accompanied by Private McIntosh. That night, the two men received an urgent message that there had been a breakout and they were to begin searching the coastline until reinforcements arrived.

Atkinson cursed as they hurried along the rough ground. 'Bloody typical,' he moaned. 'As soon as we're not there to keep an eye on things, the bastards escape and *we're* meant to recapture them.'

'Why would they make for the Moray Firth?' queried McIntosh. 'What good's that going to do them?'

'Hey! Look there!' Atkinson thrust an arm out in front of him, pointing at a figure in the distance.

Toni had appeared around a cluster of bushes, moving quickly towards them. The soldiers immediately levelled their rifles at the sight of an unidentified man heading in their direction. Toni stopped when he spotted them, waving frantically.

'Captain Armstrong needs help,' he yelled, but his words were carried away on the wind. He continued to wave his arms above his head.

'It's a POW,' said McIntosh. 'What the hell's he doing?'

'The bastard's mocking us,' Atkinson said furiously.

Their weapons were difficult to hold steady, so Atkinson went down on one knee as he had done so often during practice. Toni watched with a growing sense of unease. There was something about the stance of the man on the ground that felt more than just threatening.

'Don't shoot!' Toni shouted. 'I need help for a British officer. He's badly injured.'

Atkinson adjusted his sights. 'This is going to be like ducks at the fair.'

'Christ, you can't just kill him, Tom,' McIntosh cried. 'Keep him covered and I'll go closer.'

Toni suddenly realised the identity of the men and was overcome with the dreadful certainty that he was about to be fired upon. He turned and sprinted back the way he came, zigzagging as best he could on the narrow path. He didn't hear the shot. He didn't even feel any pain as the bullet tore through flesh and muscle. Instead, it was as though an enormous hand had shoved him hard in the back, sending him sprawling.

'Bullseye! Those target discs are a bloody brilliant idea.'

'Fucking hell, Tom.' McIntosh froze, his expression aghast. 'What have you done?'

Atkinson got to his feet and took hold of the other man's jacket. He pushed his face close. 'You're a witness. He's an escaped POW. We shouted at him to stand still, but he turned and ran. The fact that he's shot in the back is proof. Now, come on, let's finish the job.'

When they reached the Italian, McIntosh turned his body over.

'It's young Toni,' he said. 'I can't imagine him hurting anyone.'

'What's he doing out here then?'

Toni couldn't speak. His body was going numb and he was finding it difficult to breathe. Atkinson kicked his leg and, from the ferocious expression on his face, looked as though he might do more. This time it was McIntosh who was the more forceful of the two.

'That's enough,' he said, grabbing Atkinson's arm. 'You've done for him. Let the lad die in peace. Our orders are to search the shore.'

The other man paused, uttered a curse and set off once more. McIntosh looked down at the figure at his feet, then he too turned and followed his companion.

Toni tried to move, but he couldn't even lift an arm. When he attempted to shout Effie's name, no sound came out of his mouth. He wanted so much to say goodbye properly; he didn't want it to end like this. Both of them lying on a cold, dirty path. He hoped she would realise that he had genuinely sought help for Christopher.

There was still no pain. Instead, the numbness spread, until only his mind appeared to be functioning. Then that too felt like it was numbing. Darkness crept over his vision and he felt his mind clearing of all thoughts, until there was nothing ... just nothing.

★

Walter's journey to the bothy was a nightmare of white-hot agony. It felt as though the blade was sawing through his insides with every jarring step. When he finally reached the hut, he collapsed against the wall, panting and sweating. The torch was still tied to his belt, but his hands were shaking so much that Walter fumbled for several minutes trying to retrieve it and send the signal.

His vision was blurred and he wasn't certain if the dark shape out on the water was real. However, the flashing light replying to his message was clear enough. The boat was near. Despite his horrendous injury, Walter was going to make it.

Then the shot rang out, the unmistakable sound of a .303 Lee-Enfield rifle, standard issue for the British army.

★

The two privates ran around a bend in the path and came across the bizarre sight of a young woman cradling an injured officer. Reaching them, McIntosh bent down. He gasped.

'Blimey, it's Captain Armstrong. He looks in a bad way.'

'Did you see Toni, an Italian from the camp?' Effie asked, overcome by dread. 'I heard a shot?'

'Don't worry, miss,' Atkinson said. 'He won't be bothering anyone ever again.'

'We better go,' said McIntosh. He looked scared and kept nervously running a hand through his hair. 'The balloon's gone up. This place will soon be alive with military. There'll be plenty of help for the captain shortly, miss. Just hang on.'

Atkinson kneeled down and spoke to Christopher. 'We'll get the bastard who did this to you, sir. I promise we will.'

'Come on, Tom!'

The two soldiers ran off, following their orders to get to the beach. Once they were out of sight, Effie closed her eyes and wept, a cascade of tears rolling down her frozen cheeks.

'No ... Toni,' she moaned, her chest heaving with sobs. A few moments later, she realised that there was something else on her face. She opened her eyes to find that Christopher had reached up a hand. It must have taken him a huge effort.

'Sorry ...' he whispered.

It was all he could manage. Effie hugged him tightly, her wails of grief whisked away on the icy wind.

★

Walter wiped the sweat from his eyes, unsure of what he was seeing. He could just about make out the boat, his salvation, bobbing nearby on the water. Yet it appeared that the craft was drifting.

No!

Walter realised with a sinking dread that the men on board had been spooked by the rifle shot. The boat was turning around and heading for the safety of the firth.

'Halt! Come back!' Walter shouted, but his voice wasn't much more than a croak.

Walter left the cover of the bothy and stumbled down to the water's edge.

'Halt! I have the secret!'

The cowards.

He refused to be caught, not now, not after everything he had endured. He sobbed in pain as he waded into the icy sea. However, the tide was in his favour. It was still possible to reach the U-boat. When the water reached his thighs he let his body fall forward. He immediately went under, pulled down by the thick clothing and his inability to make any of his limbs work properly. The amount of effort it took to get back to the surface was frightening and he only managed a few weak strokes before discovering that his ankle was tangled in seaweed.

'Nein!' he cried. 'Nein!'

Then he realised that his other ankle was also caught and he couldn't move at all.

'Where do you think you're going, sunshine?'

It was a man's voice, right behind him. It wasn't seaweed holding him back but strong hands that gripped his legs. Walter was pulled toward the shore, powerless to do anything about it. He screamed as he was dragged up the beach and the knife's handle caught on rocks and pebbles. Then he was roughly turned over.

'Bloody hell, it's the local minister,' said McIntosh.

Atkinson sneered. 'I never trusted him.'

'You don't trust anyone,' McIntosh pointed out.

'Well, he was far too matey with the Italians.'

'This is one bloody strange night.'

Walter stared up at the soldiers, struggling to follow their conversation. He thought he was going to pass out. He desperately wanted to; he wanted oblivion to rescue him from the utter despair of his failure. But there was a message he needed these men to know, the one truth that had given him hope and determination through all the lonely, difficult years.

'Hitler ...'

'What's he saying?' asked McIntosh, leaning down to listen.

The men kneeled either side. Walter weakly took hold of the nearest jacket.

'Hitler ... is ... a ... genius.'

'Is that right, reverend?' Atkinson said. 'Well, I'll tell you what, you don't look too fucking clever at the moment.'

'Hey up, here come the cavalry.'

With disgust, Atkinson removed the German's hand from his jacket and stood, following McIntosh's out-stretched arm. The cliff edge came alive with running figures carrying torches and shouting.

'About bloody time!' Atkinson said.

★

Effie heard loud voices and was suddenly blinded by a light. She held up a hand to shield her eyes and was aware of several people around her. Some rushed past, and others grouped around where she sat, cradling her sister's fiancé. A man crouched down beside them.

'Christopher needs help,' she said.

'Let me see,' said the sergeant briskly, using his torch to examine the officer's face. When he spoke again, his voice was gentler. 'There's nothing more you can do for Captain Armstrong, miss. I'll take him now.'

'No!' Effie cried. 'He just needs a doctor.'

'Private McGuire,' the sergeant called.

'Yes, sergeant,' one of the men nearby replied.

'Get his woman safely home. Use the jeep.'

Effie felt a hand on her shoulder. 'Come along, miss,' said the soldier, helping her to her feet. The sergeant respectfully laid Christopher out nearby.

'There are so many dead,' Effie said. It didn't feel real.

'Let's get you back to your family,' the soldier said kindly. 'I'm sure they'll be worried.'

'They're all dead ... all of them.' Effie stumbled, and the soldier had to put his arm around her waist. He half-carried her along the path.

'I'm sure it will be sorted, miss.'

'All I did was to love someone. I never meant for anyone to be hurt.'

'These things always appear better in the morning.'

'How am I going to explain to Ina?'

They were almost out of sight when the sergeant turned and spoke to another of his men.

'Stewart.'

'Yes, sergeant.'

'Go with them. I want to know exactly who that girl is and where she lives. Tell McGuire he's to stand guard outside her house. She doesn't leave for any reason until he has new orders. That girl has one hell of a lot of explaining to do before this night is over.'

40

Effie's parents and sister cried out in alarm when she appeared in the kitchen doorway, covered in blood and looking like a terrifying vision from the underworld, a wicked person damned for all eternity, as described by some of the more 'fire and brimstone' ministers they had heard preaching in the kirk over the years.

'Dear God above!' shouted Mr Ross, jumping up from his wicker chair near the range. 'Are you hurt?'

'It's not my blood,' Effie replied in a hoarse whisper, unable to meet his eyes.

'Whose is it?' he asked.

Effie's heart had been broken into a thousand pieces and she didn't believe it could be hurt any more, yet she couldn't bring herself to speak the words that she knew would cause so much pain to someone else. Slowly, unbearably slowly, she shifted her gaze to Ina. In the end, there was no need to say anything at all.

'No!' Ina screamed, a hand flying to her mouth.

'I'm so sorry, Ina,' Effie said. She was afraid to go any closer to her sister after all that had happened between them, but wanted to run to her more than anything.

'He didn't die alone. I held him in my arms ... until the end.'

Martha hugged her daughter, and Mr Ross sank back into his seat, his mouth agape.

'I can't believe it,' he said. 'What's happening to us?'

Effie slumped into a chair at the far end of the table. She hesitated before speaking again. 'There's more ... I ... I killed the Reverend Smith.'

Even Ina's grief was momentarily overshadowed. For a moment there was just silence, as everyone stared at Effie in utter disbelief.

'What?' Mr Ross struggled to get his words out. 'I don't understand. What are you talking about?'

'He was about to murder Toni. I joined in the fight and we pushed a knife into him, until he stopped struggling ... stopped begging us not to.'

Effie spoke without emotion, as if she was merely recounting an event on the farm. Her expression was unreadable. However, her words had the rest of the family reeling.

'I don't believe I'm hearing this!' cried Mr Ross, what little colour there was left in his face rapidly draining away. 'You've *killed* the minister?'

'He was a German spy.'

'That's nonsense!' Mr Ross snapped. 'He was a good person and our minister. He was my friend.'

'This is your fault, Effie!' shouted Ina. 'I was going to spend the rest of my life with Christopher and now he's dead and you're responsible!' She drew herself up to her full height, staring at Effie with such anger. 'You've destroyed me ... you and your Italian lover.' Her face contorted as she spat out the words, before she crumpled into her mother's arms.

For a long while the only sound in the kitchen was Ina's weeping and the ticking of the clock. Effie didn't cry, at least not visibly. She just sat, staring straight ahead. Gradually, she became aware that her father had come over and sat in the seat beside her.

He made no attempt to speak or offer any comfort. Instead he looked at her, and there was a coldness in his expression that Effie had never seen before. She knew it wasn't her blood-soaked clothes that prevented him from holding her. No, she realised that he felt she had become contaminated by something much worse – by sins that could never be washed away. Across the room, Martha stood and helped Ina to her feet before leading her out of the kitchen and up the stairs. Several minutes passed before Effie broke the silence with her father.

'There was another death, Father. Toni died.'

The farmer stared at her as if he was in a trance, seemingly unable to take in the horror unfolding around him. Effie yearned to be held by him so much that she physically ached.

'Didn't you hear me, Father? Toni is dead.'

Her father sighed. 'There's no need to worry about that now. We have to think about Ina's loss and what we can do to help ... and we must consider what's to be done about your involvement with the murder of a minister of the kirk.'

The fragments of Effie's heart turned to ice ... they turned to stone ... they turned to dust and were blown away on the wind, across the firth and out to sea where

275

they disappeared beneath the waves. In the place where her heart used to beat there was only a crushing emptiness. Her love for Toni meant nothing to her father. His death was not even worth mentioning.

'Ina wants to be left alone for a while,' Martha said, returning from upstairs and joining her husband and daughter at the table. 'I'll go to her later on.'

They sat in stunned silence, no one sure what to do or say. However, it wasn't long before they heard the front door open and footsteps come into the house. Constable MacKay entered the kitchen, followed by two men in dark suits and overcoats.

He nodded at Effie's father. 'Mr Ross, these gentlemen are from the authorities.' He didn't expand on what he meant by 'authorities' and appeared completely out of his depth.

'Are you Effie Ross?' said the older of the two men, a powerfully built man who looked as if he'd forgotten how to smile a long time ago. Effie nodded. 'You have to come with us, miss.'

'Who are you?' asked Martha.

'We're from MI5, Mrs Ross,' he replied, holding up an official-looking document, although no one had a chance to read what was on it. 'Your daughter has some explaining to do.'

'Surely it can wait until morning,' said Martha.

'We have to go now.'

'Where are you taking her?' Martha continued. 'How long will she be away?'

'We're going to the military base at Tain. How long for depends on what she has to say.'

Martha opened her mouth to argue, but Effie held up a hand to cut her off. 'It's all right, Mother. I'll go with them.'

'You can't go in that state,' said Martha forcefully.

The man had seen the revolting mess Effie was in and conceded that her mother was right.

'You've got five minutes then we're leaving.'

Effie went upstairs. Ina was lying on their bed, curled up in a ball and quietly crying. She stopped when her sister entered. There was a dim, golden glow from the dresser where their mother had lit a paraffin lamp.

'I would give anything not to have hurt you,' Effie said, standing just inside the door.

'I'll never meet another Christopher.'

'No ... and I'll never meet another Toni.'

'Did he suffer?'

'A bit. He told me to say that he loved you.'

'I loved him.'

'I tried everything I could to save him.'

'It should have been me with him at the end,' said Ina, starting to cry again.

'I'm sorry, more than I can possibly say.'

'What good is that to me?'

'Tell me what I can do?'

Effie stepped forward, but Ina spoke sharply. 'Stay away.'

Effie knew that Ina's emotions were raw. There was nothing that could be done tonight to mend the huge chasm that had been wrenched open between them. She went to the corner and stripped off her bloodied clothes, before putting on a clean, dry outfit. Leaving the dirty items in a heap on the floor and her sister in a heap on the bed, Effie went back downstairs and followed the strangers outside. She did not speak to or acknowledge her parents, pausing in the porch only to put on her coat.

★

The older man sat in the back of the car with Effie as the other drove through the dark, the part-covered headlights providing just enough light to steer by. Effie felt so numbed in spirit and body that she didn't care where they went or what happened to her. She just wanted the nightmare to end, although part of her feared that worse was yet to come.

No one spoke during the journey and after about twenty minutes they stopped at the gates of the base. The car was allowed through immediately when the guards saw the identification and moments later they parked up in front of a squat, single-storey, brick building. The driver came quickly around to the back door and took her arm, gripping her firmly as if fearing she might attempt to escape.

Everything felt surreal. Only an hour or so ago Effie had experienced more fear and anguish than she had ever known in her life, yet now she felt strangely detached from the unfamiliar surroundings and people... from everything. She was led to a small, bare room. The two men sat opposite her and a man in uniform deposited three steaming mugs of strong tea on the table between them.

'Right, Miss Ross,' said the senior of the two men. 'You better tell us exactly what you know about the events leading up to tonight – and don't leave out a single thing.'

★

It was around three o'clock in the morning when Effie returned to Kirk Farm. Her father was sitting in his wicker chair by the range, holding his pipe though not smoking it. There was no sign of anyone else. Although she was almost fainting with fatigue, Effie remained standing, keeping a few yards between them. He stayed silent for a long while, studying her with an expression that she couldn't fathom.

'So they let you out.'

'Yes.'

'I thought they might have locked you up. What did you tell them?'

'Everything.'

'I see.' He paused to examine his unlit pipe. 'A couple of soldiers arrived earlier with an officer. He told me a little of what's been happening tonight. They've taken away all of Christopher's possessions. It's almost as if he had never been here. All Ina has is a small photograph of him in uniform ... and her engagement ring.'

'How is she?'

'Ina's in bed with your mother.'

'She won't sleep with me?'

'No.'

'I understand.'

'Do you! Well I wish that I did, girl! How could you have done such evil? You've betrayed your country ... put at risk the lives of our men.'

'All I've done was to love someone.'

'Love!' he shouted, standing up, his pent-up rage suddenly bursting out. 'You only knew him for a few weeks. Ina has spoken to me. I can't even begin to understand

279

what you were thinking to take an Italian upstairs and let him into Christopher's bedroom.'

'I never meant any harm. Toni only wanted to see my puppets.'

'How can you stand there talking about *puppets* when you have the blood of others on your hands? Because of your stupidity... your wickedness... people are dead, including a man of God.'

'He was a spy who would have taken a dangerous secret back to Germany.'

'He wouldn't have had a secret if it hadn't been for you. He was a good man. The war would have eventually ended and he would have continued as a minister. Now he's gone, your sister is broken and our family is in ruins.'

He suddenly hurled his pipe across the room and took two large steps towards her. He was trembling in his attempt to control his anger.

'If you're able to speak one word of truth, then tell me this... did you shame yourself with the Italian before or after Duncan died?'

He was so close that she could smell the tobacco on his breath and see the wildness in his eyes. She knew that the truth would be the worst thing she could possibly utter.

'After.'

'Damn you!' He was screaming now. 'Your brother was still warm in his grave and you're disgracing yourself with the enemy, letting a dirty foreigner pleasure himself with you. How many of them did you whore yourself with? How many?'

'That's not fair.'

'FAIR!'

The word seemed to tip the balance of his mind, as if the letters had the power to release a demon that now took over his body. The man in front of her was a frightening, deranged stranger with no hint of the person who had cherished and cared for her since she was born. There was nothing of the gentle farmer who loved his land, who would stay up all night with an ill animal, who would defend his family at all costs. Yet even so, Effie wasn't prepared for what was about to happen; neither of them were.

The impact of his hand sent her staggering sideways and it was only because she caught hold of a chair that she didn't crash to the floor. Waves of nausea washed over her as she leaned across the table, panting and trying not to be sick. Everything was spinning so fast that she couldn't focus and had to remain still for several minutes. There were tears in her eyes, but she wasn't crying. People without a heart have no reason to cry.

Mr Ross had never hit anyone in his life and was shocked at the explosive force he had used. It had almost been as though his arm had momentarily belonged to someone else. He stood, rigid, with no idea what to do other than wait for a reaction.

Her legs felt as if they wouldn't support her and the room continued to spin, but somehow Effie slowly straightened up with an enormous effort of will. The farmer took an involuntary step backwards. He would never have believed it possible that his daughter could look at him with such hate.

'You will never touch me again.'

The voice didn't sound like her own. It was cold and full of bitterness. Effie didn't mean that he would never strike her again. She meant exactly what she said. He would never touch her again, never hold her hand or put an arm around her shoulders, never kiss her goodnight or cuddle her. The bonds of love and blood had been shattered and they were all drifting apart on a sea of loneliness and misery.

Effie turned around and walked with an unsteady determination out of the house, leaving Mr Ross standing in the kitchen, aghast at the tragedy that was tearing his family apart.

41

The moon had disappeared behind dense, angry clouds and the night was wild and black. Effie groped along the low wall outside the kitchen before setting off towards the barn where Toni and she had made love. It was the only place that held any sense of belonging.

The door was difficult to open against the wind, but she made it inside and up the ladder. The piles of straw in the hayloft were still there and she buried her way into the biggest mound, seeking safety and warmth. It was only when Effie was deep within the straw that the enormity of the encounter with her father struck her.

Then the horrifying images that she had been suppressing flooded her mind ... pushing the knife into the Reverend Smith, holding the dying Christopher, that last look from Toni before he went to find help and instead found his own death.

Effie started shaking and although she wrapped her arms tightly around her legs, the movements became more severe and uncontrollable. She cried out in alarm as one scene after another flashed in front of her, so real that it felt as though she was back on the path, covered in blood and hearing the rifle shot. It wasn't long before she was shouting, pleading and calling out into the darkness for Toni to save her.

As the storm howled outside, Effie's anguish filled the barn in an endless, agonising lament.

★

As the day broke, Effie felt herself climbing out of a deep, dark well to become aware of her surroundings ... and her grief. Slowly, she emerged from her straw nest. It was daylight, morning.

The side of her face felt hot and tender and one eye was partly closed. Movement hurt every part of her body and she had to hold on to a beam until the nausea and dizziness faded away. Yet this was nothing compared to the ache in her soul.

Her foot had just reached the bottom of the ladder when the door opened and the barn was flooded with light. Her father looked drawn, and it was clear that he was even more shocked at her appearance. They studied each other for a while before he broke the silence.

'Alastair has come over with the bogie. He'll take you to Tain station. Your mother has packed a suitcase and there's an envelope with your ration book and other documents, plus money to keep you going for a few weeks. There should be plenty of work in the bigger towns without risking the cities.'

So that was his solution ... he was exiling her from Kirk Farm; she was being disowned by them all. Well, it was no great surprise. What other option was there for her except

284

to leave and begin a new life elsewhere? But there was one innocent person in this hellish nightmare.

'I want to say goodbye to Hugh.'

'It's because of him that you have to leave!' her father shouted, his anger bursting to the surface. 'He's only a boy. What sort of future does he have growing up here with everyone knowing that his sister betrayed her country, killed the minister and disgraced herself with the enemy only days after her brother's funeral?'

He would deny her even this small comfort. What story would be told to Hugh to explain her departure from his life?

'Shame on you, Father, for using Hugh as the excuse when it's your own inability to forgive that lies behind all this. Well, I'll go and I swear to you that you'll never see me on Kirk Farm again.'

She walked past her father, leaving him standing where he was. He didn't turn around to watch her leave.

Alastair was sitting in the cart, staring straight ahead as if made of stone. He must have heard everything that had just been said. He didn't acknowledge her when she climbed up beside him and a few seconds later he flicked the reins and the horse walked on.

Effie glanced back only once. There was no sign of her family. But when they passed the far side of the horse chestnut tree she caught sight of Hugh, hiding so that he couldn't be seen from the house. Effie wanted to tell Alastair to stop, but something prevented her and the cart trundled on along the drive.

Hugh slowly raised his arm. He had the puppet of Effie on his hand and when he moved his thumb the tiny arm waved goodbye.

His sister made no sound, but in the shell of the body that once was Effie Ross of Kirk Farm a grief-stricken wail of anguish sounded. No living soul would ever hear that cry, but it would echo inside her for years and years to come.

PART THREE

42

Effie gently laid her fingers on the ivory keys of their grandmother's harmonium and recalled how Ina and she perfected the technique of operating one foot pedal each so that they could sit side by side to perform. She wondered if Ina had taught Hugh how to play the instrument, or even played it again herself.

Now Ina was dead, her funeral taking place in the morning. If Hugh had not written the previous week, then this part of the family's story would also have passed without Effie knowing. Over the decades, whenever she had moved house, Effie had written to Ina. There had never been a reply. However, much to her surprise, the letters had been kept and when Hugh had started going through Ina's paperwork he had found them. Assuming that the last correspondence contained Effie's most recent address, he had written. And so there she was, at seventy-nine, walking around the empty building that had once been her home.

She went upstairs, one part of her compelled to tread these footsteps of the past and another part reluctant. She paused in the doorway of her old bedroom. It was immediately apparent this room had remained Ina's. The double bed that she had shared with Ina had been replaced by a modern single. Effie remembered the varied conversations they used to have in the dark, the fits of giggles they'd burst into, cuddling together in the cold ... always being there for each other.

Effie picked up a small silver frame, which had pride of place on the dresser. The black and white photograph inside showed Christopher in his captain's uniform, smiling and so handsome he could have been a Hollywood film star. For a moment, Effie was thrown back to that terrible night. She felt the weight of the dying man as she cradled him, the wetness of his blood on her clothes. She held the frame to her breast, but the tears for those lost that night had been shed long ago.

Hugh's letter hadn't given any information about a surviving husband or existing family. Had Ina never married? Had she gone to sleep alone every night, with only her fiancé's image for company?

Effie turned to leave and gave a small cry of surprise at the sight of the garment hanging behind the door. It was the army greatcoat that she had thrown off before hurrying back to find Toni, while Ina continued raising the alarm. She laid a hand on the sleeve of the heavy, grey material and thought about the last words she had spoken to her sister before running off into the night.

'Whatever happens, I'll always love you, Ina.'

It was true. She always had.

Effie walked along the corridor. Of course, the whole house had been refurbished, probably several times since she left. However, there were pieces of furniture that she recognised – a lovely mahogany chest of drawers in her parents' old bedroom, Duncan's sturdy wardrobe. It was from that wardrobe that Toni, with his childlike curiosity, had retrieved the secret documents.

In the tiny room that Hugh had used as a child she was astonished to find the shelves still full of puppets. There was Constable MacKay beside Mr Lawson the Home Guard, who rested against Doctor Gray with his little medical bag. On one shelf were her parents, along with Hugh and Duncan. Further along, sat by themselves, were Ina and Christopher.

Effie didn't see one of her and assumed it had been thrown out. Then she spotted it, on a lower shelf, near a figure in a POW uniform. Her breath caught in her throat as she picked up the latter. The bright red target disc on the jacket seemed an obscene feature now. Is this what the soldier had used to shoot Toni that night? Aiming for the centre of the circle to cause maximum injury? Tenderly, she laid the puppet so that his head rested on the girl's knee.

'Just toys,' she said, sighing. 'Not flesh and blood.'

The kitchen had been completely modernised, the dresser and cabinets replaced by built-in units. Where the ancient solid fuel range used to be there was a shiny blue version that presumably ran on oil. Nobody today would choose to regularly feed wood or coal into a cooker that still went out overnight and had to be constantly cleaned and black-leaded.

However, the grandfather clock continued to tick away in the corner, still five minutes fast, and the big table stood where it always had, as if the passing of time was of no consequence and ageing was something that only occurred in the outside world.

They had eaten so many meals and discussed so many topics sitting around those thick oak boards. Before Duncan had joined the army, the six of them would laugh, tease, question and listen, enjoying each other's company and their mother's excellent food. How often had they heard their father say grace? She wondered if Ina had eaten at the table alone after their parents died.

'Fee.'

Effie hadn't heard anyone enter and turned in surprise. Across the room stood a man in his late sixties. There was only one person who had ever called her Fee.

'Hugh!'

She put a hand to her mouth and stared, trying to recognise some feature, perhaps in the eyes or the shape of the face. There was nothing. What could be expected after so long apart? And what did he see? An eccentric, grey-haired woman, shuffling around an empty house stirring up memories, dust and ghosts. Hugh was carrying a box. It took a moment for her to realise what it was.

'My sewing box from Duncan. I never expected to see that again.'

Hugh seemed on edge. Bizarre as it was, Effie was surprised that this meeting had made him so anxious. He fidgeted from foot to foot.

'I wasn't sure if you would come,' he said hesitantly.

Effie smiled, trying to put him at ease. 'I didn't know myself until yesterday, which is why I never replied to your letter. I just woke up in the morning and decided that I would. I'm staying in Tain. I'm sorry, but I was too tired and it was too late when I arrived last night to make contact.'

Hugh dismissed her apology with a wave. 'That's all right. I saw a strange car and I assumed ... well, hoped it was you. I built a new house just up the hill.'

'I saw it.'

'I took over running the farm and when I got married I moved out and left Mother, Father and Ina here. For a long while now there was only Ina.'

They fell silent. Effie had thought often about this moment, this reunion with the brother she had loved so much. It was one of the main reasons she had returned. But there was no rushing into each other's arms, no screams of joy or tears of delight. The little boy who used to climb into her bed was gone and it felt as though the table between them was a barrier that neither was able to cross.

'Anne, my wife, would love to meet you,' said Hugh. 'Maybe, when you've finished here, you will come over and stay for a meal?'

'That would be lovely.'

'I've got two sons and a daughter, plus five grandchildren.'

'It's difficult to believe. I look forward to meeting them very much.'

'There's tea in the caddie and the milk in the fridge is fresh, if you want to make yourself a drink.'

Effie sensed that Hugh was holding back, that he was hesitating to impart some information. He had always been sensitive and considerate of other's feelings. She waited, letting him find his own way.

'Fee … there's something else you have to look at. I think it's best that you do it here.' He had been clutching the old sewing box as though it contained his most precious possessions, but he now laid it carefully on the table. 'Take as long as you want. I'll be at the house whenever you need me.'

'Goodness, whatever is it?'

For the first time since entering the room Hugh began to get visibly upset.

'I didn't know, Fee! I honestly had no idea. I only found out a couple of days ago, after I had already written to you.'

Effie was utterly baffled. However, it was obvious Hugh wasn't going to explain so she just nodded and agreed to come along later. For a brief moment, Hugh appeared to consider coming around the table to take her in his arms, but then he simply turned away without speaking and left.

★

Hugh didn't go home. Instead he sat on the low wall outside, just out of sight of the kitchen window. He had worked on the land all his life and was still a strong man, not prone to being nervous or outwardly emotional, yet as he hugged his arms around his chest his legs were trembling.

There were always noises around a farm, but it seemed to him that everything had grown quiet and still. No cattle mooed, no birds sung. Even the wind stopped blowing, turning the trees into statues. It felt as if the entire world was holding its breath, waiting for his sister to lift the lid of the box and discover the greatest tragedy of all the tragedies that had befallen the Ross family.

'I'm sorry, Fee,' he whispered.

The piercing scream that followed ripped apart the silence. It ripped apart his heart.

'I didn't know … I promise I didn't know.'

Then Hugh began to cry. He cried as though he was that small boy again, watching his beloved Fee being taken away, never to be seen again.

43

Effie's scream echoed around the empty house. In her hand, she held a letter. The sewing box was full of envelopes, dozens and dozens of them, all addressed to her.

26 March 1946

My darling Effie,
My soul has been tormented by not being able to write before now ...

'He lived! My Toni lived!' Effie wailed into the empty house.

With great effort, she forced back the tears that threatened to blur her vision, and continued to read.

I have thought of you every day since that night. I promise that I did try to find help for Christopher. I came across a British patrol, but they didn't appear to understand what I was shouting. I was a figure appearing out of the dark and I suppose they were nervous. One of them shot me.

I honestly believed I was going to die. The soldiers left me lying on the ground in the cold and I blacked out. The next memory I have is waking up in hospital. I didn't know at the time that nearly a week had passed. I was very ill and the doctor later told me it had been 'a very close thing'. For a long while I wasn't aware of much. As I got better I realised I was in a room by myself and discovered it was on a military base.

One day two men in suits came to see me. They were some sort of secret police and knew a lot about me and the escape. They wanted to hear my account. It seemed that the best thing was to tell the truth, exactly as it happened. So I explained how we had fallen in love, how it was my fault I ended up in Christopher's room and that I looked at the secret papers (Effie, I wish with all my heart that I'd never done that). I told them about Mirko and how he said we were going to Germany with a local man who was a spy.

Talking about those events while lying in my hospital bed made them feel unreal. They feel even more so now, as I write these words sitting on the porch at my parents' house in Termoli. Only you remain real, Effie. My love for you is as strong as ever. I will only ever love the girl on the farm who made me sing to a pig.

I'm sorry. I should finish my story, so that you can understand what happened and why you have not heard from me until now.

The two secret police had to visit on several occasions because I wasn't strong enough to explain all that occurred in one interview. As the days went by I told them what happened after Mirko and I had escaped from the camp, that I killed him with a rock to save Christopher and then stabbed the 'minister' later.

(Effie, I clearly remember the fight and stabbing the man who was the spy. You arrived a short while afterwards, before we went to try and help Christopher. I explained this very precisely to the two men.)

Although they seemed to believe my explanation, they wouldn't answer any of my questions – they wouldn't even tell me if you were all right. Did Christopher survive his injuries? I really hope he did and was able to marry Ina. They seemed very much in love.

I wonder if perhaps the British authorities went to so much trouble to save my life because they needed to find out what I knew and what information might have been passed on to the enemy. I accepted that, having escaped from a POW camp and killed two people, I would be executed. After all, the war was still raging.

However, when I had recovered sufficiently, I was transferred to solitary confinement. I never found out where this was. The only people I saw for months were the same few guards. Then, one day, without any warning, I was taken to an Italian camp in England. It was 7 June 1944. Of course, I soon understood that the information I knew about Normandy no longer mattered. The D-Day landings had begun.

I wanted to write while I was still in Britain, but the military wouldn't let me. I was only allowed to contact my parents in Italy. With the country in need of labour, a great many of us were kept on after the war ended. During my last six months in Britain, I worked in London, helping to clear rubble from buildings that had been bombed. I only arrived home yesterday. Today, almost two and a half years after we were last together, is the first opportunity I have had to write.

I don't have the words to describe the agony I have felt during this time – not being able to let you know what happened and how I am, and not knowing how you are.

I love you, Effie Ross, and I will do so until the day I die. I hold true to what I said. Until you release me from my promise, I will remain yours and yours alone. I wait only for the day that I can see your beautiful face once more.

Love,
Toni

Effie's hand trembled as she laid the letter on the table.

'Oh, Ina, if you hated me so much, why did you keep these?'

However, for the moment Effie's need to find out more about Toni outweighed anything else, so she buried her emotions and instead focused on the contents of the box. She took out the next letter and began to read.

13 May 1946

My darling Effie,

I have not received a reply, but I am writing again as I cannot be certain that my first letter reached Kirk Farm. I will continue to write until I can no longer do so or we are together as we planned so often.

Italy is in a very bad way. Hardly anyone has work and everything is in short supply. However, I am united with my entire family again now that my brother Luca has finally returned. My two sisters never left home, and so although we are poor, we are happy to be together. We've always been close – typical Italians, you might say!

I have told them that you are the girl I intend to marry. They are all so eager to meet you and send their best wishes to Scotland...

Effie didn't finish, and instead pulled out another envelope about halfway down the pile. The correspondence appeared to have been filed neatly in date order. She discovered that Toni had written every year on her birthday. The third letter she read was full of news about his success as a cabinetmaker and how he was now an uncle several times over. His brother and sisters lived near by and their family was closer than ever.

He asked lots of questions about her life and what she was doing, enquiring what was happening on Kirk Farm. He still sent his love and repeated that until she released him from his promise, he would continue to wait for the girl he loved.

Effie was going to select another envelope just a little further along the timeline, when some instinct made her pull out what she assumed was the last letter. She had to fight back her sobs when she noticed the handwriting was different.

2 February 1994

Dear Auntie Effie,
I have grown up hearing Uncle Toni talk about the girl he fell in love with while in the Highlands of Scotland. Although we have never met, you have been so real to all of us that we consider you to be part of our family. I know he wrote regularly and you were always in his heart and thoughts. I am very sorry to say that our lovely uncle died recently after a short illness. His health never fully recovered following the injury he received while a prisoner of war.
　　Uncle Toni was a man who loved life and

301

people. He was extremely popular yet never married, although there were many women who would have walked down the aisle with him. I want you to know that he was greatly loved and an integral part of our lives. He was a second father to my cousins and me (I am the daughter of his brother, Luca) and a grand-father figure to the next generation.

I do not know where the years are going. My eldest daughter is twenty-two. She was a particular favourite of Uncle Toni. I hope you do not mind, but I called her Effie, in memory of the woman that my uncle loved so much. It pleased him greatly.

Shortly before he died, he asked if I would send my contact details. If my letter should arrive where his have not, I want you to know that you have a family here in Termoli, who will welcome you warmly into our homes ... you are already in our hearts.

With love from all of the Mario family,

Cristina

44

Hugh and his wife, Anne, stood at the entrance to the kirk and welcomed people as they arrived for Ina's funeral. The building was almost full when they joined their family, who sat in the front two pews. He kept the seat next to him free for Effie. So far there had been no sign of her.

The day before, Hugh had sat on the wall by the kitchen for a long time. However, after that one heart-wrenching scream the house had been quiet and he had finally returned to his own home, although he kept looking out of the window for any sign of his sister. It was late evening when he noticed that her car was no longer there. He had walked back to the farmhouse. Effie and the sewing box had gone, and the rooms felt even emptier than they had when Ina died.

He became aware of Anne nudging him, and he turned to find someone sitting in the empty seat next to him. Effie looked pale and tired, as if she hadn't slept at all. Neither of them spoke. Instead, she reached over and took hold of his hand. He couldn't stop the tears streaming down his face.

★

Effie had sat in the kitchen for hours the previous afternoon, reading and rereading the letters, crying, remembering, realising that she could have had a completely different life if Ina had only let her know that Toni was still alive. What had prevented her sister from writing or calling?

Over the years there had been other men and Effie had even loved a couple. Yet whenever Effie compared those feelings to what she and Toni had known, they had faded into insignificance. Now she was no longer concerned about such matters.

Ina's coffin was plain, with a simple wreath of red roses on the top. It was difficult to imagine her sister lying within those planks of wood. Ina had been such a beautiful, vibrant young woman.

As they waited for the service to begin, Effie couldn't help analysing her life. Funerals did that to people, particularly if they were of a certain age. She feared that so much time had been spent living in loneliness; it had swamped her during those first years after leaving Kirk Farm. From Tain railway station she had taken one train after another, with no particular plan other than to head south and as far away from the Highlands as possible.

Eventually, she ended up in London, where she got a job at a hospital. There, she buried herself in work and the misery of others so as to hold at bay the despair that threatened to overwhelm her. There was plenty of misery in the capital during the last year and a half of the war in Europe. However, when the fighting ended, she no longer had the energy to keep going. The depression she had staved off ate her up.

Then one day she saw an advertisement for a children's

short story competition. It stirred distant memories of producing plays for Hugh. She felt as though it was beckoning her not only to write, but also to return to the living. She sat down that evening and a few days later sent off her entry. Along with winning first prize, a published article and a cheque for five pounds, Effie had found a new hope and purpose.

She created a pseudonym and threw all of her passion and energy into writing. As the decades went by, she had become an established novelist and writer of short stories – the most popular being about a group of children growing up on a farm during the war. But her loneliness had always been there, like a shadow she couldn't escape no matter how fast or how far she ran. Finally she had accepted it as an unwelcome, though familiar, companion.

Her thoughts returned to the present at the sight of the minister. He looked far too young; he couldn't possibly have gained the experiences required to provide guidance to others. So many professionals looked too young these days.

Seeing him standing in the same pulpit the Reverend Smith had used for Sunday services brought memories flooding back. Sometimes she couldn't prevent an image playing out in her mind: the steel blade pushed inch by inch into his withering body, the minister begging her to stop, calling out her name until he went limp and could call no more.

'We have gathered here today to celebrate the life of someone who was known and loved widely within the community.' The young minister had a good, gentle voice and an appealing manner. 'Ina Ross dedicated her life to teaching. Many of you will have spent some of your school days in her class and benefited from her enormous enthusiasm and amazing ability to instil in others a desire to learn.'

Effie listened to the stranger give a history of her sister's life and it felt as though she too was a stranger. It seemed wrong that other people should have knowledge and experiences of her immediate family that she did not have herself. She had been robbed of something precious that could never be returned.

'Ina loved Kirk Farm and the surrounding area. She lived here for the whole of her life, never travelling far away. Ina dedicated her life to helping those who needed it. She became a prominent figure in several local organisations and enjoyed playing the kirk's organ and leading its choir.'

Effie thought that Ina's life seemed dull. She wondered if Ina had sought solace by staying close to those she knew, choosing a 'safe' career, being heavily involved in religion and the community. As a young woman, Ina had had the potential to go out into the world and be anything she wanted.

But then what had Effie done? She had travelled a great deal, yes, but she was forever moving on, never settling anywhere long enough to make friends – at least not real friends who she could turn to for help. She had certainly never found anywhere that felt like 'home'. On the surface, she was a highly successful woman, in great demand for book festivals and literary events. But when the front door was locked and she settled down for yet another evening alone, the demons would be waiting patiently.

You had to hand it to them, they were always patient.

Effie and Hugh followed the coffin out of the church still holding hands, everyone else giving them a little extra space, as though the brother and sister were walking a path that no one else had the right to tread. Slowly, the congregation emerged into the bright summer sunshine and made its way respectfully to the freshly dug earth. Here, Hugh had to let go of Effie's hand, as he and his sons each took the end of a cord to help lower the coffin.

Oh Ina, what have we done to each other?

When the coffin was in the ground and the ceremony over, Hugh led Effie to the grave of their parents.

'Edward Ross ... nineteen sixty-one ... Martha Ross ... nineteen seventy,' said Effie, reading out the inscription on the headstone. 'Father would have been sixty-eight and mother seventy-five.'

'Father was found lying dead in the top field,' Hugh explained. 'It was a heart attack, completely out of the blue. Mother was ill for many months. Nothing was ever diagnosed for certain. She just seemed to fade away until there was nothing left to fade. I'm sorry you were never told when they died.'

They stood in silence for a while. The cemetery was empty and quiet, apart from the birds singing in nearby trees.

'None of us were ever the same after those few weeks,' Hugh said. 'Duncan's death, followed so soon by Christopher's ... and then you leaving. We were drowning in grief and simply didn't know how to deal with it. I guess we were lost souls, particularly Father. He felt the betrayal by Walter Smith very deeply. It was ages before another

307

minister was appointed, but Father was never close to him or any of those who followed.'

'When did you return to Kirk Farm?'

'It was the May of 1944. Having initially been so eager not to leave, we found coming home worse than living away. Every corner of the place was full of memories. It was after we returned that Father started saying he hadn't intended for you to go forever. He regretted it terribly, Fee. I think the pain had simply overwhelmed him. He needed someone to blame and you were too convenient ... too close.'

Effie nodded. 'I couldn't write to let you know where I was. I fell into a black hole and it took years ... and a writing competition ... to find my way out. I wrote to Ina then, but I never heard back.'

'She didn't tell any of us that you had made contact.'

'All these years, she kept it a secret that Toni was still alive.'

'Yes.'

'For about six months, before he was sent back to Italy, we were both in London. Can you believe that we might have been only a few miles apart, maybe just around the corner from each other? If fate had only made one of us walk around that corner.'

'I don't know what prevented Ina from replying,' admitted Hugh with a sigh. 'Perhaps, because she didn't reply straight away, it just got harder as time passed.'

'So many people died that night, including many of those who walked away,' said Effie.

'Afterwards, I pestered everyone for ages about where you had gone and why,' said Hugh. 'Nobody would tell me anything. I eventually stopped asking.'

'You were only a child.'

'When I turned twenty-one, Ina asked me what I wanted for my "special" birthday. I said I would like to know why you had gone.'

'Did she tell you?'

'Well, probably not everything. However, it was enough for me to put most of the pieces together. Fee, there's something that I want you to see.'

She followed him to an older part of the cemetery. The last time she had been there was when they had all visited Duncan, the afternoon of that fateful day. They stopped at a well-tended grave with fresh flowers by the headstone.

'Christopher!'

'When he died there was only his mother left. He had told her a lot about the girl in the Highlands he had fallen in love with. His mother said that her son should be buried near Ina. Ina came here every single day, regardless of whether it was snowing or blowing a gale.'

'That's why she never moved away … Christopher was here.'

'She didn't feel the need to go anywhere else. Everyone and everything she loved was around Kirk Farm. There was only one person who wasn't.'

'I don't think I was on her list of people to love,' said Effie sadly.

'No, Fee, you're wrong. She never forgave you, not until the last few weeks of her life, but she always loved you. That was Ina's dilemma. It was part of the conflict she carried within her.'

They remained silent, each lost in their own thoughts.

'Hugh, did you know Toni and I killed the minister in a

fight? We pushed his own knife into him. It was horrible. In the end he was begging us to stop, but we kept on until he went silent. The sound of his voice haunts me. The last thing I did with the man I loved was kill another human being.'

Hugh looked at her in surprise. 'Fee, you didn't kill him.'

'What? He didn't die?'

'Not from being stabbed.'

'I don't understand.'

'Several of Christopher's fellow officers attended his funeral, including a huge guy who Ina had met before. She pleaded with him to tell her about the person who murdered her fiancé. He must have seen how much she needed to know, because he agreed to come back. I'm sure he broke an entire regiment of regulations, but he kept his promise and returned several weeks later.

'The official version was that Captain Armstrong and the Reverend Smith were murdered by a deranged Italian POW who had escaped from a nearby camp and who was himself killed soon afterwards by an army patrol. I think the authorities considered it would be bad for public morale if it came out that the enemy had infiltrated British society so completely that you couldn't even trust your minister.'

'So no one knew he was a spy?'

'Nobody ever had reason to suspect that things weren't exactly as they appeared to be. His real name was Walter Möller and he was a proper minister. In fact, most of what he told people was true. His mother was Dutch, as he claimed. It was his father who was German, and it was with Germany that his loyalties lay.

'In the dark and confusion of that night the U-boat sent to pick up Möller escaped, but he was taken to a military hospital and recovered well enough to be interrogated. When the authorities thought they had learnt everything they could, they put Möller against a wall and shot him.'

Effie almost collapsed against the headstone in relief. Hugh quickly stepped forward and, for the first time, took his sister in his arms. She buried her head in his chest and wept.

'All these years I believed I had been responsible for killing someone ... all these years.'

'Forget about the spy. He got what he deserved. People died because of him and those who survived have all been punished enough. Anyway, you're wrong ... the last thing you did with the man you loved was try to save Christopher.'

'Oh, Hugh ... I would give so much to have peace of mind.'

'Ina once said that to me, one evening when we were sitting alone by the fire. She didn't often talk about her feelings. It was a rare glimpse into her innermost thoughts.'

'Did Ina really forgive me?'

'Yes. When she knew the end was near. By doing so, I think she finally found a contentment of sorts.'

They stood beside Christopher's grave, reflecting on what had been said.

'Fee ... do you think it would help to be at Kirk Farm?'

Effie pulled back in surprise and looked up at him.

'You mean, to live at Kirk Farm?'

'The house is empty and it's mine to do what I want with it. I don't need a decision anytime soon. I just want you to

311

consider it. You have a family here and I know they would all love you as I do.'

'I don't know what to say.'

'Well, say nothing then,' he reached out and squeezed her hand. 'Take as long as you need to consider it. Come on, let's go to the reception and rescue poor Anne from having to be the host.'

45

For more than sixty years, Effie had feared that if she ever returned to the Tarbat peninsula people would be hostile towards her. She was the girl who had slept with the enemy only days after her brother's funeral. She was the girl whose actions had almost led to Germany learning one of the country's greatest secrets, which would have resulted in the death of thousands of Allied troops. She was someone never to be forgiven.

But no one outside of her family knew that she had loved Toni. Anyone who remembered the minister believed he had been killed by an escaped POW. Christopher had died in the line of duty, and the friends and neighbours who knew of his betrothal to Ina considered his death just another tragedy of the war. Effie wasn't thought of as the scarlet woman, the would-be traitor, the disgraced daughter who had destroyed a good local family. She was simply Hugh's older sister who left during the war and never came back. It wasn't that unusual a story.

Those she met were keen to introduce themselves and express their sympathy for her loss. Effie even came across a few of her old classmates. Now they were grandmothers and grandfathers. She was surprised to find that she

313

enjoyed speaking to them. Some of her happier childhood memories came back and she was interested to hear what had happened to old friends and neighbours, and to learn about the new generations.

Nobody knew she was a writer. When people asked about her career, Effie simply said that she always seemed to end up having to do lots of typing, the faintest echo of her old, mischievous character creeping into her words. Everyone assumed she had been some sort of secretary and didn't ask any more.

After the reception, Effie wanted to be alone, so she returned to the church. It was empty. She walked slowly down the aisle to the third row from the front, which had once been the Ross family pew. Hugh would always sit between his sisters. He had been such an affectionate little boy and they had all been devoted to him. It was difficult to think of him with his own grandchildren.

Effie looked around. The interior of the building didn't seem to have changed at all from those far-off days when they would sit listening attentively to the minister. Even the organ appeared to be the same one that she and Ina had played to accompany the congregation in hymns. She recalled how they used to dare each other to speed up the music or add an extra verse to confuse everyone and try to keep them singing.

Attending Ina's funeral that morning was the first time she had entered a church since leaving the area. While Ina had sought comfort in religion, Effie had shunned everything to do with it, as she had done with so many of the things that were important to her father. She had been sitting for about thirty minutes when the door opened and someone entered. Effie sighed as the footsteps drew closer. It was the young minister who had taken Ina's service.

'I'm sorry for disturbing you,' he said, bowing his head. 'I'll leave you to your prayers.'

'They're hardly prayers ... memories perhaps.'

'I thought I knew Ina well, yet I never realised she had a sister.'

'I'm the black sheep of the family, reverend.'

'Please, call me Matthew. May I?' he stretched out a hand, indicating that he would like to sit beside her.

'It's not for me to tell you where to sit in your own kirk.'

'Well, it's really God's kirk. I just help out now and again.' He slid into the pew.

'I'm afraid God and I haven't seen eye to eye for a very long time,' Effie said. 'Anyway, I'm not surprised Ina never mentioned me.'

They were both quiet for a while and he left the silence between them hanging, as if it was a question.

'I'm here to seek forgiveness, Matthew, but the people I seek it from are all dead. I'm too late ... a lifetime too late.'

'Perhaps what is needed is forgiveness much closer to home ... in here,' he said, putting a hand over his heart. 'We can be the most critical judge of our own actions, reluctant to be compassionate and kind to ourselves, even though we may show these qualities to others on a daily basis.'

'You're rather wise for one so young.'

The warmth of his expression unexpectedly made her think of Toni, and the beautiful smile he had given her when they had first met.

'For a moment you reminded me of someone I knew

long ago. A young Italian. He was called Toni. Your lovely smile is so like his.'

'And Toni died?' the minister asked.

'Yes ... and no.'

Matthew didn't respond immediately to the ambiguous answer. As silence settled between them again, he sensed that Ina's sister was either going to tell him something extremely important to her, or she was going to leave.

'If you want to talk, I will listen without judging,' he said eventually. 'Anything you say here will never be repeated.'

He had made the offer and could do no more. It was up to Effie. They sat for a long time, until Matthew began to think she would not speak further.

'In a few months I'll be eighty years old. In all that time I've never told anyone my story. Perhaps, Matthew, it's time I did.'

So the elderly spinster and the young minister sat side by side in the quiet of the kirk, and Effie told her story.

46

Effie returned to Kirk Farm later that afternoon. The weather was glorious, so she parked near the gates and walked slowly up the drive. When she reached the horse chestnut tree, she stopped and put a hand against the bark, as if laying it on the shoulder of an old friend.

When Hugh was a boy he would play for hours on the tyre hanging from a sturdy branch. How many times had she pushed her brother, laughing at his cries of delight and shouts of 'Higher!'? There was no sign of the rope or tyre now, and Effie wondered if children still played such simple games.

The pigsty was empty. She didn't know what livestock Hugh kept. Since her arrival there had been no opportunity to talk of such things. She sat on the wall and thought of the day she'd met Toni, when he had chased the pig, singing love songs to it. Those weeks in 1943 were forever seared in her mind. They had ended in pain and anguish, but also marked a period of the greatest joy she had ever known.

Effie went to the barn where she and Toni had made love. It was strange, looking back. She had felt such passion for Toni; the lovers that she had known since had all paled into vague memories, but she vividly remembered everything about Toni, their conversation, the tenderness of his touch, the entwining of their souls along with their limbs. As she walked slowly past the disused stalls, Effie felt that Toni was close by.

She returned to the kitchen and stood very still, as if straining to hear something. On the day she was disowned, it had seemed like every nook and cranny in every room of the house screamed at her in anger. Her family had blamed and rejected her, and Effie had felt that the walls of their home also shunned her with disdain and distrust.

Yet, now, decades later, all she heard was the clock ticking. All she felt was contentment. Effie laid a hand on the clock's case. She smiled, remembering how no one was allowed to touch it except Father. Even Mother wasn't permitted near.

Effie looked inside the clock and saw that the weights had dropped almost out of sight. The winder was on a nearby ledge, in the same spot it had always been kept. She picked it up and opened the glass face, surprised moments later at how much effort was needed. She left the clock running five minutes fast.

Effie walked around and ended up by the harmonium. Since leaving Kirk Farm, she had not played any instrument. Playing music was another experience that had grown alien to her. On the music stand was the *Scottish Psalter and Church Hymnary* that Father had given to Mother one Christmas; his large, scrawling handwriting was still visible on the first page.

To Martha,
Wishing you a very happy Christmas and a
peaceful New Year. Edward. 25 December,
1930.

There had been a great deal of love within the family. Over the years it had become too easy to forget, too tempting to believe that what had torn them apart was hate and anger when really it had been love ... Ina's for Christopher, Effie's for Toni and everyone's for Duncan. There had been hurt, not hate. There had been anguish, not anger.

If only Effie had returned, maybe after a few years, when everyone had had some time to reflect and recover. But she never did. Too stubborn, too frightened of what she might encounter, unable to endure another rejection.

Effie sat on the sloping wooden stool at the harmonium and picked up the book. It opened naturally at her father's favourite hymn, 'Eternal Father, strong to save'.

Effie took a deep breath, then she started to play. She recalled how her father would tell to let the rafters sing with the music of God, so she slipped her thin legs between the swell-pedals just below the keyboard and pushed them outwards. The volume increased, until it felt as if every single part of the house was vibrating and alive with the sound.

Hugh was nearby with the cattle. The sound of the harmonium carried clearly across the field. He knew there could only be one person playing and one reason for it. For a few moments he was transfixed by the music, then he let out a booming shout of joy that made Bella, his favourite cow, raise her head in surprise. Hugh wanted to run, to shout, to hug his wife, to hug everyone, but there was no one around.

'Bella,' he said, putting his hands firmly on her head, 'I love you!'

He gave the animal a huge kiss on the forehead. Bella mooed loudly and Hugh laughed in a way he couldn't remember doing since he was a child. Then he kissed the cow again.

When Effie finally stopped, the silence was absolute. She was breathing so hard that she had to sit quietly for a while to regain composure. Effie was surprised that she could still play, by how much the music had moved her. Playing again had dispelled the last of any doubts.

From her handbag she took out a small package wrapped in tissue. Carefully, she removed the paper to reveal the wooden box that Toni had given her. She held the token of their love to her lips and kissed it tenderly.

'Oh, Toni, I've gone from having no one for so long, to two families ... yours in Italy and mine at Kirk Farm,' she said, gently placing the box on top of the harmonium.

Effie had come home.

A NOTE ON THE HISTORY
OF *Effie's War*

The story of *Effie's War* was inspired by real events in Scottish history. On 11 November 1943, approximately nine hundred people in Scotland's Tarbat peninsula were given four weeks to vacate their homes, crofts and farms. Some farmers faced the enormous task of selling their entire livestock and processing crops.

Residents were informed that the military needed the land for battle practice. This wasn't the full story – they wanted the beach to the west of the fishing village of Portmahomack to rehearse for the D-Day landings, destined to take place on the French coast of Normandy. Operation Overlord, the campaign to free Western Europe of German control, was one of the greatest secrets of the Second World War. The D-Day landings began on 6 June 1944 and were the largest seaborne invasion ever undertaken. The British government went to enormous lengths to convince the enemy that this anticipated invasion would occur somewhere other than Normandy.

Of course, the Highland folk receiving their eviction notices knew nothing of the momentous events scheduled for the following year. The affected area was roughly fifteen square miles, stretching from east of the Hill of Fearn and north of the Seaboard village of Hilton to south-west of Portmahomack and Rockfield. The orders resulted in the closure of two schools, plus the evacuation of the village of Inver. No one knew when they would return and some elderly residents feared that they wouldn't live long enough to be able to die in their own beds. Sadly, a few of them were correct.

People were expected to organise their own temporary accommodation. Many families moved to Tain, which was the closest town with the capacity to absorb them. Others went further away and some never came back.

Farmers had little alternative but to sell their entire livestock. To help with this, the authorities arranged transport for the animals – more than a thousand cattle, eight thousand sheep and fifty pigs – to sales at the Dingwall auction mart. Maintaining secrecy was paramount, so only selected farmers were invited to attend the auctions. Special trains were laid on to take away purchased stock.

Those living north of the evacuation zone were not forced to leave, but once restrictions were imposed they needed a special pass to travel and could only do so during limited times, as determined by the military. This made it difficult for someone to visit – even a doctor making a call – particularly as these brief windows could be changed with no warning.

Although the harvest had been gathered, crops such as wheat, barley, oats and potatoes still needed to be processed. Equipment, including mobile threshers, balers and potato dressers, was rushed to the area from different parts of the country. Some of this was operated by the Women's Land Army. There were three 'land girls', as they were fondly known, living in Portmahomack.

Italian prisoners of war based at Kildary were also brought in to help, with the Home Guard providing manpower at weekends, when the POWs were sent back to their camp for a break. Italy's capitulation in September 1943, which involved the Badoglio government changing sides and allying itself with Britain against Germany, subsequently resulted in significant conflict between inmates.

The situation sometimes became so fraught in some camps that men had to be moved to separate those who were loyal to Mussolini from those who were not. After the war the Kildary camp was used for a while for German POWs previously held in America.

People were allowed to return to their homes from May 1944 onwards, once the army had declared the area clear of unexploded bombs. However, farmers continued to dig up live shells for years.

Some properties suffered damage, ranging from slight to severe. The problem that most people faced was that their houses were damp and cold after being unoccupied throughout the winter. The soil in many fields had been compacted by heavy tanks and other vehicles, and it took a long time for farms to repair broken fences and dykes, restock and regain a semblance of normality.

The family of my wife, Catherine, moved into a building a hundred yards outside the Tarbat peninsula evacuation zone in the 1970s. Catherine grew up hearing all about the area's history. When she passed the tale on to me, I tucked it away in that mental filing cabinet in which writers store interesting information. It was a visit to the Tarbat Discovery Centre and the purchase of Dr James A. Fallon's excellent booklet *Evacuation: Tarbat Peninsula 1943–1944* that shone a light on these events once more and set the writing boulder rolling down the hill. I became fascinated by the story, my imagination suddenly set alight.

Apart from Lord Rosebery and General Sir Andrew Thorne, who did indeed hold a meeting at Inver hall on 11 November, the characters portrayed in *Effie's War* are entirely fictitious, and settings such as Kirk Farm, the kirk and the manse also came from this author's imagination. There was never a German spy living in the area of the Tarbat peninsula during the Second World War – at least, not as far as anyone knows …

Philip Paris
www.philipparis.co.uk

ACKNOWLEDGEMENTS

My very grateful thanks to all those who helped me to understand Highland life during the 1940s ... from farming to funerals! In particular, I would like to acknowledge Douglas Gordon, George and Isabel Ross, André Saunders and David Scott. A special thanks to Iain Ross and Philip Ward for reading and commenting on the manuscript. As ever, my thanks, love and gratitude to Catherine, without whose support little would get written.